In Love and War

A novella collection by:
Miralee Ferrell
Kimberly Rose Johnson
Debby Mayne
Trish Perry

MBI

In Love and War

Published by Mountain Brook Ink
White Salmon, WA U.S.A.

The website addresses shown in this book are not intended in any way to be or imply an endorsement on the part of Mountain Brook Ink, nor do we vouch for their content.

These novellas are a work of fiction. All characters and events are the product of the authors' imagination. Any resemblance to any person, living or dead, is coincidental.

Scripture quotations are taken from the King James Version of the Bible. Public domain.
ISBN 978-1-943959-01-3
© 2016 Miralee Ferrell, Kimberly R Johnson, Debby Mayne, Trish Perry

The Team: Miralee Ferrell, Nikki Wright, Cindy Jackson
Cover Design: Indie Cover Design, Lynnette Bonner Designer

Mountain Brook Ink is an inspirational publisher offering fiction you can believe in.
Printed in the United States of America

Contents

LASSOED BY LOVE

By
Miralee Ferrell

CHAPTER ONE

LINDSEY MORGAN GAZED AT THE BEAUTIFUL log lodge with the massive stone chimney, flanked by Ponderosa Pine. Peace and country living were fine, and she thanked the Lord for her new job, even if it wasn't what she'd expected. But regardless, she'd be happy living in the country if she could save enough to get a used car in the near future—besides, a fancy resort wasn't really like living in the country, even if it did have a bit more rustic feel.

Riding the bus all this way then walking here from town hadn't been fun, but that's what happened when you had to sell your car to pay bills. Squaring her shoulders, she strode toward the front entrance. Good thing her friend Melissa helped her score this job at the Red Butte Resort's gift store, or she might be homeless by now. And no way would she ask her parents for help, unless she truly became homeless, then she might consider it.

Time to meet her new boss. She breezed through the front door and entered a wood-paneled lobby. An office door with *Dixie Sanderson, Manager—Human Resources*, was off to the side and stood cracked a few inches. A masculine voice blended with the higher pitched tones of a woman. Lindsey hated to eavesdrop, but her only other option was standing outside in the cool spring afternoon.

She sank onto a chair and picked up a travel magazine. Opening the front cover, she flipped through the pages and found an article on Red Butte Resort. Nice. She'd almost forgotten the conversation going on a few yards away when the man's voice increased in volume.

"Our groom broke his wrist, and this leaves us in a bad fix for the tourist season, Dixie. I'm already shorthanded."

Prickles ran up Lindsey's back. She'd heard that voice before, but she couldn't quite put her finger on where.

The gentler pitch of the woman's voice drifted out. "I know. But we have a new girl coming in, and I'll assign her to the stables."

The very masculine voice responded. "I looked at her resume, and her name is familiar. If she's who I think, she's a pampered, spoiled, city girl. No way will she want to get her hands dirty working with horses or mucking stalls. Honestly, I doubt she'd last the week out."

"She's all I can offer right now. Maybe something will change in the next day or two. I'll keep you posted."

The sound of chair legs scraped the floor, and the door swung wide. "I'll cut her a little slack when she starts, then I'll have to work her like anyone else. You'd better keep the employment agency in town on call just in case."

Lindsey ducked her head and concentrated on her magazine, but couldn't resist a quick peek after the man strode past. A pair of dusty cowboy boots covered by blue jeans. She raised her gaze a few inches. A muscular but slender build with sun-bronzed skin and tawny blond hair. His back was to her as he marched toward the front doors, but his irritated tone had done little to impress Lindsey. That man needed a confident woman to set him straight.

She jerked her thoughts back to where they belonged. The woman he was describing might have been her a few years ago, but she'd run into too many hurdles the past couple of years to take any chances of jeopardizing this job.

At least according to what she'd understood when she'd been hired, *her* job was secure. The last thing she'd want was to work in a barn with *that* man as her boss. In fact, the very thought of working in a barn with any boss made her shudder.

Miss Sanderson—at least she assumed it was the woman whose name was on the door—stepped out of the office and beckoned her way. "Miss? May I help you?"

Lindsey stood and tugged at the hem of her jacket. "I'm Lindsey Morgan. I know I'm not due to check in till tomorrow, but I arrived early. But we spoke on the phone a couple of weeks ago, and you hired me to work as the assistant manager in the gift shop. I was hoping to get settled tonight."

A solemn look covered the woman's face, then her mouth pulled down in a frown.

Sudden apprehension gripped Lindsey, but she pushed it away. "If that's all right?"

"Pardon my manners." The woman waved toward a chair in the office. "Please, come in and have a seat. I'm Dixie Sanderson, the manager of Red Butte Resort, and all the employees call me Dixie. We tend to be a bit informal here."

Lindsey released her pent up breath and perched on the edge of the leather seat. "I'm so happy to be here. My friend Melissa told me a lot about the resort, and I appreciate you hiring me for the spring and summer."

Dixie's face tightened, then she placed her elbows on the desktop and clasped her hands under her chin. "Did you read your acceptance letter thoroughly, Miss Morgan? All the way to the fine print at the bottom?"

Lindsey's mind scrambled as she tried to visualize the letter. She'd read the first couple of paragraphs saying she'd been hired for the season, and that living accommodations came with the position, along with her arrival date. The rest had appeared to be legal mumbo-jumbo, so she'd barely skimmed it. "I think so. Is there a problem?" She laced her fingers in her lap and squeezed.

"I'm afraid so. I'm not one to mince words, Miss Morgan, and I'm sure you'd prefer I get to the point. It states in your contract, which you signed and returned, that we retain the right to make changes in your employment or job description as needed."

Lindsey leaned forward and opened her lips to protest. She couldn't lose this job. The bus fare took a chunk of her small savings, and she'd let her apartment go. She had stored most of her belongings, content in the knowledge her future was secure, at least for the summer. "But I don't have anything—"

Dixie held up her hand. "Please. Give me a moment. You still have a job. That's not the problem."

"Oh." Lindsey's shoulders relaxed, and she mustered a smile. "I'm happy to hear that."

Dixie twisted her lips sideways in concentration. "We had to make some changes. When we offered you the position in the gift shop, we assumed our long-time assistant manager who'd had family problems, couldn't come back. She notified us a week ago, saying her situation was resolved, and she'd like to work for us again. Since she's a favorite with guests and staff, as well as highly experienced, we hated to turn her away."

Lindsey met Dixie's gaze. "Are you saying you gave my job to someone else?"

"Not entirely. That's why I asked if you read the contract. Once we signed it, we can't terminate you without cause, but we can shift you to another position. You're still working for us, simply in a different capacity."

A vision of the angry voice and stiff shoulders she'd glimpsed as the man stalked out of the entry flashed across her mind. "I see. And that would be?"

Dixie drew in a short breath then sighed. "Working at our barn in the trail riding and lessons program."

Lindsey willed her voice to remain calm, even though rising panic threatened to swamp her. "But I don't know anything about horses."

"Don't worry. You won't be riding. We have other employees who take our visitors on the trails and give the lessons. You'll be working in the barn doing odd jobs—feeding, grooming, cleaning stalls and tack—that sort of thing."

The woman might as well have spoken a foreign language. Feeding she understood, but what did grooming entail or cleaning tack, whatever *that* was? And stalls. Did that mean she'd be required to scoop up horse droppings? "I don't have any training." She kept her voice firm, praying the woman would see her mistake. "Surely there's got to be another job on this resort. I'm an excellent swimmer, and I understand you have a large pool. Maybe a swim instructor for children or even a waitress? I've worked at both jobs during summer vacations in college."

"Sorry, no. We're fully staffed everywhere. We might have a dishwasher position open, but it's less pay and doesn't come with housing. Would you care to consider that?"

Lindsey's mind raced, sorting through her options. The business she worked for had closed, and few people in her town were hiring.

She'd come hoping to get back on her feet and maybe even enjoy a few hours by the pool. Washing dishes for minimum wage wouldn't allow her to put anything in savings for a car or her future. She shook her head. "No, thank you. I don't have the funds to secure housing right now, and I was counting on the promised apartment."

Dixie gave a slight nod. "You'll still have housing, but I'm afraid the employee returning to the gift shop is taking the condo we'd planned to give you. But we have a cabin near the barn. It's a little more rustic, but comfortable and has its own bathroom and kitchen. The position at the barn pays a little less, but since you won't have the apartment we'd planned, I'll keep you at the higher pay level. I can take you to your quarters, if that's agreeable?" She pushed back her chair and stood.

Lindsey sat unmoving for a full ten seconds, then rose and squared her shoulders. "May I ask who I'll be reporting to and when?"

Dixie waved her hand toward the door. "I'm sorry you missed him. Your new boss was here a few minutes before you arrived. His name is Steve Graham, and he's very pleased we've found someone to take the position. He'll be eager to meet you tomorrow. We'll have you start right at 8 a.m., and it will be 8 to 5 with an hour lunch and weekends off. I should say, though, we may need you an occasional Saturday. If that happens, you'll get overtime."

Lindsey bit her lip to keep from breaking out in a wild laugh. If Steve Graham was pleased, then she was a grandmother of ten. Now she knew exactly where she'd heard that voice before. High school. But there was no way that could be the same Steve Graham from eight years ago. The boy she remembered was a quiet country kid who loved horses and the rodeo, and he'd asked her to the prom their senior year. She blushed at the memory.

That was where the similarity ended. The man she'd seen was filled out, muscular, and much taller than the Steve she remembered. Besides, Red Butte, Oregon, was hundreds of miles from her old home in Montana. What were the odds two kids from a small city high school would end up at the same resort years later? Not great, that's for sure. She shrugged—she could easily be wrong. Thinking she'd recognized his voice meant nothing. From what she remembered, the old Steve's voice hadn't echoed with such depth or passion.

There was only one thing to do. Pray hard that she'd survive the ordeal, then go in swinging. She'd show her new boss she didn't know the meaning of the word quit. He thought she'd cut and run within two days, did he? She smiled. "The hours sound fine, and I could use the overtime, so that's not a problem. I look forward to meeting the boss, as well." And proving to that man she wasn't the type of woman he could drive off, no matter what he threw at her.

Dixie grabbed one of Lindsey's bags, and she hefted the other two, following the older woman to a sedan parked on the curb. "It's a bit too far to walk dragging your bags." She popped the trunk and waited for Lindsey to settle her bags before shutting the lid and walking around to take her place behind the wheel.

Dixie waited for Lindsey to fasten her seatbelt then backed her car out of the parking area. "We'll drive through the main part of the resort then hit River Road so you can see more of the area. You don't own a car?"

Lindsey shook her head, unsure of how much to say. Losing her car hadn't been easy, but she didn't want to appear needy. "I sold it before leaving home. It wasn't in good enough shape to chance driving it from Missoula to Oregon, and I didn't want to put it in storage." She looked out the window at the number of buildings they passed, amazed at the distance they'd already covered from the lodge. "I didn't realize Red Butte was such a large resort. Is a lack of transportation going to be a problem?"

"Not if you don't mind riding a bike or using a four-wheeler—both of those will be at your disposal. When you go into town for groceries, we can loan you one of the Lodge vehicles, just sign up for it a few hours in advance. You're covered under our employee insurance." She pointed off to the right. "The marina is down that road, along the Deschutes River. We rent watercraft, do guided raft trips, and there's a dock for visitors who bring their own boats."

Dixie cranked the wheel to the left and turned into a narrow road. "The airport is a little farther past the marina, and the stable is ahead. It seems overwhelming now, but you'll get the lay of the land in no time." She drew the car to a stop next to a rustic, wood-sided cabin.

"This is your new home, and it's only a short walk to the barn. You hit the trailhead here, and you can see it in the distance."

Lindsey peered the way Dixie pointed. A two-story structure with a dark brown metal roof towered in the distance. Most of the barns she'd seen in Montana were red with a steep pitch to the roof, rather than mostly cream and brown with a barely sloping gable. Of course, this was the dry side of Oregon, and they probably didn't get the snow load that could destroy a flatter roofed barn like they did in Montana.

She swung her attention to the cabin, and her heart sank. She'd lived in Missoula all her life and was more used to living in a modern structure than something like this—even if her hometown was in somewhat of a rural area. It didn't even look as big as her apartment back home. Smoke spiraled out of the chimney at the edge of the roofline, and a compact, covered porch lined the front of the single-story dwelling. A window was set on each side of the door, and the outer walls were covered with weathered strips of boards.

"Did they forget to put on the siding?"

Dixie laughed, then turned twinkling eyes on Lindsey. "No, that's called bat-and-board siding. It's quite popular in this area, especially for cabins. The narrow strips of wood that cover the seams where the boards meet are decorative now, but before insulation was invented they helped keep the wind from whistling through the walls." She waved an airy hand. "No worries about that here. You'll be snug and warm and should have everything you need—there are even basic groceries in the cupboards and fridge, to keep you until you can shop for yourself. Come on, let's unload your things and get you settled."

CHAPTER TWO

STEVE HEFTED A BALE OF STRAW onto his shoulder and headed down the barn aisle, wondering where Jon had stored their wheelbarrow. If only their long-time employee hadn't broken his wrist with the tourist season so close at hand. He turned a corner and ducked his head, hefting the bale to a more comfortable position.

"Ouch." A female voice sounded not far ahead.

Steve lifted his head and slowed to a stop. A slender young woman with auburn hair drawn into a ponytail stood with her back to him, rubbing her bare arm.

"May I help you? Are you hurt?" An angry red streak ran from her elbow half-way to her wrist, and he saw blood oozing from the wound. He dumped the bale on the ground and reached out. "I'm sorry, miss. Let me take a look at that."

She swung around, clamped a hand over her arm, and glowered. "I came around the corner too close and fast, and I ran it into a thing-a-ma-jig sticking out of the wall." She pointed at a bolt with a hooked end, then met his gaze and gasped. "It *is* you." She slapped her other hand over her mouth then sighed. "Sorry. I mean, how are you, Steve?"

He gritted his teeth to keep something unkind from slipping out. He'd suspected there might not be two Lindsey Morgans who hailed from Missoula—although it wasn't a totally unique name, and he'd hoped he'd been mistaken. "Hello, Lindsey. What are you doing here, besides running into walls and hurting yourself?" He reached out a hand, knowing he'd asked a stupid question. "Here, let me take a look at that—it looks like it might need attention. Are you up on your tetanus shots?"

She pulled away and stepped back. "First, I work here, which I'm sure you know. Second, the application didn't say anything about health requirements. And I think I'm current on my tetanus, so I'm sure I'll be fine."

He had all he could do not to roll his eyes or snort. This girl had caused him no end of grief when he'd been a skinny ranch kid, and she'd been the ever-so-popular cheerleader that all the boys chased and the other girls envied. In all fairness, she hadn't been exactly mean to him, but the one or two times he'd tried to talk to her, she hadn't put out much effort to reply. He'd had a major crush on her and had even mustered up the courage to ask her to prom in their senior year.

It hadn't helped when he'd overheard one of Lindsey's girlfriends giggling about his physique. Lindsey had shushed her, but he was sure he'd seen her condescending smile while doing it, and she turned down his invitation and attended with one of the jocks. After graduation, she'd gone off to college, and he'd stayed working on his family's ranch, putting on a few pounds and a lot of muscle.

He gave a wry smile. Not without a lot of hard work, but the thought of that smirk had driven him—and what came after. Steve cleared his throat. "I understand you initially applied for the gift shop position, so that wouldn't come with any health requirements. But working around horses is different. We recommend our employees are caught up on their tetanus shots, and we require a certificate from their doctor saying they are. And if you get injured, you aren't given a choice unless you can provide that proof. Sorry, but you'll need to run into the clinic and get a shot."

Lindsey bit her lip. "Oh. Is that covered by the resort? And is the clinic nearby?"

He shook his head. "You don't have health insurance as a temporary employee, if that's what you're asking, but it might be in this case, since you got hurt on the job. The clinic is a couple of miles away on the edge of town. It won't take you long to drive there."

She gave a slow nod. "Right. What do you want me to do first, boss?"

That was the last thing he'd expected to hear from this pampered girl. Was she mocking him? If so, she hid it well behind her calm expression. "Come to the office with me and get salve on that then call the clinic."

She shrugged, lifted her hand from her arm, and peered at it. "It's really not a big deal. The cut has stopped bleeding. Can't you just tell me what my first job is?"

He stifled his frustration and held out his hand. "Let's go. No arguing. The owner of the resort would have my hide if I ignored this and you contracted tetanus." Steve wanted to bite his tongue at how that had come out. It wasn't that he didn't care what happened to this girl—no—she was a woman now, not the girl he remembered. It was simply that he didn't want to care, and the effort made him gruffer than he'd planned. He softened his tone, keeping his hand extended. "Please?"

She started to reach for his hand then hoisted herself to her feet instead. "I'll make the call." She pivoted and headed the direction he pointed, her mouth and chin set in a determined line.

What had he been thinking, accepting Lindsey Morgan as an employee? Of course, Dixie hadn't given him much choice, but there was no way this would ever work. He'd had plenty of experience with the hurt a woman could cause, and not only from Lindsey. If she stayed any length of time, he'd make sure he guarded his heart.

CHAPTER THREE

LINDSEY WANTED TO GROAN IN HUMILIATION, not to mention the fact that her arm was throbbing. She still didn't know how she'd managed to cut it like that. She'd had her head down, marching down the long aisle between the stalls and the indoor arena headed for the barn office to check in, when she'd rounded the end of a stall too fast and skidded along the wall.

What would she do about getting a shot? She was terrified of needles—had hated them for as long as she could remember. She'd do almost anything to avoid the experience—and no way would she let them stitch up her arm. She wasn't destitute yet and could pay the clinic, but it would take another bite out of her remaining savings. Besides, she didn't have a car and wasn't about to ask Steve Graham to drive her. It was enough she'd been forced to work as his employee after the things she'd overheard him say to Dixie.

Her face flamed with heat as she remembered him saying she wouldn't last long and was too pampered to work in a barn. She drew herself up straighter. She'd do her best to prove him wrong, whatever it took. Even if it meant shoveling horse poop.

He stopped at a door marked office and pushed it open. "We keep a few first aid supplies in here. Also, the number for the Clear Water Clinic is posted on the wall by the phone. Give them a quick call while I get the hydrogen peroxide, gauze, and salve." He waved toward the old-fashioned wall telephone then disappeared into a small room in the back.

Lindsey glanced around her, wondering if this was his office or used by someone else. She pulled a Kleenex out of a box on a shelf and dabbed at her arm. Better already.

A large wood desk sat against the side wall, with a tall file cabinet behind it and shelves lining two walls. They were filled with books and a couple of trophies. She stepped closer to one with a running horse and calf and peered at the plate on the base. Calf-roping championship, Steve Graham.

Her eyes widened. What had happened to the kid who'd blushed nearly every time he'd looked at her in high school? She'd liked him — even wished they could be friends, but she didn't have a clue how to talk to him. Steve had turned away back then, his face redder than ever. She'd already had a date when he asked her to the prom, but her friend had appeared, giggling about something that happened that day. Before Lindsey could explain, Steve had stalked off, shoulders thrown back and head high. He'd never tried to talk to her again.

She touched the trophy, then jerked her hand away as he stepped into the room. "Is this your office?"

"Yeah. Why do you ask?" His tone held a gruff edge.

Lindsey bristled. What was with him? He'd gone from scared kid to a man with a chip on his shoulder. "So, this trophy is yours? I didn't realize you were into rodeo."

He hunched a shoulder. "For a couple of years. I'd hoped to make a career of it, but it didn't work out." Bending his head, he began to rummage through the box he'd brought with him.

"What happened?" She pointed at the trophy. "This says you won a championship, so you must have been good."

"An injury. Nothing I care to talk about." He pulled several items from the box. "Let me get that cleaned up. Have you called the clinic to see when they can get you in?"

She bit her lip, unsure of how to deal with this. "Not yet. I'm just not sure . . ."

He shook his head and reached for the phone, scanning the list on the wall next to it, then punching in a series of numbers. "Hi, Claire, it's Steve Graham. We have a new employee who cut her arm out at the barn today, and she's not up on her shots. Can she come in this morning? A half hour? Great, I'll tell her, thanks." He hung up the phone and turned toward her. "You're all set. I'll show you on the map how to get there. It won't take long to run in and come back."

Lindsey drew in a deep breath and let it out slowly. It looked like it was time to swallow her pride. "Then I'll need to leave soon. I should be able to walk a couple of miles if you tell me where to go."

He scrunched his brows. "Why wouldn't you drive your car?"

She turned away, not wanting him to see her embarrassment. Now she was the one who felt like a gawky kid. Is this how it had been for Steve in high school? "I don't have one. But I remember Dixie saying I could use a company car if I needed to go to town, so I'll ask her."

"You have to sign up for that in advance, as there are only two, and they're often in use." He pointed at the chair next to his desk. "Sit down and let me disinfect that cut and stop the bleeding, then we'll figure out what to do."

"All right. Thanks." She could be gracious, even if she was nearly broke and didn't own a car. "Does the resort have a bike I could use?"

He plunked a first aid kit onto the desk. "Probably." A full minute passed as he opened a bottle of hydrogen peroxide and soaked a cotton ball. "This might sting. Hold still while I clean and wrap it. It looks like it bled enough to flush out the wound, but we can't be too careful."

She didn't flinch as he cleaned the cut, but she almost jumped from her chair when his knuckles made contact with her bare skin. What was wrong with her? Sure, he was handsome, and yeah, she'd thought he was nice when they were kids, but this was ridiculous. Besides, as far as he was concerned, she was an inept, spoiled city girl who'd already made her first mistake. He was probably already counting the hours until she did something else and he could send her packing. "Thanks." She shifted in her seat as he finished. "Hardly felt a thing. I'd better get going. Should I go to the office to ask about a bike?"

He scratched his chin then glanced at his watch. "Tell you what, I'll run you over there then come back and pick you up. Or better yet, I'll sit in the waiting room while you get your shot. It sounded like they'd get you right in."

Panic at being trapped in a car with him, even if it was for only a couple of miles, warred with relief that she didn't have to ride a bike over there. Not that she'd never ridden one before, but it had been years, and no matter what they said about never forgetting, she didn't need another accident on the heels of this one. "That's very nice of you, but I'm sure you're busy. Seriously, it's only a couple of miles. I can jog over there pretty quickly if I leave now, or grab one of the bikes."

He slid the first aid kit back in a cupboard. "Nope. Not busy at all at the moment. The season is barely getting started, and we don't have anyone coming in to ride today. We're mostly cleaning up, grooming the horses, and doing light maintenance." He walked toward the door and swung it open, giving her a slight smile. "Come on. No more argument. And your arm is apt to be sore after the shot, so you might not want to tackle riding a bike back to the barn."

She stood and walked toward him, trying not to let her body shiver at the thought of a needle plunging into her muscle. Who cared about a sore arm or a deep scratch, for that matter—sure, it had bled a bit, but it looked worse than it was—it wasn't like she'd need stitches or anything. The thought of even seeing a needle coming at her nearly made her sick to her stomach.

CHAPTER FOUR

STEVE INSERTED THE KEY AND WATCHED as Lindsey clicked the seatbelt into place. What was it with this woman? She'd gone all silent on him, and as soon as she could, she'd turned her head away. This was taking the whole stuck-up thing a bit too far, if you asked him. It wasn't like they were still teenagers.

He'd made a couple of attempts at conversation on the way to the car, and she'd kept her lips pressed tight. Lindsey Morgan needed to grow up and get over herself. He'd tried to help with her arm, made the appointment at the clinic and offered to drive her there and back, and all he got was cold silence. He gave a half shrug and swung the car out of the parking lot and onto the road. Whatever. If she didn't want to talk, he wouldn't push her.

Forty-five minutes later, he rose from his chair in the waiting room of the small country clinic as Lindsey exited an exam room and walked toward him. Her normally happy face appeared pinched and pale. Had they found something wrong while cleaning the wound and giving the shot? He stepped forward and held open the front door as she neared it. "Everything okay?"

She nodded but didn't reply, simply continued walking toward the car.

He took three long strides to catch up, not sure what was going on. This didn't feel right, but he still wasn't sure why. As she stepped off the curb in the parking lot, she wobbled and tipped sideways. Steve grabbed her arm and steadied her. "Whoa, there. I don't want you to move another step until you tell me what's wrong."

Lindsey simply shook her head and pinched her lips more tightly together, then blew out a puff of air. "I'm being a baby. I'm sorry. Can we get in the car before someone sees me?"

"Sure. But I'm not letting go until we get there." The sensation of her warm, soft skin under his palm almost made him break out in a sweat. He couldn't be attracted to this woman again—no way—he wouldn't allow his heart to get broken a second time. Of course, he'd been a foolish teenager back then, hoping for something that wasn't possible. But Lindsey Morgan was as much out of his league now as she'd been then—and well he knew it. Designer jeans, name-brand shoes, the whole works. Hadn't his last girlfriend made it all too apparent that a man working as a cowboy was a loser with nothing to offer? Lindsey came from a good family with a ton of money, and she'd never give him a second look.

He opened the door and waited until she seated herself, noticing the slight tremble of her body before he released her arm. Rushing to the other side, he worked to figure out the change that had come over Lindsey. She'd said she hated shots, but no one would react like this over something as small as a shot, would they?

She faced the side window, and he couldn't help but notice her hands gripped tightly in her lap and her shaking shoulders. Had he been too hard on her, pushing her to come to the clinic when she hadn't wanted to? But rules were rules, and it was for her own safety. Surely she could see that. He buckled his seatbelt and leaned toward her. "Are you angry with me that I forced you to come?"

"What?" She kept her gaze averted. "No. Not at all. It's not your fault I didn't watch where I was going and sliced my arm."

"Then what is it?" He tentatively touched the bandage on her arm. "Looks like they wrapped it up and did a nice job."

Lindsey turned her head and met his eyes. With a jolt he saw tears glistening there. "Lindsey? What is it? Did I do something wrong? Or did the doctor find something that upset you?"

She gave a weak laugh and shook her head. "None of the above. I feel like a silly goose is all. I've been sitting here thinking you'd fire me for sure, for being a sissy."

He sat back against his seat and stared. He had absolutely no idea what she was talking about. "If I promise I'm not going to fire you, will you please explain?" The anxiety oozing out of every pore made him want to reach over and hug her, but he held himself rigid. He wasn't taking that kind of chance.

"I suppose I should, even though you'll wonder how I'll be able to work at a barn after you hear me out." She drew in a deep breath and let it out slowly. "I almost fainted while the doctor worked on me. That's why I was shaky when I came out. Remember I told you I don't like shots?"

Steve nodded but didn't speak.

"Yeah. Well, I don't just not like them, I hate them. Shots, needles, anything like that. I'm not even sure why, although I suspect it goes back to one of my earliest memories of a nurse taking me away from my mother at the pediatrician's office and holding me down while the doctor gave me my shots." She shivered. "Silly, huh? That something so many years ago could impact me now? But honestly, as a little kid who didn't understand what was happening, I felt like that nurse was some evil monster trying to keep me away from my mom while the doctor tortured me. I saw that needle coming toward my arm, and I screamed. The nurse shushed me and almost shook me from frustration."

Steve stiffened. He knew how his mom would have reacted to that kind of treatment—grabbed him into her arms and told the nurse a thing or two. "How about your mother? Didn't she say anything?"

Lindsey gave a small shrug. "She's always been somewhat of a follower when it comes to authority—besides, she prefers to keep up appearances. The nurse told her to let her handle me, and it would be over faster. It's all burned into my memory. I didn't understand what was happening, and it's never left me. I see a needle now . . ." She wrapped her arms around herself and shivered. "Not only did I get a tetanus shot, but they had to deaden my arm so they could stitch it up." Biting her lip, she turned her head away.

Steve couldn't stand it a minute longer. He didn't dare hug her, but he had to do something. He gathered her small hand in his, noting how cold it felt, then started to rub it, not knowing what else to do. "I'm so sorry. If I'd known, I'd have gone in with you. Forgive me for not being more sensitive to you not wanting to come? I had no idea . . ."

She straightened, then suddenly seemed to realize he was holding her hand, and gently pulled it back to her lap. "It's not your fault. I'm an adult now, and I need to grow up and get past it—my gracious, people deal with so much worse, and they aren't scarred for life."

Steve gave her what he hoped was a comforting look. "Don't be so hard on yourself. A rattler almost struck me when I was a kid running down a hill. I barely cleared it as I launched myself into the air to miss stepping on it. I still turn to ice now whenever I see a snake."

Her eyes widened. "That's a whole lot worse than getting a shot. I'd be freaked, too." She glanced at her watch. "We probably should get back to work, right?"

He stuck his key in the ignition. Somehow he didn't want this conversation to end. He felt as though he'd never known the real Lindsey Morgan at all. She'd allowed him a glimpse into her heart, and in spite of his resolve to not get involved again with a girl who'd been the belle of the ball, he wanted nothing more than to learn what made this lovely girl tick.

CHAPTER FIVE

A WEEK LATER, LINDSEY STOOD IN the large, airy barn, watching an instructor giving a child a lesson in the arena. She'd always thought it might be fun to ride a horse, but she'd never had the opportunity. Besides, they were much bigger and more intimidating in person than they appeared to be in pictures. Oh well, time to get back to shoveling stalls. She pivoted, then grabbed the handlebars of the wheelbarrow she'd parked off to the side, and took a step forward.

"Ugh! What did I step in?" Something slid under her foot, and she didn't even want to look. "Please, don't let it be horse poop." She whispered the words under her breath, not wanting anyone to hear—after all, she did work in a barn where droppings abounded—but somehow she's been able to avoid stepping in it. She lowered her gaze to her new tennis shoe.

Until now.

The horse in the arena had been tied in what Steve called cross-ties—two ropes snapped, one each, to a post on each side of the alleyway running in front of the stalls. A rider could bring their mount out of its stall and saddle or groom the horse in the alleyway, as long as they were willing to move if another horse needed to come through. Lindsey hadn't even thought about the mare—at least, she thought it was a mare—depositing a little gift while it stood there not ten minutes ago. That was what she got for leaning on the half-wall separating the spacious arena from the alleyway and daydreaming, instead of paying attention to her work.

She wheeled to a stop in front of the next empty and still dirty stall, then slid open the door. In fact, the stall belonged to the mare being ridden in the arena. Trundling the wheelbarrow containing a pick for cleaning shavings into the stall, she tried to ignore the glob on the bottom of her foot. She'd scrape it off once she got out of sight. Lindsey glanced at her watch and groaned. She shouldn't have spent so much time watching that rider, as it had put her behind schedule. She'd barely have time to finish this stall before the instructor brought the lesson horse back.

Oops. She'd forgotten the rake outside the last stall she'd cleaned. She wrinkled her nose, debating whether to take the time to scrape off her shoe first or dash down the alleyway and do it when she returned. That would be best—she might step in another pile, anyway. Blasting through the door with her mind on making up for lost time, she kept her eyes on the ground, determined to watch where she stepped this time—until she saw a pair of cowboy boots and tried to slow.

"Hey!" The deep, masculine voice hit her ears right before she impacted with a solid chest.

Lindsey stumbled and felt strong hands grip her shoulders as her manure clogged foot came down on top of a clean cowboy boot. She didn't even want to look up. How many times could she make herself look foolish in the course of a few days? Please, Lord, don't let it be Steve. Anyone but Steve. But of course, she already knew that voice. She sighed.

Slowly she raised her gaze and met the inquisitive, slightly humorous gaze of her boss. Yep. Steve. "Sorry, boss. I was watching where I was going, really I was, only . . . only . . ." She bit her lip. How to explain she'd hoped to avoid stepping in another pile, and that had been more important to her than not running into a client—or her boss. "I'm afraid I've ruined your nice shiny boots."

A chuckle broke from between his lips, and Lindsey's eyes flew to his. "Why would you laugh at that? It's all over my shoe, and I stepped on your boot." She tried to suppress a shudder but didn't quite succeed. "Personally, I don't think it's particularly funny." Nor was the fact that he was still gripping her shoulders as though he thought she'd fall if he released her. Well, maybe she would, based on how things had been going, but she wasn't going to act even more the silly goose than she'd done already. She took a step back.

Steve released her, the chuckle replaced by a grin. "When you've been raised on a ranch, you don't worry too much about your footgear and what gets on it. Or should I say, what you step on. It's not the first time I've had to clean these boots."

She shrugged. "If you say so. I certainly can't see anything humorous in the situation, but to each his own." She gave an inward groan as soon as the words left her lips. Why did she always have to say something snippy to this man, when what she wanted to do was make a good impression? He'd formed a bad enough opinion of her when they were seniors in high school. There was certainly no reason to strengthen it now and prove he'd been right.

Although for the life of her, she still didn't understand why he'd snubbed her so completely after asking her to the prom. Sure, she'd told him no, but she'd already had a date. She'd secretly kind of liked Steve. He'd been one of the most down-to-earth, honest, cute guys she'd known, even if he was a bit aloof.

Steve's face lost the relaxed smile from a moment before, and he raised one brow. "So what's the hurry? You came flying out of that stall like something was pursuing you."

Lindsey felt warmth rush into her cheeks. "Uh, yeah. Sorry. Again. I got a little behind schedule when I . . . well, never mind that . . ." She pushed a tendril of hair that came loose from her ponytail out of her face. "I forgot the rake at the last stall. I wanted to make up for lost time, so I figured I'd run down and grab it and run back." She started to dart around him. "Excuse me, I'll get back to work." After two fast steps, she skidded to a halt. "Would you like me to clean your boots? It's the least I can do."

He took one stride toward her, closing the distance until he was almost invading her personal space. "So . . . what got you behind schedule? Not that it's a big deal, although we do like to have the stalls clean before the horses come back, but I'm curious. Did you have a problem this morning?"

What should she tell him? That she'd always been afraid of horses, but intrigued and drawn to them at the same time? That would sound stupid to a man raised on a ranch and practically born on a horse, from what she'd been able to see. "Um, not a problem exactly." She flicked her fingers in the air. "It's no big deal. I should get back to work. The riding instructor will have the lesson horse back soon."

Steve shook his head. "Nope. There's another lesson after this one. We rarely book only one, and we try to put them back to back, so the horse doesn't have to be tacked up twice."

Lindsey scrunched her brows. Oh yeah. He meant saddled and bridled. "Right. Okay then." She started to move away.

He held up his hand. "Hold it. You didn't answer my question. You said 'not a problem exactly,' which doesn't tell me a thing. Please explain." He leaned his shoulder against a nearby post and crossed his arms. "This is your boss asking."

Lindsey kept from rolling her eyes. Not a cool thing to do to your boss, especially after mucking up his clean boots. But she couldn't keep from glancing down.

He gave a hoot of laughter. "Quit worrying about my boots! And by the way, I'd suggest you wear the oldest, rattiest pair of shoes you own, until you can buy a pair of boots. There's no sense in ruining a good pair. Besides, it's safer wearing boots in case you ever get stepped on."

Her eyes rounded in surprise. "Stepped on? You mean, by one of the horses? Yikes! That could break my foot!"

"If they only stepped on one toe, yeah, it could. But if you have boots on, they generally protect your foot enough that you'd only get bruised at worst. And you learn pretty quickly to watch your feet and theirs, as well as how to move them backwards quickly if they do make a misstep. Now. Please answer my question."

Lindsey's heartrate increased as she looked into his intense eyes. All she wanted was to run for the rake and not look back. "It was stupid." She shook her head emphatically. "And now that you told me about getting stepped on, I don't think I'd ever want to, anyway."

He straightened and let his arms fall to his sides. "Want to what, Lindsey? Out with it. What does wanting something have to do with running behind on your work?" He held up his hand, palm out. "Wait. Before you answer that, let me assure you that you are not in trouble. When you work around animals, all sorts of delays can happen, and we factor that into the schedule. Go ahead. You were saying?"

There was no help for it. She sighed. "Ride a horse."

He gave her a blank stare. "Ride a horse." He gave a slight shake of his head. "I don't get it. What does that have to do with anything?"

Now she did roll her eyes. "And I'm getting even farther behind schedule while we talk about something that doesn't matter." Her hand flew to her mouth. "Oh my. I'm sorry."

"Y..e..s..s? And? Explain please."

"Fine." She planted her hands on her hips. "I was watching the instructor and wondering what it would be like to ride."

"You've never ridden a horse?" He removed his hat and slapped it against his leg, then placed it back on his head. "Of course you haven't. You were Miss Cheerleader and one of the most popular, richest girls in school, about the farthest thing from a cowgirl I'd ever met. So, before you came here—had you even touched a horse before?"

Lindsey bristled at his slightly sarcastic tone. What was with this guy? He was all grins and chuckles one minute, then appeared to be making fun of her in the next. "No. I was raised in town and never had the chance." She took a step around him. This time she was getting that rake and no one was stopping her. "I really do need to get back to work, so if you'll excuse me?" She didn't give him a chance to reply but marched down the alleyway to where she'd left the rake propped against a wall. That wasn't smart, either. A horse could have stepped on the tines and been slapped with the handle, causing an accident or injury to the horse or rider. When would she ever learn?

She grasped the rake and swiveled, squaring her shoulders to meet his disapproving gaze, but Steve had disappeared in the time it took her to walk a few yards. Was he completely disgusted that he'd been forced to hire someone who kept making mistakes and who'd never been near a horse? Probably. But at this point she didn't care. She gritted her teeth and strode toward the dirty stall waiting to be cleaned. She'd make good here and prove she wasn't a helpless imbecile. In fact, she'd even see that Steven Graham ate the words he'd said to Dixie when she'd told him the name of his new employee.

CHAPTER SIX

THE FOLLOWING WEEK, STEVE WAITED IN his office until he'd seen Lindsey push the last load of dirty shavings down the alleyway to the refuse pile, then slipped out and across the arena. The second lesson was well under way now, and he needed to talk to the instructor.

Thirty minutes later, with the horse tied in the stall, he went looking for Lindsey. It was nearing the end of her shift, and she might be too tired for what he had in mind, but he had to try. He could barely fathom someone wishing they could ride a horse—not to mention never having the chance to touch one during all her growing up years. All week he hadn't been able to get it out of his mind. Hadn't her parents ever taken her to the county fair, for Pete's sake?

"Lindsey." He found her perched on a bale of straw in front of a stall. No sign of the wheelbarrow. "Done for the day?"

She nodded and started to stand.

He waved her down. "Sit. You've done a lot of work today for a rookie." He sucked in a breath and said something that two weeks ago, he'd never believed would come out of his mouth. "I'm proud of you. I honestly didn't think you'd make it this far."

Guilt flooded him when he saw the look of shock replaced by pleasure that suffused her face. He'd been a jerk when she'd come that first day, but it had been so hard, remembering what Janney, one of Lindsey's friends, had said after he'd asked Lindsey to the prom. She'd found him at his locker after everyone else had gone to class, and told him, sweetly and as though she really cared, that Lindsey thought he was a nice little country bumpkin, but she'd never give him the time of day.

She assured him that, while he *was* a nice guy, he wasn't Lindsey's type, and if he didn't want to be even more embarrassed in the future, he should leave well-enough alone. She'd left with what appeared to be a genuine smile, after giving his hand a gentle squeeze. The balance of the year, Janney had put out an effort to be kind, and even acted interested, and it wasn't long after graduation that they started dating.

He pushed the memory to the back of his mind, not wanting to revisit yet another painful event. After Janney, he'd sworn off girls for a long time, and even now the idea of getting serious didn't appeal. Not that he didn't have hopes and dreams like a lot of guys to get married someday. He held out his hand to the only girl who'd ever really impacted his heart in a way he found hard to forget. "Actually, if you don't mind coming with me, I've got something I'd like to show you."

She gazed at him for a long moment, uncertainty hovering over her face, then she placed her hand in his and allowed him to pull her to her feet. Awareness jolted him at her touch. He'd worked hard to get Lindsey Morgan out of his life, and here she stood next to him, still holding his hand as though she belonged. He released her and took a step back. "Ready?"

"Since I have no idea what you're talking about, I'm not sure if I am or not." She gave him a tentative smile. "But sure. Lead the way."

LINDSEY FOLLOWED STEVE DOWN the alleyway, her hand still tingling from his grip. A sense of safety and belonging had surrounded her in those few seconds before he let go, something she'd not had a lot of as a child. Growing up in a wealthy family wasn't all it was cracked up to be, especially when your father was a top-notch, wealthy executive who was rarely ever home, and your mom enjoyed spending time with her ritzy social circle more than her own daughter. Then there were the trips around the world when she was a child and leaving her to be raised by a nanny.

That was another reason Lindsey refused any financial help as an adult. They still wanted to interfere in her life, as they'd done all the way through high school and college. But their idea of life was making the social rounds among the jet set. She'd finally grown a backbone and told them she'd decided to discover who she wanted to be and who God meant her to be. They definitely didn't get that.

She'd be forever grateful to her college roommate for introducing her to Jesus during her freshman year. It had taken the first two years to figure out there was more to life than being a socialite, following in her mother's footsteps. But once her friend introduced her to the Lord, that was it. She'd closed the door on her past, while still hoping to show her parents how she'd changed and what made the difference. They didn't get it, and she wasn't sure they ever would. At this point, all she could do was love them and pray.

Steve stopped in front of an open stall door.

Lindsey halted beside him, wondering what she was supposed to see. "Uh—the horse is still saddled and in his stall. Isn't that the lesson horse? Did you want me to unsaddle him and rub him down?"

Steve raised his brows at her and shook his head. "Nope. He's all yours for the next thirty minutes, then I'll help you untack him and put him away when we're done."

"Mine?" Her voice squeaked on the word. "Why would I want a horse for thirty minutes? What am I supposed to do with him?" Her heart pounded in her chest—whether out of excitement or fear, she wasn't sure. Horses weren't quite as scary as when she'd first arrived, but she'd yet to unsaddle or lead one completely alone. The thought gave her the shivers.

Steve grinned. "I'm going to give you a riding lesson. Your very first, right? You said you'd always wanted to try, so I'm going to make it happen."

Lindsey took a step back, unsure how to respond. From the look on his face, Steve thought he'd handed her the moon. She hadn't even said she'd always wanted to ride, only that she wondered what it would be like. That didn't mean she was *ready* to climb up on this giant beast and maybe fall off. Uh-uh, no way. She took another step toward the middle of the alleyway. "Um, I'm supposed to be working, right? I mean, I don't really have time for this, and I'm sure you're busy too. Maybe another time?" She could have bitten her tongue at that last sentence. Why give him an option of there ever being another time? Scary wasn't the word for considering climbing onto that tall back.

His grin slowly faded, and he leaned against a post, not removing his gaze from hers. "You're frightened, aren't you." It wasn't a question. He must be able to read her face like a roadmap.

"Well . . ." She bit her lip, attempting to stuff down the anxiety threatening to choke her. "I guess riding looked interesting from a distance, but . . ." She waved her hand toward the gelding . . . "he's just so big when you get up close."

Steve straightened and reached out his hand. "Give me your hand."

She folded her arms across her chest. "Why?" She wasn't going to get tricked into entering that stall and getting on that horse. No way.

"Please trust me. I won't do anything that will hurt you."

"All right. I guess." She placed her hand in his and felt his strong, warm one close around hers. "Now what?"

"Move closer to me."

"To you? Not to the horse?"

"Yes. To me."

"I guess I can do that." She shot him a quick grin and moved up beside him. "Although you have your scary moments as well, you know."

He laughed, and the sound unthawed her partly frozen heart. "Right. Do you see old Soldier here? He's almost asleep. Does he really look that bad?"

She gazed at the horse with his head drooped almost to his knees, his eyes nearly closed, his breathing even. "I guess he doesn't seem like he's going to buck or kick or bite or anything. Yet."

Steve shook his head. "How did you manage to move a horse out of the stall before you cleaned it?"

She tried to suppress a slight shiver and almost succeeded. "I keep saying over and over, I'll go to heaven if I die, I'll go to heaven if I die. And I always pray before I enter the stall. Besides, I can usually wait and clean most of them after an instructor or trail leader takes them out."

Now his brows nearly reached his hairline. "You're a Christian? Or are you being facetious?"

She stiffened and tried to remove her hand from his grasp, but his grip tightened. "Just because I was a silly cheerleader in high-school doesn't mean I couldn't change. My college roommate led me to the Lord, and it changed my life completely."

"Wow." His voice was so soft she almost missed the word. "I had no idea."

"Why? Are you?"

He nodded. "And I'm sorry if my attitude or actions since you've arrived haven't reflected that fact. And I'm sorry if you felt I was calling you a silly cheerleader. I was raised in a Christian home, but I struggled to maintain my faith during high school. Then later, something tough happened that made me take a hard look at my life, and I recommitted my life to the Lord." He drew her closer to the horse who still stood with his head down, practically snoring. "Come on. If I help you and show you what to do, and promise I'll stay right by your side through every minute. Will you at least try?"

She couldn't shake the awareness of her hand still gripped in his. Or the depth of his warm eyes as he gazed down, his face entreating, willing her to say yes. How could she deny this man when he was trying to make her happy—even if it was slightly misguided. She sighed. "All right. If you promise. But I have a question first." It was difficult to believe this man was the same kid she'd known in high school.

His smile had returned. "Sure."

"What happened to you?"

CHAPTER SEVEN

STEVE ALLOWED THE FOUR WORDS TO bounce around inside his brain for several seconds, trying to decipher their meaning, before he replied. "Excuse me? I don't follow? When? What?"

Lindsey's cheeks turned a softer pink than usual, and she averted her gaze. "Since I saw you last." She sucked in a long breath and faced him again. "You were a shy, skinny kid with few muscles and even less confidence. You were always nice, and kinda cute, but . . ." The color deepened in her cheeks.

He almost laughed at that last part, but he didn't want to scare her off. "Uh-huh. But now? I'm what?"

She shook her head and tried to pull away, but he didn't let go. She'd taken this too far, and he intended to see it through to the end, come what may. "A totally different person." She blurted the words. "I mean, I get it that people can put on weight and work out, but your personality changed. You're in charge of this barn, you seem to know what you're doing and what you want out of life, unlike me. And you're not a bit shy anymore." This time she succeeded in removing her hand, and Steve instantly felt the loss.

He cocked a grin at her. "Am I still kinda cute, or . . ."

Lindsey swatted his arm. "I am *not* answering that. But maybe I'll add conceited to the new list. But hey, our lesson time is speeding by—not that I mind, but I probably should get to work instead of bombarding you with questions. Besides, I know it's none of my business. It's not like we were ever friends, or anything."

He sobered. "No, we weren't, were we? Although I would have liked to be at one time." But that wasn't a door he intended to open again, without a lot of encouragement from Lindsey, and he didn't see that happening. Her friend had made it clear what Lindsey thought of him. "I don't mind telling you, but I'm going to give you the short version, if that's okay?"

She shrugged, trying to appear nonchalant, but he could see the gleam of interest in her eyes. "Sure. Like I said, not really my business, so don't tell me at all if you'd rather not."

Steve bumped her with his shoulder. "Don't go getting up on your high horse, lady. It isn't that big of a deal. I worked on the ranch doing chores all my life, but after we graduated, I worked full-time for my dad for a couple of years. I grew a few inches those two years, and packed on muscle tossing hay bales and toting grain bags—more than I had while I was growing a blue streak through high school. I figured I'd take over the full operation someday and needed to learn all I could. But Dad had other plans. He said Grandpa had just assumed Dad would run the family ranch, and Dad never had the opportunity to go out on his own and discover what he wanted to do with his life. Dad didn't want the same for me. He wanted it to be my decision, but only after I did something else for a few years."

Lindsey leaned against the post opposite him and nodded. "Right. So he kicked you out of the nest?"

"Yeah, with me kicking and screaming. All I ever wanted to do was ranch. But he said I couldn't come back to work for him for eight years." He hunched a shoulder. "That was seven years ago—almost eight, as I'm sure you know. After I left the ranch I decided to try my hand at rodeo and discovered I was good at it, especially calf roping. Dad taught me to toss a loop as a kid, and I was always roping something on the ranch. I had to start on weight training to build my muscles and started running to keep up my stamina. The rodeo life is actually more strenuous than you might think."

She nodded. "I can't even imagine. So an injury sidelined you? Was that super disappointing?"

"Yeah. I rode the rodeo circuit for three years, and worked at physical therapy for another, trying to recover from surgery after I tore my rotor cuff. I never got the full strength back in my arm—at least, not what I'd need for all the hours of practice I had to put in throwing a rope to lasso the calf, not to mention throwing and tying a calf. I landed this job not long after." He had no intention of telling her about dating

Janney for the two years he'd spent working on the ranch. He always wondered if she'd thought he'd inherit and have money one day, because she dumped him when he went into rodeo. He'd never quite figured her out. One minute he thought he was in love and had a future with her, and the next his head was spinning at the speed she'd departed. No way would he get suckered like that again.

"I'm sorry to hear that. But I can't imagine being on the road all the time with the rodeo was a comfortable life. Now that the eight years is almost up, I suppose you'll return to the ranch?"

Was that a glint he saw in her eyes? Right on the heels of thinking about Janney's actions and attitude, and Lindsey had to say that. Sure, his dad had a big ranch by any standards, and their family made good money, but that wasn't why he wanted to go back. He loved the life, and after Janney, he'd made the decision he'd never marry someone who couldn't be happy in the country. And from all appearances, that definitely wouldn't be Lindsey.

He reeled his thoughts in, shocked at the direction they'd taken. Whoa now. He had no plans to marry anytime soon, even if she did meet the criteria of being a Christian, which still surprised him. "I'm not sure. I mean, I haven't talked to my dad about it recently, to see if he still wants me or if there's even a place for me. It's been a long time."

She touched his arm, and electricity traveled straight to his heart. "But you're his son. It wouldn't matter if he'd hired ten people to take your place, I'm sure you'll always come first." She gave a wry laugh. "Unlike my family."

His head jerked up. "Your family? But your mom and dad are wealthy, right? I can't imagine you lacked for anything growing up." Certainly not from what he'd seen in the four years they'd been in high school together. She'd always been the envy of the other girls, with her expensive clothes and later, a fast car. It hadn't only been her looks that made the boys swarm around her. He was stupid to think he had a chance with her.

"Wrong. I got pretty much anything I wanted from them, except the one thing that mattered most."

He met her gaze full on this time and held it there. "And what was that?"

"Their love and acceptance." She bit her lip and turned her head. "Now shouldn't we get to that lesson? It's getting late."

Steve felt as though he'd been punched in the gut. His parents hadn't given him a lot, even though they probably could have, because they wanted him to learn the value of work and earning a wage for himself. But he'd never lacked for love. He reached out to touch her hand, but she drew away. Better not push it. This wasn't the time or the place, and the last thing he wanted right now was another rejection.

CHAPTER EIGHT

THIRTY MINUTES LATER, LINDSEY WAS STILL burning with humiliation at how much she'd revealed to Steve, but he'd been so nice. She shoved the memory away and concentrated on the final instruction he was giving her.

"All right, I'm going to wrap the lead rope around the saddle horn, and you're going to sit there exactly as you've done since you got on. Nice and relaxed, allowing your body to move slightly with his motion as he walks. You're doing great!"

Panic welled up inside. "You can't let go of the lead rope. What if he runs away on me?"

Steve chuckled. "Have you noticed I've had a totally loose rope for the last ten minutes? Since you picked up the reins, you've been doing it all yourself, anyway. Trust me, Lindsey, you can do this. I'll stay right beside you after I loop the rope around the horn."

She worked hard not to hyperventilate. "Why beside me and not next to his head? Don't you need to grab him if he starts to run, or whatever it is they do when they aren't walking?"

Steve laughed outright this time. "Quit worrying. Soldier is tired. Believe me, you'd have to really urge him to get him to move out of that walk and into a trot. I'll stay beside you to give you more confidence, but I want you to keep doing what you're doing. Keep the reins steady, sit up straight, look between his ears, and take slow, deep breaths. Okay?"

She gave a quick nod. "Right. Okay. I can do this."

"Tug on the reins and ask him to stop."

"All right." She pulled back and Soldier instantly stopped. "Hey! He did what I asked him to! And it wasn't even hard."

"Exactly what I've been trying to tell you all along. You got onboard beautifully using the mounting block, you have very steady hands on the reins, you haven't accidently booted him in the side with your heels once—I'm telling you, Lindsey—you're a natural at this—if you can get past your fear, you're going to enjoy riding. I'm proud of you."

Lindsey beamed. All her father had ever done, the occasional time he was home, was criticize. Her music was too loud, her friends were too messy, she ate too much. It didn't take long to learn to fade into the background and leave him alone—and starve herself from time-to-time in hopes he'd notice. He didn't. She couldn't remember a single time he'd praised her or told her he was proud of her. What an amazing feeling. She could get used to this. She shot a look at Steve as he looped the lead rope around the horn. If only . . . dare she allow herself to dream about this man? "Thank you. I'm not as frightened as I was to start." She reached forward and stroked Soldier's neck. "He's a nice horse, and I'm glad you insisted I try to ride him."

He patted her leg. "Well, I didn't insist, you agreed. I wouldn't have forced you to do it, but I'm glad you did. Now, squeeze his sides with your calves and cluck to him like I showed you. And keep your reins just about that length. Good."

She concentrated on following his instructions, but her mind wanted to keep straying back to his hand touching her leg and his fingers brushing hers when he'd placed the rope around the horn. Somehow she must have pressed too hard, because Soldier suddenly moved out faster than his normal slow walk. She let out a squeal. "Steve! Stop him. He's going to run away."

"No, he's not, he's simply doing a slow trot. You're fine. Stay relaxed and move with his stride."

Every muscle in her body did the opposite and froze up. Soldier came down with a slightly harder stride, and her body lurched to the side as her foot slipped out of the stirrup. She released the reins and launched herself at Steve, certain the horse would tromp on her leg if she hit the ground. "Help!"

All she saw was his wide eyes before his arms wrapped around her, and he pulled her close.

STEVE'S BLOOD THUNDERED THROUGH his veins as he held the shaking girl in his embrace. He'd barely kept his balance when she'd flown out of the saddle, and he couldn't believe he'd caught her and they were both standing. "Lindsey, are you okay?" He took a half-step back, but kept an arm around her shoulders as he used his other hand to brush a wisp of hair out of her eyes.

She nodded and tried to smile. "Yes, I'm fine, thanks to you."

"Whatever possessed you to jump off?"

She withdrew, breaking the contact with his arms and leaving him feeling alone. "I'm sorry. I thought Soldier was going to run, then my foot came out of the stirrup on the other side, and I started to bounce. I guess I panicked. I'm afraid I'm not exactly the natural you thought, huh?" Her chin was quivering as though she were going to cry.

"Hey, don't be so hard on yourself." He reached out and gave her a quick hug then stepped away. "I meant what I said about being a natural and being proud of you." He'd seen the look of amazed gratitude when he'd uttered those words not long ago, and he didn't want her to think he planned to take them back.

"I guess we'd better unsaddle him and get to work, huh." She scuffed her toe in the dirt of the arena.

"Nope. There's a rule of riding that every beginner has to learn, and we might as well start now. If you fall off, and you're not seriously hurt, you have to get right back on."

"You mean now?" Lindsey's eyes widened.

"Yep. No delay. If you don't, then this episode will grow in your mind and become way bigger than it is. You don't have to ride any more, but you do need to get on, sit there, relax, then get off. Think you can do that?" He studied her closely, praying she wouldn't bolt for the exit. Lindsey had been nothing but game since taking this job, and he hoped he wasn't pushing too hard.

"To tell you the truth, I do feel a bit silly. Soldier didn't do anything wrong, and I got scared for nothing. But I'm not sure about getting on again." She looked from him to the horse. "Only for a couple of minutes?"

Pride filled him at her guts and determination. "Yes. I won't make you stay on longer if you don't want to." He led Soldier to the center of the ring to the mounting block and waited for her to catch up.

A couple of minutes later, she sat in the saddle as though she'd never left it. "Now what do I do? Just sit here?"

He gave her what he hoped was a reassuring smile. "If that's all you want to do, it's fine. Totally up to you."

She pursed her lips for a moment. "I want to walk him forward a few steps. Is that okay?"

Joy blossomed in his chest. "Absolutely! Now this time, squeeze very gently, and make sure you don't bump him with your heels."

She followed his instructions and rode Soldier around the entire perimeter of the large indoor ring with Steve walking beside her, then reined him to a halt, grinning. "I did it. And it felt much better this time. Can we ride again someday?"

Steve wanted to pull her off the horse and back into his arms, but he controlled himself and simply smiled. "You bet. Anytime you want to, let me know, and I'll find time for another lesson. You're going to make a first rate rider before long."

CHAPTER NINE

A FEW WEEKS LATER, STEVE WAS even more amazed at the progress Lindsey was making. She'd ridden several more times, and each time she'd grown in confidence as her fear had lessened. He'd heard her laugh more often, not to mention the way she'd joked with him. He could talk to her more easily than anyone he'd ever met—and they'd lingered more than once after work, sitting on hay bales, talking over their day, and occasionally, shared things from their lives. Why had he ever thought this young woman was a stuck-up rich girl? He still had reservations, after the fiasco with his last girlfriend, but somehow he felt the Lord was opening his heart to Lindsey. The question was, did she have any feelings for him?

He hadn't asked the question he was dreading—what were her plans and where would she go when the fall riding season ended? Back to the city? And did she feel that was where she truly belonged? There was no way he'd ever live in a city, and he was still praying about returning home to help his dad run the ranch.

Best to take one day at a time where Lindsey, and his future, were concerned. Sure, they'd known each other all the way back to junior high, but this was the first true relationship they'd had a chance to develop, since they'd gone their separate ways after high school. He returned his attention to the bridle he was oiling. Having all the lesson equipment in top condition was high on his list of priorities.

"Steve?" The HR manager's voice swung him around. Her face wore an expectant look, as though she had news to share. "Do you have a minute? I'd like to talk to you privately in my office."

"Sure. Let me put this up, and I'll be right there."

She gave a small wave of acknowledgement and headed out the tack room door.

Steve took a little longer than he needed to replace the cap on the can of oil, hanging the cleaning rag on a peg, and returning the bridle to its place. In spite of Dixie's relaxed appearance, he couldn't shove down a sense of dread, which didn't make a bit of sense. He'd never known Dixie to be rude or uncaring with the resort's employees, and he'd been told she was the best Human Resources head they'd ever hired—but she'd never appeared unannounced in the barn, either. *No reason to put this off any longer.* He strode down the alleyway at a quick pace, hoping Dixie wouldn't be annoyed at the delay.

She stood next to the coffee pot, a mug poised in the air, her brows raised as she watched him enter. "Is this decaf, or something with a bit more of a jolt?"

He couldn't hold back a laugh at the serious tone of her voice. "It's the real thing. I don't make it strong enough to curl your toes, as not all our clients like it that way, but it should do." He left the door slightly ajar, so he could hear if anyone called for him, then he headed across the room to join her.

"Good." Her smile hadn't returned.

His heart sank. So it was bad news, and she'd been putting on a happy face in case any clients were in the vicinity. "I hope you won't mind if I don't chit-chat. You've got me curious, since you rarely visit the barn. What's up?"

She inclined her head, took a sip of the hot coffee, released a sigh that sounded like contentment, and sank into a nearby chair. "I don't have a lot of time to spare, either. Have a seat? I'm not comfortable with you hovering over me." Her lips gave a slight up tilt. "You're too tall."

He snorted but sat. "Like that would bother you. I've seen you boss bigger men than me, when they tried to get out of line."

She gave a sheepish grin. "Guilty as charged. All right, I'll get straight to the point. One of the employees in our restaurant is quitting in a few days. She wasn't the best waitress we employed, so the manager of the staff there isn't too heartbroken, but it will leave a hole."

Steve chuckled and leaned back in his chair, placing one booted foot across his other knee. "So you think I'd make a good waitress, huh? Sorry, that's not quite in my wheelhouse."

Dixie's eyes sparkled. "What I wouldn't give to see you in one of the waiter uniforms." She sobered. "But no, that's not why I'm here. I understand Jon's broken wrist is healing well. He called yesterday and told me he'd like to return to work soon. Maybe in another week or two. He can't do heavy lifting, but he can help the instructors, groom horses with his other hand, and do odd jobs. I doubt it would be long after he returns before he'd be back to full strength."

Steve's tense shoulders started to relax. "Sounds good to me. We have plenty to do around here, and it's always nice to have another set of hands—even one hand for now, until he's able to use both. As far as I'm concerned, he's welcome." He started to push up from his chair. "That was easy."

She held up her hand. "I'm not finished. As I recall, your newest employee, Lindsey, was emphatic about not wanting to work here when I hired her. She came believing she had a job in the gift shop, and I had to break the news to her after she arrived that the girl we thought we were losing wasn't leaving after all. I had nothing else open at the time besides this position with you." She spread her hands wide. "Now I do."

Steve stared, unable to take in what she'd shared. Dixie wanted him to let Lindsey go? What if he didn't want to?

"I see I've taken you by surprise, but as I recall, you were not happy that I sent her to you. In fact, you made it quite clear you felt she was unsuited for the job and wouldn't last long. I believe she'd be much happier earning steady, good tips and working as a waitress in a quality restaurant, than mucking stalls. Don't you?"

Steve's head was spinning. He didn't know what to think, but he blurted out the first thing he could think of that wouldn't sound too contradictory to what he'd told Dixie when he'd taken Lindsey on. "Uh, yeah. She's worked out better here than I'd expected, but I'm guessing she would be a lot more suited as a waitress with her background."

"So it's settled. She'll come to work at the restaurant as soon as Jon returns next week."

Steve hesitated several long seconds. He hated this. Hated

everything about it. He didn't want to lose Lindsey. Didn't want her somewhere he'd rarely, if ever see her, unless he took his meals there and sat at her table. They'd never get to talk anymore—he couldn't continue giving her lessons. And what about *her* feelings? Was there a chance she might not want to take the job?

He slumped as the next thought hit him. Of course, she'd want it. She'd only worked here because she didn't have a choice. She was a city girl, after all, not a ranch-bred girl. What more could he expect? But regardless, he still needed to give her a chance to make the decision for herself. "No." He shook his head. "It's not settled yet. I'll give you a decision in no more than three days." That would at least buy him a little more time with her.

Dixie's mouth pulled down in a frown. "I don't see why that's necessary."

Steve struggled to come up with something more plausible. "Lindsey needs to make this decision, not me. She's grown a lot in this job and faced some of her fears with horses. It might not be the best time for her to leave. I've noticed a different attitude the past few weeks, and she's become a steady, dependable employee." Now it was his turn to hold up his hand before Dixie could interrupt. "I'll keep an eye on her for a couple of days, then I'll talk to her—see how she feels about working here, and if she'd like a change. I'll tell her about the other position opening up. Since Jon's not returning for a week and the waitress isn't leaving yet, we have time, right?"

"I suppose, if that's the way you feel you want to handle the situation. But I'll need an answer within three days, tops. If Lindsey doesn't want the waitress job, I'll check with the employment agency and see if they can send someone out who's suitable. Plus, I'd prefer Lindsey have a few days training before we throw her to the mercy of our more particular patrons."

"Right." He nodded and rose to his feet, then another thought hit him. "You said if she doesn't want the job—what then? Is there enough in the budget to allow her to stay here and still have Jon come back, along with the other two part-time employees who help clean stalls and take horses out to pasture and back? I've pretty much taken Lindsey off stall-mucking duty, and given her other jobs with more responsibility. I don't feel comfortable handing those off to one of the temp workers."

She gave a slow nod. "If Lindsey decides this is where she wants to be, then we'll probably cut one of the temp workers. She and Jon will have to share their chores, but that's up to you. Structure it how you'd like, it's your barn, not mine." A genuine smile lit her eyes. "We're blessed to have you, Steve. And I'm praying this won't be the last season you're in charge of the barn."

"Sorry. I don't follow." While relief at her decision about Lindsey had eased his mind, it now started to whirl, trying to decipher her newest declaration. "Why wouldn't I?"

Dixie spread the newspaper on the desk that she'd kept tucked under her arm. "I assumed you'd seen this. You might want to read it before you do anything else." She gave him a warm look then pivoted and left the office.

CHAPTER TEN

LINDSEY'S HAND FELL BACK TO HER side. No way was she knocking on that door after what she'd heard inside. Clearly Dixie and Steve were discussing her, and the last thing out of Steve's mouth had been, "I'm guessing she would be a lot more suited as a waitress with her background," and Dixie's clear reply that it was settled.

Disappointment warred with anger as she strode down the alleyway to her next assigned job. She'd finished the last horse sooner than she'd expected, and she'd wanted to ask Steve when he thought they might schedule the next lesson. Riding wasn't nearly as scary as she'd thought at first, and in fact, she was riding around the perimeter with Steve staying in the middle and had even tried a trot a couple of times.

But apparently that was over, along with her job. She stopped in front of the next stall and kicked a small pebble out of the way. Maybe she should march back in there and tell them she didn't want to quit—they couldn't force her to be a waitress, could they?

Surprise hit her like a slap in the face of a horse's tail swatting at a fly. Sudden and unexpected. Since *when* didn't she want to quit working in this barn? She'd hated the idea of giving up the gift shop position and resented being sent here. In fact, she'd done a little waitress work on summer vacations between her college years and actually enjoyed it—not to mention the extra income from tips that a place like this was apt to generate.

Since Steve gave her that compliment about riding and told her he was proud of her, that's when. Not only that, but his kindness, and the gentle understanding in his eyes when she'd almost fainted after the tetanus shot—her entire attitude had changed from proving herself to an antagonistic boss, to making this man proud of her. This man she was coming to care for more than she should. Their lives were too different—he was right when he said someone with her background wasn't suited for this type of work.

All of a sudden, resentment rose at the thought. Why couldn't she do as good a job as any country girl? Did being raised in a city disqualify her from doing ranch or barn work? Maybe Steve meant something deeper—more internal. It was possible he still saw her as a shallow city-girl with no depth or ability to stick to a hard job.

She swung open the stall door and stepped inside, bringing Brandy's halter along. No fear choked her at entering a horse's stall on her own. Not even a tiny bit. She'd changed. A lot. And much of it was due to Steve. Stroking the mare's neck, Lindsey thought it through. Was it only Steve?

No. She was sick of her past. Sick of the shallow, mundane lifestyle her parents lived. Trips to Europe instead of parenting— constant parties within their high-brow social circle—living for what they owned, instead of for their family. She'd come to understand since meeting Jesus that a lot of what her parents believed wasn't true. Jesus expected more. In fact, He expected her all. Her best and nothing less.

Sure, she could stay in the city and find a job. Her college degree must be good for something—but was that what she wanted? To live in the city and fight the rat race of corporate life every day? She shuddered at the thought. It wasn't in the least appealing.

Lindsey leaned her cheek against the mare's soft neck. "What do you think, girl? What other alternative do I have? If Steve wanted me here long term, would I want to stay? Could I ever live on a ranch and not be bored out of my mind?" She suddenly laughed at the thought— she hadn't been bored once since starting here, and she imagined life on a ranch as even more complex. But what a foolish place to let her thoughts stray. That obviously wasn't something Steve would even consider, and a ranch? Where did that come from?

She slipped the halter over the mare's nose and fastened the buckle. "Come on girl. Let's get you groomed and ready for your rider. It sounds like this might be one of the last times I get to do this, so I'm going to enjoy it."

ALMOST TWO HOURS HAD passed, and Lindsey still hadn't heard a peep out of Steve. She wasn't going to put this off any longer. Why drag out the decision when she could go to his office and give him the opportunity to tell her? Of course, she couldn't very well let him know she'd overheard part of his conversation, but surely he'd blurt it out himself, since he appeared anxious to get rid of her.

She marched down the alleyway, glad all the clients and riding instructor had departed for the day. Glancing up, she thought she saw the hem of a skirt disappear into the office. She slowed her pace, but didn't hear anything, so she pushed on, determined to get this over with.

The office door was ajar, and Lindsey stopped, stunned. A blonde woman with her back to Lindsey flung her arms around Steve with a loud squeal. She couldn't see his face, but he didn't seem too anxious to disengage himself from her embrace. Maybe she *would* take that job as a waitress. All this time she'd assumed Steve was free, but this seemed to give lie to that assumption. She took a step backward at the same time Steve raised his head.

STEVE HAD NO IDEA what hit him. A woman had flown through the door and launched herself at him with a squeal, enveloping him in a hug before he had a chance to get his defenses up. He felt more than saw another person start to enter the room and pause at the door. He repositioned himself so he could see around the woman's head to discover who'd entered, all the while trying to gently free himself.

A groan almost ripped from his throat. Lindsey. And if the look of surprise and hurt on her face meant anything, she planned to flee as quickly as she could turn around. "Lindsey." He carefully gripped the blonde's shoulders and moved her to the side. "Please don't leave." He still needed to find out who the tornado was who'd pounced on him.

The woman raised a radiant face—one he'd had the great misfortune to fall for in the past—and smiled—then arched her brows at Lindsey.

Both he and Lindsey said her name at the exact same time. "Janney?"

Lindsey leaned against the doorway as though her legs wouldn't hold her up. And maybe they wouldn't. She and Janney had been friends in high school, but Janney told him that Lindsey got too stuck up when she went off to an expensive private college and ditched Janney. That had been one more strike in Steve's book against Lindsey, but now he wondered how much he could believe of what Janney had told him. She hadn't turned out to be the girl he'd thought at first, and Lindsey certainly wasn't the girl he'd remembered.

He took a step away, wanting more distance between them, but she edged closer. "Steve, aren't you happy to see me? I drove hours to get here. I've missed you so much, darling, but seeing you today feels as though no time has passed at all." She reached out and stroked his arm, shooting Lindsey a glance at the same time. "In fact, I've made us dinner reservations at the resort restaurant. How soon can you shut this place down and get out of here? I'm dying to take up right where we left off." She almost purred the words. "We were so close. And it was silly to let distance come between us. Believe me, all the reasons I had for breaking up with you are a thing of the past."

Janney swiveled to Lindsey. "Hey there, friend. Long time no see. What are you doing here—staying at the resort and taking riding lessons?" She snickered. "Isn't shopping more up your alley?" She sobered and looked Lindsey up and down, more than likely taking note of the dirt smudging her face and dirty jeans. "Huh. I guess not. Don't tell me your darling parents have disowned you and left you with no money? I'm so sorry!"

Steve hadn't been able to interject a word through this long monologue, but Janney appeared to be finished for the moment, as she stared up at him with an expectant gaze. He drew in his breath to reply and . . .

"Steve." Lindsey stepped forward and completely ignored the other woman. "I came to tell you that I accidentally overheard Dixie telling you about the position opening in the restaurant. You hadn't shut the door all the way, and I was ready to knock when I heard my name mentioned. I apologize for listening, but I think it's just as well. Dixie said she needs an answer quickly, so she'd have time to hire someone else, but I don't want to make her wait. I'd like to take the job, and I want to be released now, so I can start the training. Besides, you always said I wasn't suited for this work, and I guess that's true." She didn't wait for his reply, but pivoted and disappeared out the door.

CHAPTER ELEVEN

Lindsey fled along the alleyway as fast as she could without bursting into a dead run—as well as bursting into tears. That could not happen. At least not until she'd reached the safety of her apartment. She didn't care that her shift had another hour to go. If Steve decided to call Dixie, so be it. She'd already told him she would report to the head of the dining staff tomorrow, regardless.

She slowed as her feet took her through the doors. Should she at least talk to Dixie and see if she was ready for her tomorrow? Maybe she'd been too hasty when she'd told Steve she wouldn't be back. She groaned. What if her decision backfired and both he and Dixie were disgusted enough to let her go? Planting her feet in the gravel, she looked toward the office far in the distance. Talk to Dixie or apologize to Steve and tell him she'd work the three days Dixie gave him, and allow *him* to make the arrangements with the head of Human Resources?

Right now it didn't matter. Besides, she didn't feel up to the long bike ride to the office. Of course, she could call, but if she talked to Dixie, it might be better in person. What *mattered* was getting away from this barn and into the safety of her own space to have a good cry. She'd figure the rest out later. Stomping across the gravel parking lot toward her little apartment, she worked to discover why she'd reacted so harshly to Janney's appearance.

She pushed open her door into her living area, which also included a miniature kitchen and dinette off to the side, all in one open area. A bedroom and tiny bath completed the area, but surprisingly, she'd been happy here. Probably happier than she'd been most of her life, even in the mansion her parents called home.

Lindsey sank onto the comfortable plaid couch and kicked off her shoes, then pulled a soft pillow into her arms. No way would she allow herself the luxury of a good cry. She had nothing to cry about, and what Steve did was his business. Sure, seeing a woman in his arms was unexpected—especially Janney—but what did she think, that he'd never had a girlfriend before? She pressed her cheek down into the oversized pillow and sighed. No. Just that he didn't have one now, but that was obviously a mistake.

Although she was sure she'd heard Janney say she'd broken up with him in the past, and she wanted him back. Hope stirred in her heart for the first time since the shocking event.

When had she started caring about Steve to the point it would devastate her world if he was dating Janney again—or any girl for that matter? It had snuck up on her slowly, although she shouldn't be so surprised. There was something different and special about him even in high school—a young man who barely talked to her, but he was always kind when he did. Not once had he hit on her the way some of the football players had done. Always the gentleman, that was Steve. But everything ended when she'd turned down his invitation to the prom. She'd never understood that and probably never would, but it was in the past—what mattered was now.

Maybe Steve didn't want Janney back. But if Lindsey remembered anything at all about her old friend from high school, it was that the pretty blonde was tenacious when it came to getting what she wanted—especially where guys were concerned. If she decided to hook Steve again, he'd probably be hooked, whether he wanted it or not—she'd make him believe it was his idea and have him loving it.

Ugh. What had she ever seen in that girl as a friend? That's one reason they'd drifted apart. Lindsey had never cared for the underhanded schemes Janney used when dating a guy, including lying when it benefited her. She hated lying with a passion.

She closed her eyes, mulling over one of her favorite Bible verses found in Psalm 46—Be still and know that I am God. It was as powerful now as the first time she'd read it as a college freshman, stressed about something she didn't even remember. But she recalled the peace that swept over her heart as she quieted herself before the Lord and let her thoughts dwell on Him instead of the problem. That was something she hadn't done lately. She pushed the pillow aside, ready to be done with her pity party, and reached for her Bible on the table nearby. Time to listen and wait on the Lord. She had no direction and no wisdom of her own to fall back on at the moment, but thankfully His direction and wisdom was all she needed.

STEVE SHUT THE OFFICE door behind Janney after she'd flounced across the threshold, angrier than he'd ever seen her. It hadn't taken long to get to the bottom of why she'd returned and literally thrown herself into his arms. He picked up the newspaper he'd only barely had time to read before she'd burst through the door. Apparently, she'd seen it when it hit the stands yesterday—or more than likely, she read it somewhere on the internet.

His gaze drifted down to the bottom half of the social page to reread the headline.

Wealthy Rancher Names Son as His Heir and Announces Retirement

Yep. That announcement would send Janney running here quicker than anything. Even back then Janney had expected to live a comfortable life in a spacious ranch house with a maid that came to clean three times a week, and money to spend however she wanted. Not that all of that would have happened immediately, but believing he was set to inherit a small cattle empire had done more than gotten her hopes up. Until they crashed when he walked away at Dad's insistence.

Steve loved his father more than anyone in his life other than his mother, but it didn't make sense that Dad allowed this to appear in the papers without calling him. His father had to know what a shock it would be to find out this way. Especially after being told to make his own way in the world and find out what he really wanted to do before tying himself to the ranch. He shook his head then raised the paper to read the article for himself.

Several minutes later, after reading and rereading, he set the paper aside. So Dad hadn't called the paper and made a formal announcement. An 'unnamed source' had contacted a reporter and given him a scoop—and who knew if they'd even bothered to verify it with his father before going to print. It could have been a new cowhand who overheard something and blabbed to the paper for money. No doubt Dad would be livid at the invasion of his privacy.

And what about Lindsey? He groaned anew at what she'd walked in on and what she must believe. He wanted to race over to her apartment right now and set things straight, but the best thing might be to wait and see if she turned up in the morning and talk to her then, rather than barge into her home when she was obviously upset. He doubted she'd simply show up at the dining room for work, when she hadn't talked to Dixie. And if she'd overheard their conversation, she knew Dixie wasn't expecting an answer from him for another three days.

He needed time to think about all that had happened, regardless. His father might be planning to ask him to come home and run the ranch, he had to make a decision about working at the barn and resort—and what would a possible move do to any chance of a future with Lindsey? He still found it hard to believe he'd gone from not trusting her as a shallow rich girl, to falling for her, in only a few weeks' time. But she'd more than proven herself with her grit, spunky attitude in sticking with the work, and tackling learning to ride in spite of her fear. Lindsey wasn't the woman he thought he'd known in high school at all. And she was nothing like Janney.

He'd still like to understand why Janney said that Lindsey made fun of him. More than likely that was a lie, based on what he'd learned about Janney and about Lindsey. He could see Janney pulling a stunt like that—both the ridicule and the lie—but not Lindsey.

Steve blew out a breath, staring at the wall, trying to decide what to do. More than anything he wanted to talk to Lindsey. He pushed his rolling chair away from the desk and was stopped from rising when the desk phone rang. He glanced at his watch while reaching for the phone. Probably Dixie, asking if the reports were ready to fax over yet.

"Son? It's your father. Sorry to call you at work, but I tried your cell, and you didn't answer. By chance have you seen the paper?" Worry and a bit of irritation laced his tone.

Steve smiled and settled back in his chair, glad he'd finished the last report for the week so he could talk. "Yeah, Dad. Saw it and planned to call you, so I'm glad you did. Fill me in, would you? I'll admit I'm a bit rocked on my heels."

CHAPTER TWELVE

AFTER A HALF HOUR READING HER Bible and spending time in prayer, Lindsey had come to at least a partial decision. She couldn't simply show up in the dining room prior to breakfast and expect to be put to work. She didn't have a uniform, didn't know their protocol or menu, and she clearly remembered Dixie mentioned training.

She took her bike from the rack and pedaled to the main building, hoping to catch Dixie before she left for the evening. Oh man—tomorrow was Friday, and Dixie might not want Lindsey to start until Monday—hence the three-day allowance for Steve to talk to her, and Dixie to get her into training. She sighed. It definitely hadn't been a good idea to storm out of Steve's office after telling him she quit. She braked to a stop in front of the main lodge that housed Dixie's office. Go in or turn around and head back?

Losing a day's pay wasn't too enticing, and it would be hard to go crawling back to Steve after she'd walked out in a huff. Her only real option was to talk to Dixie and pray she'd allow her to start sooner rather than later. She parked the bike in the rack and headed for the expansive front doors. Reaching for the ornate handle, she jerked her hand away and stepped back as the door swung open.

Dixie walked out then paused a few feet away. "Lindsey. What a surprise to see you. I think this is one of the first times I've seen you at the lodge since we hired you. Can I help with anything?"

Lindsey tried not to gape. "You mean Steve hasn't called and told you anything?"

Dixie's brows scrunched in tight grooves. "I didn't expect to hear from Steve for a few days. Is there something going on that I'm not aware of?" She didn't wait for an answer, but turned and swung the door open again, beckoning Lindsey to go in first. "Please. Step into my office where we'll have a bit more privacy."

Lindsey did as directed, her heart hammering in her chest. She'd fully expected Steve to call and warn Dixie about what happened. What a surprise he'd kept quiet. Maybe he didn't believe her and figured he'd see her at work in the morning. She almost groaned aloud. Too late now. She'd come this far, and there was no going back. She'd have to leave her future in God's hands—and Dixie's. She perched on the edge of a solid, blue-pine chair across from the desk, lacing her hands in her lap, and waited for Dixie to sit.

The manager smiled and sat. "Please, fill me in. I have an idea why you're here, but maybe not the details of the timing."

Lindsey's heartbeat had started to rise at the nod and smile, then as quickly slowed at Dixie's comment about the timing. She leaned forward. "I didn't mean to eavesdrop, but I was ready to knock on the office door when you and Steve were talking. It was partly open, and I heard voices, so I planned to leave until I heard my name." She shook her head. "I apologize for continuing to listen, but I was afraid you might be planning to fire me for some reason."

Dixie gave another encouraging smile. "And you've discovered you enjoy working at the barn and have decided you don't want to leave? That's why you were so worried we might be letting you go?"

"Yes. No." Lindsey slumped against the chair. "I mean, yes, I've enjoyed working there a lot more than I thought. But I can't afford to lose this job." She flicked a hand in the air. "Sorry, that's more personal info than you probably want to know. But I didn't at all mind finishing the season there."

"Right. So you've come to tell me that's your decision. I appreciate that you didn't wait the three days I gave Steve. I can call the employment agency right away and see if they can send over a waitress."

"Oh dear." Lindsey was going to chew her bottom lip off if she didn't quit biting it. She drew in a long breath and tried to relax. "I'm sorry I gave you that impression. I'll start over. You asked if I'd enjoyed working at the barn, so I was only answering that part. But I didn't come to tell you I want to stay there. I'd like to take the waitress position, if it's still open and you don't mind."

Dixie tilted her head to the side and observed Lindsey for a long moment before she replied. "Why? What made you change your mind? I assume you did change your mind, based on what you said a moment ago."

Lindsey hunched a shoulder, but her gaze didn't flicker from Dixie's. "To be honest, I suppose I did. I went to the office to tell Steve I didn't want this job, and I interrupted . . ." She couldn't stop the intense heat from flooding her face. Once again she'd said too much.

Dixie leaned forward, continuing her close scrutiny. "Yes. Please go on. I can only imagine one thing that could be happening in an office that would send a flood of red to another woman's cheeks. If Steve is doing something inappropriate there, I need to know." Her voice changed from soft to firm. "Not as gossip, Lindsey, but for the barn's reputation. A client could have walked into that office." She shuddered. "If it's what I think it might be, then I thank our lucky stars it was you, and you brought it right to me. In fact . . ." she reached for her cell phone on the desk . . . "I'm going to get to the bottom of this right now."

Horror engulfed Lindsey at what she might have done. She could get Steve fired. In reality, she wasn't sure what she'd seen, but she did know the Janney of old. That Janney wouldn't have hesitated to throw herself into a man's arms, whether he invited it or not. Come to think of it, once he untangled himself, he'd been firm in the way he'd set her to the side and ignored her. What if none of this was his fault, and he was an innocent victim? She almost bolted out of her seat as she impulsively reached toward the phone. "Please don't! I'm probably wrong. Please. Steve has been nothing but honorable the entire time I've worked for him, toward me and everyone else. I'm sure there's a misunderstanding."

Dixie hesitated, then placed the phone back on the desk and heaved a sigh. "I think you need to tell me what happened, then I can make an informed decision. I respect Steve a lot, and frankly, I'd be shocked if he did anything inappropriate. Proceed."

Lindsey filled Dixie in as honestly as she could, trying not to allow her own emotions to color the explanation, and throwing in a few comments about Janney's behavior in high school, in the hope of swinging the manager's displeasure away from Steve. When she finished, she collapsed into her chair, not realizing until this moment how tense she'd been through the telling. "So that's it. Thinking back, I don't believe it was Steve's fault." She'd keep to herself that she what she didn't know was if Steve would have welcomed or allowed Janney's display if it had been in a more private place. After all, she couldn't guess whether he was still in love with his old girlfriend or not.

"I see." Dixie steepled her fingers and tapped them against her chin. "Now I'm going to get a little more personal, as I'd like to understand your motivation for taking this new position. By the way, I reviewed your application, and I see you had a full summer of work as a hostess and another as a waitress, so we'd be happy to take you, if that's what you decide."

Lindsey opened her mouth to say she'd already decided, but Dixie forestalled her with a raised hand. "No, Lindsey. Hear me out before you say anything more. I'm curious. Are you running away from the barn and Steve, because that scene in the office made you realize you're falling in love with him yourself? Steve mentioned to me that the two of you had history, so it's not like you were strangers when you started to work there."

Lindsey gaped at the woman, wanting nothing more than to rush into a vehement denial. In love with Steve? It might be possible—but when she'd first seen him here, she hadn't felt a thing, other than a bit of nostalgia and regret for how circumstances turned out in school. And he'd made it clear he didn't feel a bit of attraction for her—just the opposite, in fact.

She snapped her lips closed as sudden awareness jolted her and widened her eyes. *Was* it possible? They'd only been reacquainted for not two months, and they hadn't even been out on a date. How could her heart be involved so quickly? But they'd spent hours with or near one another each of those weeks, and the lessons he'd been giving her had shown a side of him that she admired. In fact, that kind, sweet nature was what drew her to him in the first place. If anything, that aspect, plus his nurturing side, had increased over the years. She shook her head slowly, trying to overcome the shock. She did care, and it took seeing Janney in his arms to realize it.

The corners of Dixie's mouth tipped up slightly, and a knowing look entered her eyes. "You don't need to say a thing. I think I understand. In fact, I want you to take tomorrow off, with pay. You need to think about your decision then talk to me again Monday morning. I'm not ready to pull you out of the barn if that's where you belong." She tapped one finger on her lips. "Now I understand a bit more why Steve was so hesitant to make a decision about letting you go."

Lindsey stared at the Human Resources Manager yet again. How many surprises could her heart take in one day? "If you're implying what I think you are, then that's not possible."

Dixie laughed. "Oh really. Well, I'm not going to argue with you, but I know what I saw on the man's face when I told him I wanted to take you away. By the way, with your experience, you'd probably rise ·to assistant manager fairly quickly, as we'll be losing our manager at the end of this season, and we might be promoting our assistant. That might be something to think about, if you plan to come back next year."

She rose from behind the desk. "And since you might be working in a new position for us, and I haven't seen you eat at the restaurant yet this year, I'd like you to have dinner on us tonight, our treat. Anything you'd care to have. You can get a feel for the atmosphere and staff that way." She extended her hand. "I'll talk to you again on Monday."

Lindsey pushed from her chair, wondering if her shaky legs would hold her. "Thank you. For everything. You've given me a lot to consider."

CHAPTER THIRTEEN

STEVE PACED THE AREA IN FRONT of the barn, anxiety tugging at his gut. He'd finally worked up the nerve to knock on Lindsey's door but gotten no response. She wouldn't have left the resort entirely, as she only had a bike, but she might have made a bee-line to Dixie to accept that job, just as she'd said she'd do. Why hadn't he believed her and come to see her before she could leave?

He groaned. His dad's phone call, that's why. Their conversation had thrown him for a loop and made him sit in his chair staring at the wall far longer than he should have. Dad had asked him to come home soon and start managing the ranch. It spooked Steve enough that he'd pressed his father hard if he had a health issue he'd been hiding, but the answer had been negative. It was simply time. That's all he would say.

They'd come to the agreement that Steve would work out the balance of this season—another two-and-a-half months. His heart soared at the thought, then plunged again when he realized Lindsey might not be working alongside him here. He rammed his fingers through his hair. How could he convince her to return? And why was this intense pressure building in his chest that made him want to jump in his car and race to find her? A little under two months ago, Lindsey had been a thorn in his side, and now she was . . . what? Certainly not a thorn. More like a rose. But even if he'd come to care for her, there was no guarantee she returned the feeling.

Besides, no way would she ever want to live on a ranch the rest of her life, miles from the city—not to mention that little matter in high school where Lindsey made fun of his looks—but he'd decided that was nothing more than Janney's jealousy and lies. However, it didn't resolve his future. No, he wasn't ready to propose, not even close to it, but never again would he date for fun. He wanted to discover if they might have a future together, and something deep inside his heart told him they could—if Lindsey didn't run from the idea of ranch life.

There was only one way to find out. And he wasn't going to let any grass grow under his feet this time. As he jogged to his car, another thought hit him. He had never prayed about this—about the possibility of a real relationship, maybe even a future, with Lindsey. He slowed to a stop and hung his head in shame. Not once. At a slower pace, he approached his car, opened the door, and slid behind the wheel, then bowed his head. "Lord, please guide me and give me wisdom. Show me Your will, and give me the strength to follow it, not my own. Give me Your peace as I move forward, and please show me what to say to Lindsey that won't send her running the opposite direction. In Jesus's name, amen." He lifted his head and a flood of peace washed over him. He'd done the right thing in giving his relationship with Lindsey to the Lord. Now to follow through and give God a chance to speak through him to Lindsey, if possible.

LINDSEY FINISHED HER LAST bite of one of the best steak dinners she'd had in years, then wiped her mouth with the dark green cloth napkin and laid it beside her plate. The food, staff, and surroundings exuded quality. This was the kind of place her parents would love, if they ever took the time to come visit. A softly-lit fountain not far from the open double doors bubbled, sending a sense of peace over her spirit. "Thank you, Lord, for Your peace and provision, no matter what happens." She whispered the words, but not a person in the lightly occupied room seemed to notice.

Her waiter, an older gentleman who reminded her of a favorite uncle, appeared almost as soon as she'd finished. "How about dessert? We have a nice selection on our dessert menu, and our chef delights in making them for new patrons."

She hesitated, hating to take advantage of Dixie's generosity beyond the meal, but her mouth watered at the thought.

He waved a hand as though he understood. "Please don't worry. Ms. Sanderson told me you were to have whatever you wanted, and to encourage you to try the dessert. Besides, there's a gentleman who says he'd like to join you." He stepped aside with a broad smile. "He said he'd had to work late and wasn't able to get here when you started, but he'd like dessert if you would."

Steve appeared from behind a towering potted plant with a hesitant smile. "That is, if the lady doesn't mind the company, this late in her meal?"

Lindsey's heartrate jumped into double time as she stared up into his handsome, entreating face. How could she possibly say no, even if she'd wanted to, which she certainly did not. She waved at a seat. "Please." The word came out on a croak, and she stopped, afraid to try again.

Steve lowered himself and smiled. "I took the time to race home and shower and change, so I wouldn't offend anyone by smelling like a barnyard." From behind his back, he withdrew a lovely trio of pink roses with Baby's Breath, wrapped in deep green foil, and extended it across the table. "A peace offering, I hope."

Her pulse jumped yet again. "Thank you—they're lovely. Peace?" There was that dratted croak again.

He kept his eyes trained on hers. "For what you saw—and I believe possibly misunderstood—in the office earlier today."

She started to shake her head, but cleared her throat instead. "It was none of my business. I shouldn't have barged in. I'm sorry. If you and Janney are a couple, then I wish you well." She almost didn't get the words out, but felt better once she did.

The waiter stood off to the side, patiently waiting, a smile on his face at the sight of the flowers. "As soon as you order, I'll bring a vase for those, miss."

"Oh, thank you." She picked up the menu and held it in front of her face. She didn't have the foggiest idea what to choose and wasn't even certain she could eat anything when it arrived.

"How about I order for both of us?" Steve waited for her nod then asked for the chocolate mousse. He quirked a brow at her. "Are you a chocolate fan?"

"Absolutely. The richer and darker the better."

As the waiter moved away, she kept the menu up to hide her face, not wanting Steve to see the confusion warring with the joy that kept trying to rise to the surface to have him sitting across from her.

All of a sudden, a warm hand closed over hers and another hand removed the menu. Her eyes darted up and met Steve's pleading ones. "Hear me out, okay?"

She looked at him—she couldn't say no to those eyes. "You don't have to, Steve. I rushed out of there like an idiot, as though you'd done something to me personally."

His hand tightened over hers. "But I feel like I *did* do something to you—even if it was unintentional—and I should have followed you immediately, but then my dad called. I won't go into that now, but I wanted to come and would have, if that hadn't happened. So you'll listen?"

She squeezed his hand back and allowed him to keep holding it, not sure where this was going, but very much enjoying the feel of his hand holding hers. "Of course."

"I dated Janney for a couple of years after we graduated, and like many young men at the tender age of twenty, I thought I was in love. To make a long story short, as I don't want to bore you with details of a past relationship that went nowhere, it all ended rather abruptly. My idyllic dreams came crashing down."

"What happened?"

"To put it bluntly, she dumped me when she decided I wasn't going to inherit my dad's ranch, or at the least, not be managing it and living there any time in the near future. I think she had it in her head that she'd move my parents out of the big ranch house when and if we married, and we'd take over." He chuckled. "She doesn't know my mom too well if she thought that. Not that Mom wouldn't give up anything to help me, but she's not going to let some 'cheeky girl', as Mom called her later, run her out of her own home."

Lindsey gasped and started to withdraw her hand, but Steve held on. "I should hope not. I like your mother already."

He grinned. "I think she'd like you too. A lot."

Her cheeks warmed, and she smiled. "Not that I'm apt to meet her, of course."

He arched one brow. "You never know."

The waiter picked that time to bring the decadent chocolate mousse and set a plate in front of each of them, then held up two pitchers. "I have a thick, sweetened cream and raspberry syrup, made from local berries picked this summer. May I put a bit on either of your servings?"

"Oh, no thank you. It looks rich enough as it is." Lindsey reluctantly withdrew her hand as Steve held up his plate with his other one.

"I'll try the raspberry. Sounds delicious. Then I think we'll be good for a while." He gave the waiter a meaningful look. The man smiled, bowed, and left as soon as he'd poured the concoction. Steve turned back to Lindsey. "Now where were we?" He stared at her hand instead of picking up his fork.

She laughed and grabbed hers. "We're eating this awesome dessert, then you're going to tell me why Janney came back here after dumping you and walking away."

"Right. Then let's dig in so I can finish this pathetic story." Steve followed his words with actions, and in a few bites the rich dessert had disappeared. He placed his fork on his plate then dusted his hands and leaned forward in his chair. "All right, ready?"

She gaped at him, trying not to laugh. "How did you do that? Never mind. But I can tell you I'm going to take my time and savor every bite. So you talk, and I'll eat."

"Deal. But under one condition. As soon as you're finished, I get your hand back."

Lindsey chuckled and gave him a mock salute. "Yes, your highness, or Admiral, or whatever requires a salute. But you will not deter me from enjoying my yummy dessert, no matter what you try to bribe me with."

He narrowed his eyes and leaned forward, dropping his voice in a whisper. "Not even for a kiss?"

CHAPTER FOURTEEN

STEVE ALMOST BIT HIS TONGUE OFF after that remark. Where had he gotten the courage to say that? And what did the stunned, rather bemused expression on Lindsey's face mean? Should he apologize or leave it alone? No, he'd meant it. He'd kiss her if she'd allow him to, so he wasn't taking it back. "Don't worry, I won't do anything to embarrass you." He rushed forward, his words almost stumbling over one another. "Shall I continue with my tale of woe?"

She nodded mutely then dug into her dessert, closing her eyes as she put the fork in her mouth. "Hmm . . ."

He could only hope she was thinking of his kiss, and not simply enjoying the dessert. *All right, enough with the daydreams, Steve. Get on with it.* "So . . . Janney rushed into my office earlier today, and flung herself into my arms without the slightest warning or invitation. I literally didn't know what hit me until you walked in the door and brought a bit of reality back to the room."

She lifted her head, her cheeks tinged with pink—could she have been thinking about that kiss?

"Did you find out why she came?"

He nodded emphatically. "Oh yeah, for sure." He reached into his back pocket and pulled out part of a rolled up newspaper. "She had her own copy of this. But before I tell you what's in it, I need to ask you a very serious question. Please think about it carefully before you respond. It's important to me that I know the answer before I say more."

"Sure. I mean, I'll do my best." She dabbed her lips with her napkin.

"It's actually more than one question—or maybe a statement and a question. Anyway, here goes." He sucked in a deep breath and blew it out. "You said you've started enjoying working at the barn. Did you mean that, or were you being kind because you know I love it?"

She wrinkled her brow. "I meant it. It hasn't been anything like I expected it to be. Except maybe the smelly part—and I was afraid of the horses for the first few weeks, but I like them now. In fact, sometimes I go into Brandy's stall and groom her when she doesn't need it, because it's so peaceful and relaxing." She shot him a smile. "She's such a sweet horse."

His heart fluttered with hope. "Yeah, I agree. Okay, so here's the rest."

Her eyes twinkled. "I thought you said one question. That was one." She held up a finger.

"Don't take me too literally—on that part, at least—but please do on the rest." He rolled his eyes. "I'll get to the point, or I'll try to. So does liking the barn and horses mean you might be willing to consider living somewhere besides a big city?"

She stared at him, and he could see her wheels spinning. "I'm not trying to be dense here, but you may have to be a bit more specific. I assume you aren't asking if I'd be willing to live in a barn, or in the little cabin near the barn where I am now, for the rest of my life."

He chuckled, and a little of the tension eased from his shoulders. He extended his hand across the small round table, and she slipped hers inside. "Whew. That's better. Now I can continue."

She gave him a shy smile and dipped her head.

"So here's what I'm asking. If you were to ever . . . ah, to marry . . . and your husband didn't want to live in a city, but wanted to live on say, a ranch—do you think that's something you could tolerate?" He sat with his breath held, praying she'd give him the answer he hoped for. It wasn't that he didn't trust her, but after what happened with Janney, he didn't want her to know about the ranch and probable inheritance first—he wanted her to care about him for himself. Of course, she came from money, so it wasn't as big a deal as it had been with Janney, but his heart still longed to be loved for who he was, not what he might own.

Lindsey leaned toward him with a warm smile and placed her other hand over his. "Yes, Steven Graham. If I loved a man enough to marry him, I'd follow him anywhere. Barn, ranch, or even the little cabin I live in now. I learned long ago that a house doesn't matter—there is no home if you don't truly fill it with love."

He exhaled and grinned. "That's what I was hoping you'd say."

She cocked her head to the side. "Why? You are going to tell me now, right?"

"Yep." Now he captured her other hand in his and scooted his chair a foot or so closer to hers. "Because I want the woman who I pursue to care about me for myself, not my money."

"But you don't have money!" She blurted out the words then gasped. "I'm sorry. That came out wrong. I mean, you aren't wealthy, so why does it matter?" She narrowed her eyes. "And what do you mean, the woman you pursue? You mean date? Like you did Janney?"

"No way." He said the words slowly with emphasis. "Not even a little bit like I did with Janney. I want this time to be special. I don't want to go on a common old date, I want to enter into a relationship with a special woman who I think might have a chance of becoming a special wife someday—and I want to take my time wooing her and winning her, the old fashioned way. That is, if she doesn't mind." He gripped her hands a bit firmer.

She giggled. "And do I know this lucky girl?"

"You certainly do. I'm holding her hands right now." He loosened one hand, placed the paper on the table, and smoothed it out. "Read the circled part. It's short."

She did it quickly and silently, then raised her eyes. "This is why Janney wanted to get you back."

"Yes. But it didn't work, and I set her straight right after you left the office. She pouted and even tried tears for a while, but I ushered her to the door, told her I had work to do, and I hoped she had a good life. Oh, and I told her I had someone in my life and to please not bother me again."

Her eyes widened. "You did? But . . . "

"I know. You'd stormed out of the office and quit, but I hoped I could change your mind and talk you into returning. I'm going to finish out the season before I move back to the ranch. That's close to three months to work on convincing you that it might not be a terrible thing to have a relationship with Steve Graham. That he's no longer the scrawny little country bumpkin you knew in high school."

"Why would you say that about yourself?" She stared at him closely. "Did someone say that to you?" She hesitated for a moment. "Was it Janney?"

He shrugged. "I shouldn't have brought it up, because I've decided she lied to me at the time. And now that I know you better, I realize she had to have lied. You'd never say that about someone, or laugh at them behind their back for inviting you to the prom."

"What!? She told you that? If I'd known that when she was in the office, I'd have given her a piece of my mind. Steve, I never said anything like that. Not at all. I'm so sorry she made you believe I'd do or say that."

"So that's not why you didn't want to go to the prom with me? I was pretty scrawny and shy at the time." He gave a rueful smile.

"Not at all. Jake had already asked me to go, and by the time the prom was over, I was wishing I'd gone with you. At least you were a gentleman. If you believe me, can we go back to the part about pursuing a girl you care about? I kind of liked that part."

He grinned. "Under one condition."

She nodded and scooted her chair a bit closer to his. "Name it."

"I get one kiss now, and another one later when it's a little more private, to seal the deal. And to show you that I do care for you. More than I'd even realized." He held his breath, barely daring to hope, then he glanced around. "The waiter isn't hovering and most of the diners are gone."

She squeezed his hand and pulled him a fraction closer. "I don't care if the waiter is hovering. I'm not going to be working here, anyway, and I have a feeling he's already figured things out on his own." She tipped up her face and closed her eyes, then snapped them open before he could lower his head. "And believe me, I plan to hold you to the kiss you promised me later."

He couldn't contain his grin and didn't even look around this time, but lowered his head and captured her lips with his. A shiver ran through him, and he raised his head. "Wow."

"Double wow." She looked at him with dreamy eyes.

"So you'll really come back to the barn for the season?"

"I will. Under one condition."

His heart started to sink.

"That if there are no clients or instructors around, I get a least one of these in the morning and one in the afternoon to get me through the day."

The sinking sensation from a moment before turned to a deep joy that he could barely contain. "Deal. And I think I'll give you a little deposit now, if you want one."

She lifted her face again and smiled. "Yes, please."

The End

DESIGNED WITH LOVE

By
Kimberly Rose Johnson

CHAPTER ONE

Jessie Morgan paused as she scrolled down the computer screen. Her heart rate kicked into double time. The TV show *"Fresh and Fantastic"* was holding a landscape design competition. The grand prize was fifteen thousand dollars and a television show development deal. The runner up received ten thousand dollars minus the TV show.

"Yes!" With the prize money she'd be able to keep her business afloat. She quickly printed the entry form and rushed down the stairs of her childhood home. "Mom." She waved the paper. "This is it. This is my ticket to financial freedom." Mom had lectured her on the topic repeatedly since she'd moved back home three months ago.

Her mother pulled a tray of gluten free chocolate chip cookies from the oven. "What are you talking about?" She placed the pan on the butcher-block counter.

"You know business hasn't been great, thanks to Brendon Jacobs."

Mom nodded and held out the spatula. "Cookie? I think I finally nailed the recipe."

"Sure. Thanks." Jessie bit into the warm, gooey delight. "Yep. This is good." All those months of sampling recipes finally paid off.

A movement in the front yard caught her eyes. She leaned across the sink and looked out the window. "Why is Scott mowing our lawn?" Her friend of long ago had followed his dream to be a landscaper too, but they hadn't spoken much in recent years. Their friendship fizzled back in high school when she'd started dating Brendon Jacobs, and they'd not been close since.

Crossing her arms, she turned to face her mother. "I told you I would take care of the lawn. Don't you realize he's the competition, and it doesn't make me look good when my own mother hires my competitor?"

"I understand. But I was talking to Scott's mom the other day, and she told me he's desperate for business. Scott is such a nice boy. I wanted to do my part to help him."

"'What about helping your own daughter?"

Mom raised a perfectly manicured brow. "Does free room and board count as nothing?"

"Sorry. You're right, and I appreciate that you let me move back home. It's just that Scott is my rival."

Mom scooped dough onto the cookie sheet. "If the two of you would join forces—"

"Don't say it." Mom had been on her case for months to talk with Scott about merging their businesses. But she didn't understand their history. Scott turned his back on their friendship. She couldn't have a partnership with someone like that.

"Fine. I won't bring it up again . . . today." Mom ducked her head, but not before Jessie spotted her mischievous grin. "It's my yard, and if I want to pay someone to mow the lawn, I will. Besides, you hate mowing and everyone knows you take care of my yard for free."

"Which makes it even worse. I'm *free*, but you still hired my competition." Why couldn't her mother understand how poorly this reflected on her?

The hum of the motor stopped. A moment later the doorbell rang.

"Would you please get that?" Mom asked. "There's a check on the table beside the door for Scott. I told him I'd have it for him when he finished today."

Jessie sighed and marched through the kitchen and around the corner to the entryway. She saw Scott through the glass window beside the door. He wore a blue shirt and jeans with brown work boots. She pulled the door open. "Hi, Scott." Wide, vivid blue eyes met hers.

"Hey." He nodded. "Your mom said to knock . . ."

"Right." She tore her gaze from his and grabbed the check. As much as she'd love to tell him not to come back next week, this was her mom's house. "Here you go."

"Thanks. What's that?" He motioned to the entry form she forgot she still held.

If she told him what it was, would he enter too? Scott did amazing landscapes. If she entered, she'd be up against tons of competition, so what difference did it make. "The TV show *Fresh and Fantastic* is holding a competition to find the best landscaper in the Northwest."

"Are you entering?"

"I thought I might." What did his slight smile mean? She used to be able to read Scott's every expression, but this one she didn't recognize.

"Good for you. I sent my entry in last week." He pocketed the check. "May the best man . . . or woman win." He dipped his head, then spun around and strode down the walkway to his pickup parked along the curb.

Mom leaned against the wall a few feet away with her arms crossed, chuckling.

"What?" Jessie stomped past her.

"Nothing. Just seeing the two of you together again makes my heart happy."

She whirled to face her mother. "We are *not* together. And we were never together the way you are insinuating."

"He was your best friend until your junior year of high school. The two of you were inseparable."

"Things changed." Although she hadn't wanted to lose Scott's friendship, he didn't seem to want anything to do with her. This was the first time since she'd returned to town that their paths had crossed, and she suspected he wouldn't have come to the door if he'd known she was there.

Scott gripped the steering wheel hard. Jessie looked good, like always. Even in cutoffs, no makeup and her hair pulled into a ponytail, there was something about her that drew him—always had. He should have anticipated running into Jessie today. After all, he'd heard she was living with her mom. But he figured she'd be working, not hanging out at her parents' home—well her mom's now. He'd been more than a little surprised when Mrs. Morgan called and hired him to mow her lawn, but business was business and he'd take all he could get. Especially now that Brendon Jacobs had swooped back into Silver Springs and was stealing his clients. Was he doing the same thing to Jessie? Unlikely, considering the two had been engaged to be married not all that long ago.

The hometown hero and former high school quarterback had returned to town and opened his own landscaping business. Silver Springs, Oregon, did not need another landscaper, but this town loved its onetime football hero and eagerly supported Brendon. Everyone expected him to go pro, but an injury his senior year in college changed all that.

Scott slammed on the brake as a kid ran into the street after a basketball. The boy waved as he dribbled the ball back into his driveway. Scott waved back. He needed to pay more attention to the road and stop thinking about his nemesis, but it was difficult when the man had taken the only girl he'd ever loved then rejected her six years later.

Even though Jessie had been back in town for the past year, he'd successfully avoided her—until today. He never should have taken that job. But he needed it and any other paying job he could round up.

His business had suffered since Jessie opened *Jessie's Landscape and Design*. He hadn't minded too much though. After all, they both had always had a passion for landscaping. As teens they'd talked about going into business together, but then everything changed.

He pulled up to his next job, stepped out of his pickup, then unloaded the mower. His entire day would be one lawn after another along with some trimming, weeding, and fertilizing.

Mrs. Spencer rushed out the door, wringing her hands. "Oh dear. I see you didn't get my message."

He grinned at the nervous older woman. "Mondays are lawn mowing days, and I don't check messages until my lunch break. Is there a problem?"

"I'm really sorry, but I hired Brendon Jacobs. I have a tight budget, and he gave me a deal I couldn't pass up."

He clenched his jaw. This was the third week in a row he'd lost a client to Brendon. Something had to give, or he'd be out of business before the end of the year. It had become increasingly difficult not to hate the man who seemed to take pleasure in stabbing him in the back.

"I hope you understand. It has nothing to do with the work you do. I'm simply trying to save money." She looked at him with eyes that begged him to forgive her.

"It's fine." He'd offer to do the job for less than Brendon, except if he went any lower, he wouldn't be able to cover his overhead. How could Brendon afford to undercut him time and again? He must be charging different rates to different people.

He put the mower away then got back into his pickup. Something had to be done about Brendon, but what? The man was beloved in this town. Maybe it was time he closed up and moved to a city where there were plenty of people looking for his kind of services. But Silver Springs was home. His family was here, and he liked being a part of his niece and nephews' lives on a daily basis. But if he couldn't make a living here he'd have no choice. Could he be happy in a big city?

It was something to consider. He knew the *Fresh and Fantastic* competition was a long shot, but it looked like it might be his final hope of staying. Too bad he would be up against Jessie, but this was business, and as they say, all is fair in love and war. But he didn't want a war with Jessie. He missed her—for years, ever since she'd started dating Brendon. He hated that he'd allowed that dude to keep him away from his one-time best friend.

But what could he do? Jessie hadn't exactly overflowed with friendliness. Yes, he'd hurt her, but he'd been hurt too. Maybe there was a middle ground where they could meet. Now to try and convince her of that.

CHAPTER TWO

JESSIE WANDERED DOWN A ROW OF evergreens at Silver Springs Nursery. A gravel path wound through the three-acre lot displaying a variety of trees, shrubs, and flowers. The strong scent of evergreen mingled with roses drew her deeper into the nursery. She'd always enjoyed this place, even when her parents brought her here as a child and allowed her to choose a plant or two for the yard each spring. Mom favored roses.

Roses were her favorite too, but her next project, a new-build, required a water feature and low maintenance landscape. She would plant a privacy screen with arborvitae and incorporate several low maintenance shrubs in the planters along with some perennials that would surprise the new owners in the spring and summer when they appeared.

A familiar voice grabbed her attention, and her stomach tightened. She did *not* want to see Brendon. She looked side to side for an escape—too late.

"Jessie!" Brendon strode toward her. His broad shoulders cloaked in a tight black T-shirt that accentuated his flat stomach and large biceps. When they had been together, he'd spent at least an hour a day at the gym, and clearly he'd kept up the habit.

Brendon stopped a few feet from her. "This is a surprise." He grinned, flashing perfect white teeth.

"It's the only nursery in town. I'm here a lot." Why had she said that? "What are *you* doing here, Brendon?"

He cleared his throat, suddenly looking uncomfortable. "I usually go to one of the nurseries in Woodburn—bigger town, more selection. But I come here now and then." He kept his voice low, clearly not wanting to be overheard by the owner who stood twenty feet away.

It would figure he wouldn't have the decency to support the local economy. The man confused and frustrated her beyond words. He'd called off their engagement, claiming he'd met someone else, then six months later he'd showed up in Silver Springs—alone. When she wouldn't take him back, he'd become her competition.

Jessie turned to leave. She'd come back later. Maybe she was being petty, but their breakup was too fresh for them to be friends. She swept past him.

He gripped her arm.

She stopped, glanced at his hand on her bicep then at him with a raised brow. Her pulse thrummed in her ears.

"How's business?"

She raised her chin, then looked pointedly at his hand still gripping her arm. "Do you mind?"

He released her. "You know we could team up again. We were great together."

Her face heated. She had to remind herself she was a Christian, because what she wanted to say right now, the Lord would not likely approve. "'Bye, Brendon." She marched away on noodle-like legs. Confrontation appealed about as much as a trip to the doctor.

In the parking lot, she reached for the door to her pickup, a necessity in her line of work. She sighed when she spotted Scott walking her way. "Lord, what did I do to deserve a day like this?" she muttered under her breath.

Scott waved and headed her way. He glanced into the truck bed. "You didn't buy anything?"

"Brendon's here." She crossed her arms.

Scott frowned. She wanted to reach out and brush away the long strands of hair that swept across his forehead but kept her arms tucked close to her stomach. Nearly the same height as Scott's five-foot-eleven inch frame, she could clearly see the irritation in his eyes. They might have stopped being friends years ago, but she could still read him, and unless she was wrong, Scott didn't like Brendon. "Want me to go deck him for you?"

She chuckled. "Yes."

A slow smile spread across his face. "What happened between the two of you?"

She shook her head. "I'd rather not talk about it."

"You used to tell me everything."

"That was a long time ago—before you abandoned me."

He jerked his head up. "What are you talking about?"

Well, maybe that was exaggerating, but the result was the same. Their friendship died. "It doesn't matter." She looked around the nearly empty parking lot. It wouldn't be long before Brendon would be leaving. She didn't want to see him again. "I guess I'll see you around now that you're doing my mom's yard." She pulled the door open to her pickup and slid in.

"Yep. Unless, Brendon undercuts me there too."

So she wasn't the only one her ex was out to destroy. "I'm sorry about him. He's . . ." What excuse could she offer? The man was vindictive. There was no excuse for him. "I'm . . . just . . . sorry."

Scott nodded. "Take care, Jessie, and good luck with the competition."

"What competition?" Brendon approached, grinning like a Cheshire cat.

"Nothing," they both said at the same time.

Jessie started the engine and put the truck in gear. No way would she stick around for this conversation. Hopefully, Scott would have the same good sense. As she pulled forward and stopped at the exit before entering the main road, she checked her rearview mirror and noticed the men talking. She groaned and pulled out.

Five minutes later, she parked in front of *Java Java*, her favorite coffee shop on Main Street. The owner had become a good friend, and she could use a listening ear right now. She got out and strode inside. The whirl of the coffee grinder greeted her, and the scent of coffee beans instantly relaxed her. She loved that smell.

Taking a moment to allow her eyes to adjust, she paused in the doorway and took in the new artwork on the wall to the left. Melissa, the owner, allowed local artists to display their pieces and sell them.

In a small town, having a gallery in the coffee shop made a lot of sense. An eleven-by-fourteen framed photograph of Silver Falls grabbed her attention. She wasn't in the market for art, but she could use a good hike.

A shoulder bumped her arm. She glanced down and spotted her unlikely friend. At only five foot tall, Melissa made Jessie feel like a giant, but it didn't matter, because her friend had a huge heart that more than made up for their difference in stature.

"You look as though you lost your best friend," Melissa said.

"You have no idea."

"Uh-oh. Sounds to me like you need copious amounts of chocolate. I made a double fudge cake today. With my house blend coffee, it's the perfect balance on the palate."

Jessie forced a smile for the sake of her friend. "You know what I like."

"Have a seat, and I'll bring it out."

Jessie nodded and found a spot near the front window that looked out onto Main Street. Silver Springs was the quintessential small town from the clean sidewalks and colorful hanging baskets to only three traffic lights.

Across the street was Jack's Plumbing and Hardware and situated beside it was Kendall's Books 'N More. The shared red and white awning sparkled in the bright sunshine.

"Here we are." Melissa slid the cake and large mug of coffee in front of her, then placed a fork and napkin beside it. She pulled out a chair and sat. "What's going on? I haven't seen you this discombobulated since you first came back to town."

Jessie grinned at her friend's choice of word. "It's been one of those days." She told her how the morning had started with Scott mowing her mother's lawn and went on from there. "I don't understand why all this is happening, much less all in one day." She looked to her friend as if she had all the answers.

Melissa only shrugged. "You haven't tried the cake."

"Sorry." She forked a small bite into her mouth. Rich, smooth chocolate melted in her mouth. "Mmm . . . It's perfect."

"Good. Now back to your issue. I have no idea what to tell you except don't forget to pray. The Lord is always there for you no matter what. And I'm here for you anytime you need to vent. I'm sorry you're having such a rough time."

"Thanks." Jessie hoped Melissa, who was a few years older than her, would have words of wisdom to offer other than to pray, but the reality was sometimes life threw you curve balls. Jessie took another bite of the decadent cake then washed it down with a swallow of her favorite coffee. "What would I do without you and your comfort food?"

Melissa grinned and patted her hand. "The bigger question is what are you going to do about Brendon? Half the town thinks the man walks on water because the football team won the state championship in our division for the two years he was quarterback."

"I know. Crossing him would not be good for my business, but he's systematically stealing my customers, so I'm not sure it matters much if I make him angry or not at this point. I don't know how he can make any money with the prices he's charging, and I heard he's hired a crew to do all the dirty work."

"That shouldn't surprise you. Didn't you tell me you were the grunt, and he was the brains when you shared a landscaping business?"

"Yes, but hiring a crew isn't cheap. I guess that goes to show how much of my business he's stealing. Oh I forgot to tell you. I'm entering a landscaping contest. The TV show *Fresh and Fantastic* is holding it."

Melissa's brown eyes lit. "What do you have to do?"

"I send in a video audition along with the entry form. I'm a little late finding out about it though. The contest closes soon."

"What's supposed to be on the video?"

"I play host as I tell about a landscape that I designed. Do you think you could help me? I need someone to record me."

"Sure! Those TV people will love you."

"I hope so, but Scott entered too. And I'm not sure, but I think Brendon might have as well."

She waved a hand. "Don't worry about the competition. Just do your best and let your work speak for itself."

"Thanks." She reached across the table and gave her friend's hand a gentle squeeze. "I should be going."

"But you didn't finish your cake."

"I'll wrap it in my napkin and take it with me."

Melissa stood. "I'll get a box."

Her petite friend flounced across the tile flooring and ducked behind the counter. She came back grinning. "You should let me do your hair and makeup for the video too."

Jessie's hand shot to her brown hair that was pulled back in a ponytail. "What's wrong with it?" Her friend had an adorable short cut that framed her pixie-like face, but Jessie was far from petite and would never be America's sweetheart.

"There's nothing wrong with your hair. In fact, I think it's gorgeous, but you hide it with that perpetual ponytail you insist on wearing. Let me add some soft curls and show the world how stunning you are."

"Ha." Not that she had a poor self-image, but stunning? Not. "Sure. I'll submit to a makeover, if for no other reason than I really want to win this competition. See you after you close?"

"Absolutely." Melissa gave her a hug.

Jessie rushed from the shop, cake in hand, and smacked hard into someone solid. Her breath whooshed from her lungs. "Excuse me. I wasn't watching . . ." Him again—three times in one day?

CHAPTER THREE

Scott steadied Jessie. "You okay?" His heart beat wildly. He hadn't anticipated running into her — literally.

"I'm fine, but . . ." she held up a squished box that oozed chocolate, "I don't think my cake is."

He winced. "I'll buy you another piece." He knew how Jessie loved chocolate.

"No. It was my fault. I wasn't watching where I was going. Speaking of that. How is it we've been living in the same town all this time and never crossed paths, and now in one day we see each other three times?" She narrowed her eyes. "Are you stalking me?"

"Hardly." He might as well tell her the truth. "I thought it would be easier to avoid you, but I finally stopped trying."

Her mouth opened slightly. "I was avoiding you, as well, but I didn't realize you were avoiding me. Why?"

He shrugged. "It seemed better that way."

"I don't understand."

"Sorry. Now that I say it out loud it does sound childish. I promise from this day forward I will no longer avoid you."

She grinned. "Good. Same here. Now what did Brendon want?"

"He sure is a piece of work." His confrontation with Brendon hadn't gone well.

"Tell me about it." She hesitated. "Is Brendon going to enter the *Fresh and Fantastic* contest?"

"I think he might. He seemed very interested." Although by the questions he asked, he seemed more interested in Jessie than the contest.

She frowned. But even then, she was beautiful. He'd had a crush on her since their freshman year of high school, but he hadn't wanted to ruin their friendship by asking her out. Everything had been fine until he dared her to try out to be a cheerleader. Then things changed.

Suddenly she was popular, and she caught Brendon's eye. They started dating, and Brendon, the jock of the football team threatened to set the entire football team on him if he didn't stay away from her. He should've stood up to the punk, but he was sixteen, and the football team had practically worshiped their quarterback.

He'd convinced himself that Jessie and Brendon would eventually break up, and then Scott and she could pick up where they'd left off, but that's not what happened. Jessie and Brendon ended up at the same college and got engaged. "I was thinking."

"'Bout what?"

"The contest. I already turned in my application, but I couldn't find any place in the rules that said you couldn't enter a second time with a partner. What if you and I join forces and put something together that will wow the judges?"

"I don't know."

"You could do your own entry too," he quickly added.

"We'd be in competition with ourselves."

"True. But we'd increase our chances of getting noticed and maybe make semi-finals. I know it says one entry per person, but we'd be a team, so it'd be different." At least that was the way he understood the rules.

"Let me think about it. You might be on to something. Maybe send me a proposal for what you have in mind. I was going to use my mom's backyard for my submission, since I designed it."

"That's right. I forgot we'd have to do the design together." He didn't have a budget for that. He had let his mouth get ahead of his brain.

Jessie's face brightened. "I have a new-build contract with a decent budget. It has to be low maintenance and include a water feature, but together we could probably come up with something so great Ted will hire me for all his houses." She tilted her head to the side. "But I can't give you a cut of the profits. I bid low to beat out Brendon."

"Understood." This could work out better than he'd imagined.

"I'll send you a few pictures of the place. My mom has your number, right?"

"Yes." Jessie must really be desperate for that prize money, because after seeing her at her house this morning and then again this afternoon, the last thing he imagined was that she would agree to work together. She had an independent streak as long as the Mississippi River. A sudden thought hit him. He'd found a way back into Jessie's life. At least temporarily.

"You're entering with Scott?" Melissa's brow puckered as she pulled the curling iron from Jessie's usually straight hair.

"It's a win-win situation really. We each get an extra entry, my client is thrilled his home will be publicized for free, and it could be fun to work with Scott. We used to be friends." Jessie shrugged as her friend wrapped her hair around the barrel of the iron. "It's not like we hate each other."

She couldn't figure out why Scott suddenly stopped wanting to hang out back in high school, and it still stung a little when she thought about it. What had she done? She'd tried to talk with him about his sudden unavailability, but he always had an excuse why he couldn't talk.

"You were friends?" Melissa sounded surprised.

"I thought you knew."

"No. I only knew there was history between the two of you." She stepped back and handed her a mirror. "What do you think?"

Was that really her? Her eyes widened. She hadn't had curls in her hair since she was a kid. It was actually cute. A longer version of what Melissa wore every day, although her curls were natural.

Melissa set the curling iron on the counter. "Let me touch up your makeup, then we'll do this before the sun goes down too far and shades your backyard."

She subjected herself to her friend's treatment a little while longer.

"Voila! You're gorgeous."

No one ever said she was gorgeous. In fact, she was quite ordinary. How could a few curls and a little makeup change that? Jessie's curiosity got the best of her, and she held up the mirror again. *Hmm.* She wasn't crazy about this girly version of herself, but if it would help her get noticed by the TV people, then she'd play along with Melissa. At least her friend hadn't insisted she wear a skirt.

An hour later, Melissa and Jessie sat at the computer screen editing the footage. "I looked up the contest online. Do you realize the grand prize is your own lawn and garden show? I thought you were in it for the money."

"There's no way I will win the grand prize, so I'm not worried. I'm hoping for runner up. It has prize money."

"You have as good a chance as anyone to win the grand prize. You did great, Jess. They're sure to love you."

"Thanks. But what about the landscaping?" The lighting had changed mid-filming and cast a shadow on the flowers, which looked so much better in sunshine.

"It's practically perfect. Don't worry, you have this. If that TV show doesn't pick you to be at least a finalist, it's no reflection on your talent, but rather what they're looking for."

"Hmm. I hadn't considered that." She stood. "Thanks for your help. Scott and I have our work cut out for us over the next several days, and we hope to record our audition this weekend. Will you be free to film us?"

"Absolutely! Should we meet here again first and do your hair and makeup?"

Jessie shook her head. "I want to wear my hair the way I always do. I think I can do what you did with the makeup, so how about meeting us there? I'll text you the address."

"Okay, my friend. Tootles." Melissa breezed out the door.

Jessie pressed send on the entry then scrolled through her emails. One from Scott grabbed her attention. She opened it and grinned. "Scott, you're a genius." His design, though simple, screamed Pacific Northwest. It looked like it could be done within budget too.

The doorbell rang. Mom was out tonight, so she trotted downstairs and pulled open the door. Her stomach jolted. "Scott, this is a surprise. I just finished looking over your design."

"I was in the area and wanted to see what you thought of my proposal."

"It's perfect. I especially like the water feature and how you incorporated native plants with boulders as well as pops of color with perennials." She stepped outside, closing the door behind her. "I think the builder will love your idea. As soon as I run it by him we can get started. Actually, he's probably still at the site. I'll grab my tablet and head over there before he leaves."

"Great." Scott looked like he wanted to say more, but instead pressed his lips tight.

"What are you worried about?"

"Brendon."

Her eyes widened. "Why?"

"I have a bad feeling about him. I think he'd stop at nothing to keep us from working together."

"Why would he care?"

"You tell me," he said softly.

Jessie sighed. No one, other than her mom and Melissa, knew what had happened between her and Brendon. Maybe it was time she set the record straight. "Brendon got bored with me after we were engaged. He dumped me for someone else then wanted me to take him back a few months later. As far as I'm concerned, we're finished."

Scott tilted his head and rubbed the back of his neck. "Brendon warned me to stay away from you."

"He did what?" Jessie balled her hands and fought to control her temper. How dare he? "I will deal with Brendon. Don't worry about him."

"Are you sure there's nothing I need to know? I don't want to come between the two of you."

A sudden thought occurred to her. "Is that why you stopped being my friend in high school? You were afraid to come between us?"

"Something like that."

She stepped close to him and reached for his hand. "You were my dearest friend."

"And you were mine. I didn't want to ruin things for you. Besides,

Brendon threatened that if I didn't step out of your life, he'd bring down the football team on me."

She caught her breath. *That beast!* "If only I'd known," she said softly. "I'm so angry with that man right now, I could chase him around with my weed eater."

Scott laughed. "That's a bit extreme, don't you think?"

She pulled her hand away and crossed her arms. "No. He deserves to be scared out of his mind by a crazed woman." She chuckled at how nutty she sounded. "You know I'd never behave like that. I'm just spouting off. But I am angrier with him than I've ever been." Scott's pulling away pushed her closer to Brendon. At least now she understood what had caused him to abandon their friendship.

"I know. I'm not happy with him myself."

Good to know they still agreed when it counted. "I should take off. I'll be at the site by seven tomorrow morning."

"Sounds good. I'll arrange to have the boulders delivered then meet you there to get started on the excavation." He turned and strode to his pickup then drove away.

Time to find Brendon and set him straight, but first she'd swing by the construction site.

CHAPTER FOUR

J ESSIE STOOD BESIDE HER PICKUP WITH arms crossed waiting for Brendon to wrap up filming his contest entry. He'd gone all out with a professional video crew and lighting. She had to admit, the man was great to watch. He had charisma and charm that most people only dreamed of. He'd be the perfect host for a television program with his boy-next-door good looks and blue eyes.

With Brendon's personality and great design she didn't have a chance against him. No one besides her knew his true despicable character. He should've gone into acting. He was a true pro.

"What'd you think?" Brendon swaggered in her direction wearing a dazzling smile.

She unclasped her arms. "You're a natural in front of the camera."

He shot her a tell-me-something-I-don't-know look. "What brings you by? Spying on the competition?"

"No need. How'd you pull this together so fast?"

He shrugged. "People like me and want to see me succeed. Unlike someone else I know." He looked pointedly at her.

"Moi?" She motioned to herself. "I can't imagine why you'd think that." Sarcasm oozed from her voice. She squared her shoulders and took a step closer to him. "I stopped by to make it clear I'll associate with whomever I want, and if you ever harass anyone about me again, I will involve the police."

He blinked and took a step back. "Whoa. Where did that come from? Is this about Scott?"

"You know it is. How dare you threaten him!"

"What a loser. I can't believe he ran to you. Then again, he was clearly in love with you in high school—probably still is." He snickered. "I should have expected this. You know I warned him to stay away from you then too."

She gasped. "You admit it." She never thought he'd own up to his bad behavior.

He nodded. "You bet. We didn't need a third-wheel."

She propped her hands on her hips. "But *your* friends hung out with us all the time." Everything suddenly made sense.

He chuckled. "My friends didn't have a crush on me."

"You are so wrong about Scott. We grew up together. We were friends. Period."

"You've always been blind to things you don't want to see. That's how I was able to get away with having multiple affairs while we were together."

Jessie's stomach roiled. *Multiple?* She'd only known about one other woman—the one he'd called off their engagement for. Her hands fisted at her sides, and she took a slow, deep breath. She spun around and marched to the driver's side of her pickup.

"We were a good team, Jessie. We could be again if you'd give me another chance. I shouldn't have said I'd had multiple affairs. I'm sorry."

She stopped, her hand resting on the door, and looked at him. So many thoughts whirled in her head, including a plethora of names she'd love to shout at him, but she wouldn't stoop to his level of scum. "I don't take seconds. Good luck with the competition, Brendon." She hopped in her pickup, and seconds later, peeled away from the curb. If her dad was still living, she'd get a serious lecture about burning rubber and how it ruined the tires.

Brendon was not the man for her, so why did it hurt so much to find out he'd cheated on her, not once but multiple times during the years they'd dated? She slammed her hand against the steering wheel. The truck weaved right. She yelped and quickly corrected her mistake. She should have broken up with him a very long time ago. They were from two different worlds and looked at life differently.

Her senior year in high school she'd become a Christian, and it had changed her. She'd known then she didn't belong with Brendon, but she loved him and couldn't let him go. If only she hadn't been so blinded by love and had seen him for the scoundrel he was, it would have saved her a lot of pain and heartache, not to mention wasted years.

If only she could go back in time for a do-over. She would never have let Scott slip out of her life. He was the best friend she'd ever had other than Melissa. But Melissa had a perfect life—a wonderful husband who didn't cheat on her, a fabulous coffee shop, and a kind heart. Melissa had never been in the same position, and Jessie couldn't imagine Melissa could understand her situation with Brendon.

She needed her old friend back. Scott had always been a good listener. For that reason alone, she couldn't believe some girl hadn't snatched him up already. Maybe by working together on the competition, they could renew their friendship. She could only hope.

Jessie drove without thinking, and before she realized where she was going, she pulled into the old fashioned Burgers 'N Shakes Drive-Up. She parked and lowered her window.

Grace, the same waitress that had taken her orders as a teen, approached her window. "It's about time you stopped in."

"I know. It's been a long time."

Rather than the old pen and paper Grace used to carry, she held an electronic device to press in the orders. "What can I get for you?"

"I'd love a chocolate shake."

"You got it." She peered past Jessie to the passenger seat. "Eating alone tonight?"

"Yep."

"Hmm. Scott is too." She whirled around and strode away.

Scott's here? She opened her door and got out. She made a detour inside and waited for her shake at the counter.

"I'll bring your shake when it's done," Grace said.

"I know, but I thought I'd wait here instead. Would it be okay if I take Scott's order to him?"

Grace smiled knowingly. "Sure." A few minutes later Grace handed her the shake as well as Scott's order.

"Thanks." She slid in the straw, grabbed the tray with his order, then headed outside. The drive-up was busy as usual, but she had no problem spotting Scott.

"HI THERE."

SCOTT JUMPED at the sound of Jessie's voice. He whipped his head to the passenger side of his pickup where she stood at the open window holding her milkshake and a tray. "Hi yourself. Want to hop in?"

"Thanks." She opened the door and slid into the passenger seat. "I brought your order." She handed him the tray. "Your truck is nice. How long have you had it?"

"'Bout a year. I'm surprised to see you here, considering we have an early morning."

"I'm too keyed up to sleep. Besides it's only eight-thirty. Plenty early enough for a shake."

"Chocolate?"

She nodded. It'd always been her go-to food of choice whenever she was stressed or celebrating. Now to figure out which one she was doing. "The landscape design you presented was perfect. Ted loved it." Scott was so much better than her when it came to coming up with unique designs.

She took a long draw from the straw and savored the chocolaty goodness. "I had an interesting conversation with Brendon."

"Oh, yeah. About what?"

"You."

His shifted his body to face her. "This I gotta hear."

She smiled and drank more of her shake then rested the cup on the seat. "He admitted he told you to stay away from me. I wish I'd known. If I had I would have broken up with him."

Scott's eyes grew wide. "Seriously?"

She nodded. "I wasn't that into him at first. Then he became a habit. It wasn't until we'd been together for a while that I fell in love. If I'd known at the start what a jerk he could be, I'd have dumped him and saved myself a lot of heartache."

"Now I feel bad."

"Don't. You were sixteen, and the past is the past. I wish things had turned out differently, but I'm a firm believer that our life experiences make us who we are, and other than being broke and living with my mother at the age of twenty-three, I like myself."

He chuckled. "I like you too. What do you say we forget about the past and focus on winning this competition?"

"That's a plan I can support. Brendon said something else too, but don't laugh."

"What's that?"

"He said you were in love with me."

Shock registered on his face. "I wonder where he came up with that idea?" He looked out the side window.

Uncertainty filled her. She'd been so sure her friend never had romantic feelings for her. "Beats me. But I told him he was wrong."

He turned toward her with a look in his eyes she had never seen.

Suddenly she wasn't sure Brendon had been wrong. But he must have been. She'd know if Scott loved her. The look on his face made her want to squirm. "I should go." She opened the door and hopped out. "See you in the morning."

Although still angry with Brendon, she felt much better about things with Scott, at least mostly. Her phone lit up with a text from Ted. She pulled over and read it. "You've got to be kidding me!"

CHAPTER FIVE

Scott signed the invoice at the rock quarry. "Can these be delivered today?"

"Does one o'clock work?" Bob, the owner, asked.

"Sounds great." Scott held out his hand. "I appreciate it."

Bob shook his hand. "I'm rooting for you and Jessie. I never was a fan of Brendon."

"Me either, come to think of it. Thanks again." Scott whistled a tune he'd heard on the radio as he strode to his pickup. He'd swing by *Java Java* and pick up a couple of iced coffees and donuts. This project with Jessie was exactly what he needed, even if he wasn't going to make a penny. It would get his name out there, and he couldn't wait to be busy once again. Before Jessie returned to Silver Springs and became his competition he'd had a crew of several men, but gradually he'd laid off all but one. Lawn care was only a small portion of his business. He specialized in landscape design and had monopolized the market until Jessie put out her shingle. Then when Brendon showed up and started stealing his customers, he had to let his last man go.

He hoped to rehire that crew one day. They were hard workers and each had a specialty to contribute. He missed their camaraderie too. He'd heard Brendon had hired a few of his men, but he knew they'd come back to him.

He parked and sauntered inside the coffee shop. Melissa stood behind the counter.

"Good morning, Scott."

"Hey." He nodded. "I'll take two chocolate donuts and two large iced coffees to go." He handed her a twenty and waited for his change before dropping a dollar into the tip jar.

"I haven't talked with Jessie since yesterday. Are you headed over to the site from here?" She carefully bagged the donuts.

"I am."

"Good. Will you tell her I'll pop over at noon after my lunch crew arrives? I offered to film a little while the two of you are working. We were thinking we'd do a montage as you toil in the soil."

He chuckled. "You have a way with words, Melissa."

She handed him a cardboard tray that held his purchase. "Have fun! Tootles."

He grinned and left. Every time Melissa said tootles it put a smile on his face. Ten minutes later, he pulled up to the building site and spotted Jessie shoveling dirt like a dog chasing a rodent. "Hmm." She'd spray-painted the outline of the water feature and had made good progress on the digging.

He slid out, tucked his gloves into his pocket, then grabbed the goodies. "'Morning," he said as he sauntered toward her.

Jessie glared at him.

"Whoa. What'd I do?"

She tossed down the shovel. "Sorry. It's not you. It's Brendon." Sweat trickled down her face. She drew her arm across her forehead.

"How about you take a break and join me for coffee and a donut. I'll put the tailgate down, and we can sit there."

Her face softened. "You brought me a donut and coffee?"

He nodded.

"Chocolate?"

"Yep."

She tossed her gloves onto the dirt. "Good. Even you'll need it after I tell you the latest news." She stomped past him, released the tailgate, then sat.

His stomach knotted. "What's going on?"

"Brendon." She sipped the coffee. "Mmm. This is good. How did you know how I like it?"

"Melissa."

She nodded and reached into the bag for the donut.

He watched her profile. A few strands of hair had slipped loose from her ponytail. He tucked them behind her ear.

She tilted her head his way. "Thanks. I have some bad news. I don't know how he did it, but Brendon talked the owner of the property into not allowing us to film here."

"What?"

"And not only that, he contacted the TV station and told them what we were doing. They updated or rather clarified the rules on the website, which now clearly state only one entry per person will be viewed. Don't ask me how their lawyers missed that little detail in the wording. But now that I've re-read the original rules it's there, just not clear like now." She ripped a bite off the donut.

He was counting on the publicity from this project. Word had spread quickly around town, and people were getting excited that three of their own might be on TV. For Jessie's sake, he wouldn't show how disappointed he was. "It's okay, Jess. We still have our own entries."

"I know, but he makes me so angry. I don't have a clue how I could have ever loved a man like that."

"Love is blind." He took a bite of the donut then washed it down with coffee. Sure it was cliché, but sometimes things were said a lot because they were true. "My day is open, and the boulders and stones won't be delivered until this afternoon. How about if I stick around and help you? Just because we can't enter the contest doesn't mean I can't help out an old friend."

Her face brightened. "Really? You'd help me even though we're competitors?"

"Absolutely. And if you're really nice, I'll let you continue to use my design plan, no charge."

She blinked rapidly. "I don't know what to say except thank you." She tossed an arm across his shoulders. "You're the best, Scott."

"I know." He winked and stood. "Break's over." He slid on a pair of gloves and grabbed a shovel from the bed of the truck. Brendon must have been worried to go to such lengths to keep their duo out of the competition, which in reality was nuts since he was up against all entries in the northwest.

Jessie tugged on her gloves and attacked the dirt once more. He held in a chuckle. Clearly, she had a lot of anger to work off. In high school she'd been such a dreamer. To some degree, he suspected she still was, but the woman working across from him was not the same girl he'd once hoped to ask to prom. This one had been hurt a few times too many, and the scars showed. He blamed himself. If he'd only stood up to Brendon in high school things would be so different now.

A sweet looking silver truck pulled up behind his and parked. A man who looked to be in his early thirties got out.

"Who's that?" he asked so only Jessie could hear.

"Ted. He's the builder who owns this place."

Scott stood tall and rested the shovel in one hand. "Good morning."

The man's frown made him appear to be having anything but a good morning. He strode straight to Jessie. "I told you the filming was off."

Jessie straightened and gave the man a look Scott had only seen one other time, but he'd never forget. "We aren't filming."

"No. But why is Scott here?"

He knows my name?

"He's helping out. Is that a problem?"

"Uh. No I guess not." He turned and marched inside.

"What was that all about?" Scott kept his voice low.

Jessie's gaze rested on the front door of the house. "I'm not sure, but I have a suspicion."

"Care to share?"

She shook her head. "It's not nice to gossip, so we'd better stick to working."

There'd been a time when Jessie would have told him anything. Clearly that was in the past. His hope for renewing their friendship dimmed. "Three of the boulders I chose will be impossible for the two of us to lift."

"There's a Bobcat in back we can use."

"That'll work." He wiped sweat from his brow and studied Jessie's intense expression as she continued to attack the dirt. How did she keep up that pace? "You know, the rest of my week is mostly open since I was planning to be here. I'm happy to continue helping as time allows." He'd squeeze in his lawn maintenance customers when he could, and since he didn't have any current projects, this worked well.

She placed a hand on her hip and faced him. "You know I can't pay you."

"Did you plan to complete this project all by yourself?"

She shrugged. The look on her face told him she had.

"It would have taken you weeks to do all of this on your own."

"My design was much simpler. The water feature was a lot smaller too."

"Where's the extra money coming from?"

"My profits, or what little profits I had," she said it as if it wasn't a big deal, but he knew differently. She wouldn't be living with her mom if her business was doing well. "In that case I insist you allow me to help complete this job so you can move on to one where you'll make some money. After all, this mess is my fault."

"I won't turn down the help. Thanks."

A few hours later, a little car pulled up to the curb.

Jessie sighed. "I forgot to tell Melissa not to come." She dropped the shovel and headed over to their friend.

Scott followed.

Melissa held up a large brown sack and a cardboard tray holding drinks. "I brought lunch!"

Scott's stomach rumbled. "That was nice of you."

"Anything for the two of you. I'm on team J-Scott."

"Huh?" They both asked in unison.

Melissa chuckled. "You haven't heard? The town is taking sides between the two of you and Brendon. They've dubbed you the J-Scott team and Brendon is the QB team."

"For quarterback?" he asked dryly.

"Nope Q is for quarterback, B is for Brendon." She laughed. "Isn't it funny?" She looked around the yard. "It's pretty rough. Where can we sit?"

He motioned toward his pickup. "The tailgate works." He led the way, wondering how long Jessie would wait to tell Melissa the news—there was no J-Scott team.

Melissa stopped at the back of his truck and frowned. "How am I supposed to get up there?"

Jessie took the bag and tray from her. "The same way you used to sit on the countertop when you were a kid."

Melissa's eyes widened. "I haven't tried that in years. Here goes nothing." She rested her arms on the tailgate then whirled around and planted her hind end on the metal with as much grace as a gymnast.

Jessie laughed so hard Scott was afraid she'd drop the food. He took the tray and bag from her.

Melissa frowned. "What's so funny?"

"You." She laughed again.

"What'd I do?" Melissa looked to Scott.

"Beats me." He shrugged.

Jessie's laugher was contagious, and he chuckled. He hadn't enjoyed work this much in a long time.

Melissa wagged a finger at them. "Be nice or I won't feed you."

Jessie grabbed her stomach and took slow deep breaths, clearly trying to regain control. He guessed her laughter had released a lot of pent up emotions.

"You're a great friend, Melissa. Thanks for feeding us—you didn't have to do that, but my taste buds thank you. You make a much better sandwich than I do."

"Your sandwiches are fine."

"Exactly." Jessie grinned and took a bite.

"When we're finished, I'll film the two of you working for a few minutes then I'll need to head back to *Java Java*."

Jessie coughed and swallowed hard. "I forgot to tell you! Brendon messed everything up, well . . . I suppose we can't exactly blame him. There is no team J-Scott. He contacted the TV station and told them our plan, and they clarified the wording. More than one entry, even as a team, is not allowed."

"That's not fair," Melissa whined.

"Fair or not. What's done is done. There was a note on the website stating that only one entry was allowed from the start, but they are clarifying," Scott added.

"Is that true?"

Jessie shrugged. "I suppose the rules could have been interpreted that way. Regardless, Brendon won."

"This round," Scott said. "He may have shut us down as a team, but our individual entries are still in the running."

"That's right!" Melissa hopped off the tailgate and paced back and forth. "The nerve of that man. Why the people in this town think he's so wonderful I don't understand. He's pathetic."

"Well said. But in a way, he did us a favor. If we had entered together both of our single entries could have been disqualified." Scott bit into his ham and cheese sandwich. Not bad, although a little mustard would have been nice. He only saw mayo packs in the bag, so he washed the dry bread down with the lemonade Melissa had brought.

"Oh. I didn't think of that." Melissa stopped her pacing. "If the two of you need any help with this job, count me and Josh in. I'll bring the food, and he'll provide the labor."

Jessie smiled. "That's nice of you to volunteer your husband, but I think we'll be fine. I'd hug you, but I'm a sweaty mess."

Melissa wrinkled her noise. "Now that you mention it."

Scott tossed his head back and laughed. He missed camaraderie with co-workers so much. Now more than ever, he wanted to get his old crew back together again.

Jessie made a face at them before donning her work gloves. "Break's over."

The builder came outside and stared at them. What was up with that dude? Scott was glad he'd offered to stick around. He wasn't crazy about Jessie being here alone with that man. Something was definitely not right.

CHAPTER SIX

JESSIE STROLLED DOWN MAIN STREET AND admired the flower baskets hanging from the awning at the hardware store. It seemed odd to frou-frou up a store like this, but she liked it nonetheless. The door opened, and a man she'd known her whole life sauntered out.

"Hey girl. I'm rooting for you." The man patted her shoulder and kept walking.

"Thanks." She went in the store and directly to the aisle with work gloves. Hers had a hole worn clear through today with all that digging and then moving rock. She'd be lucky to lift her arms tomorrow.

A few friendly people smiled in her direction. It felt like all of Silver Springs suddenly knew who she was. Hopefully, that would translate into more business. Maybe she should print up flyers about her landscaping services and hang them up around town.

"Good evening, Jessie," Mr. Miller said. "You, Scott, and Brendon are the talk of the town."

"Is that so?" She pulled a ten from her wallet and handed it to him.

"Yep. Since I sell stuff to all of you, I'm like Switzerland."

She chuckled. "Staying neutral, huh? You're a wise man." She accepted her change and grabbed the gloves. "Have a good one."

"You too." Mr. Miller had been the woodshop teacher at Silver Springs High School until the year she graduated. Then he'd bought this store and retired from teaching. She stepped outside and breathed in deeply the sweet scent coming from the flowers. They'd need to incorporate fragrant flowers into Scott's design.

Melissa stood across the street in front of *Java Java*, waving.

Jessie looked both ways then crossed the two lane street. "What's up?"

"That's what I was going to ask you." The twinkle in her eyes put Jessie on alert.

"I wore out my gloves today and needed to pick up a new pair."

Melissa rocked back and forth. "That's not what I meant." She looked around and lowered her voice. "What's up with you and Scott?"

"Nothing. Why do you ask?"

Her friend stilled. "Really? That's disappointing. I thought for sure I saw a spark between the two of you."

"You've been reading too many romance novels."

Melissa rolled her eyes. "I've cut back to one a week."

"That's one too many to my way of thinking."

Melissa's brow puckered. "What do you have against reading?"

"Nothing. It's the romance part I have a problem with."

"Since when did you become so cynical about love?"

She shrugged. Since her fiancé dumped her for another woman. It didn't matter that he'd come crawling back. The damage had been done. "I'm beat. Maybe I'll see you tomorrow." She'd learned a hard lesson with Brendon. One she didn't care to repeat. Ever.

JESSIE TOOK THE COFFEE mug her mother offered as she sat on the barstool at the kitchen counter. "May I ask you a question?"

"Of course." Mom poured creamer into her mug and stood, resting a hip against the butcher-block counter.

"Did you have a boyfriend before Dad?"

Mom's eyes widened. "That was not what I was expecting, but to answer your question, yes."

"Were you serious?"

"We were, but we realized we didn't want the same things out of life and parted ways."

"Just like that." Jessie snapped her fingers. "You moved on?"

Mom chuckled. "Not exactly. I was very sad for a long time, but breaking up was the right thing for both of us. He was a Christian, and

I wasn't. He always wanted to attend church activities, and though the people there were nice to me, I wasn't interested in Christianity at that time."

"So he dumped you because he was a Christian and you weren't? Why'd he start dating you in the first place then?"

"He wasn't a Christian when we started dating."

"Oh." It was exactly like her and Brendon only opposite, but she didn't have the guts to let him go when it became clear they were too different from each other. She'd wanted to attend church and he didn't. She wanted to go to a small group Bible study for college kids, and he didn't. But more than anything she wanted to be married, so when he proposed she didn't think twice about saying yes.

Once they were engaged, her church activities became more of an issue, and they drifted apart. No wonder Brendon had found someone else.

"Jessie," her mom said softly.

She met her mother's concerned gaze.

"What's this about? Are you thinking of getting back together with Brendon?"

"No. We both changed after high school but not in the same way. We drifted apart, even though we fought hard to make things work. I thought going into business together would fix things in our relationship, but I was wrong. I didn't realize until a little while ago the reason we were struggling was because we were in a different place spiritually. He had no interest in church, and it came between us."

Mom set her mug on the counter. "That's understandable. But in my case, breaking up with my old boyfriend was the best thing I could have done. A couple of years later, another friend invited me to her church, and I really liked it there. The people were warm and inviting, and that's when I finally became a Christian. It's also where I met your dad."

"I wish I'd known your story. Why didn't you ever tell me?"

"It didn't seem important."

Jessie sipped her now lukewarm coffee. Maybe the problem wasn't love in and of itself, but rather finding the right person. "I should go. I only have Scott this week, and I want to take advantage of his help as much as I can."

"I heard you won't be entering the contest together." She clucked her tongue. "I'm surprised your *competition* offered to help you."

"He had already cleared his calendar, so it worked out. I'm grateful he did. Yesterday was a killer. I never could have done it by myself. My arms still hurt. At least all the heavy lifting is done." And she didn't have to beg any of the construction workers to help her.

"That young man is a keeper. You're always welcome to use the kitchen if you'd like to entertain anyone." Her eyes twinkled mischief.

Jessie stopped herself from rolling her eyes. Her mother actually had a good idea. She owed Scott, and a meal would be a nice gesture. "I appreciate the offer, Mom. I'll see you tonight."

An hour later she pulled up to the site and got out, forcing her sore muscles to move. The bed of her truck held all the foliage they'd be planting today. She couldn't wait to see the finished product. She looked once more at the sunlit fountain that cascaded into a small pool, and pleasure surged through her. Scott was an amazing landscape designer. She never would have come up with that. Her idea had been a simple bubbler.

This fountain would be the main feature of the yard and the plants would complement it.

Scott pulled up behind her and hopped out. "What'cha standing around for?" He tugged on gloves and marched to her pickup. "These look great. That's a beautiful Japanese maple."

"Thanks. I thought it was just the right size. It was a budget breaker though, so I had to skimp on the rest."

He frowned. "I have gallon size azaleas in pots at my place. You're welcome to them. They need a new home."

"Thanks!" She pulled on her new gloves, already missing her broken-in ones. She rested a hand on the tree. "On three?"

Scott nodded.

"One. Two. Three." She grunted as the weight of the tree transferred from the tailgate to them.

"Where are we taking it?" Scott asked as if he lifted heavy trees on a daily basis.

"To wherever you think it will look best." She liked to set

everything out before planting. She followed his lead and eased it to the ground. "Let's place the rest of the plants out before we dig any holes."

"Okay." They worked in silence, seeming to know on instinct where each plant would go. She'd had to buy a few cheaper species due to cost, but believed they would still work with Scott's plan. Twenty minutes later they stood back to study what they'd done.

"I like it," Scott said. "And the azaleas will finish off the palette. Don't you agree?" He looked at her.

She caught her breath. His smile sent a tingle racing through her. "I do. Now to get them in the ground."

The sound of shovels piercing the dirt and the echo of hammers and saws filled the otherwise quiet morning. Jessie glanced toward Scott as he backfilled a hole. "I'd like to make a thank-you dinner for you."

He stopped working, resting his hand on the top of the shovel. "I'd enjoy that. When did you learn to cook?"

"I've picked up a thing or two watching my mom. I'm sure I can whip us up a fantastic meal."

"Or we could go for burgers, fries and shakes at the drive-up."

"Nope. I want to do this for you."

"Your mom won't mind?"

"Not at all. Does next Friday at six work?"

"Sure. I'll be there." He grasped the shovel and tossed the last of the dirt into the hole he'd been backfilling.

Jessie patted the nutrient-rich soil she'd brought in to aid the lesser quality plants. She didn't even mind that she and Scott couldn't enter the contest together. The point had been to renew their friendship, and she'd accomplished that. At least it felt that way right now. They were still rivals in business, but they didn't have to go out of their way to avoid each other anymore.

The front door opened, and Ted stepped out. He strode down the driveway and stood on the sidewalk observing them.

Jessie stood resting her hands on her waist. "What do you think?"

"It's great." He ran a hand along the back of his neck. "When will you be finished?"

"Today. Once we get the plants in we'll throw down some bark and be out of here."

"Excellent. The Realtor wants to take pictures." He glanced toward Scott then back at Jessie. "May I have a word with you in private?

"Sure." Jessie clapped the dirt off her gloves then tucked them into her back jeans pocket. She followed him into the backyard which was as builder basic as homes came, with mostly grass and a planting bed along the fence—Ted's choice, not hers.

"I wanted to apologize about the other day. I had a bad morning and Brendon's interference made me angry."

She nodded.

"Why did you let Brendon railroad you?"

Ted clenched his jaw, and his face reddened.

"Forget I asked. I hope you'll give me a call the next time you need a job done."

"About that. I really like what you and Scott did, but Brendon will be getting my business in the future."

A surge of anger shot through her. "Why? We both know Brendon wouldn't have done anything half as nice as what Scott and I pulled off. What's Brendon holding over you?"

"It doesn't matter. I just wanted you to know it's nothing personal when I don't call you for the next job."

"Fine." She whirled around and marched to the front.

"Everything okay?" Scott asked.

"Brendon blackmailed Ted into giving him all future jobs. I'm sorry, but I don't want to talk about it."

He raised his hands palms out. "No problem."

But it was a problem. A big one named Brendon. What was that man up to now?

CHAPTER SEVEN

Friday, promptly at six o'clock, Scott rang Jessie's doorbell. He hadn't seen her since last week when they'd finished the project at the new build. It'd been a full week too, thanks to the publicity the contest had created. Several people near the outskirts of town had hired him to maintain their yards, which had added an extra day to his schedule—he wasn't complaining. Mowing wasn't his favorite side of the business, but it helped pay the bills, and he was grateful.

He looked at the orange roses he had cut from his garden and placed in a simple glass vase. Jessie would enjoy them. She'd always been a fan of roses.

The door swung open, and all the air whooshed from his lungs. "Brendon."

"Scott." Brendon opened the door wider, and a pungent smell smacked him in the face.

Scott wrinkled his nose. "What's burning?"

"Apparently your dinner." Brendon closed the door and stood tall, looking down his nose at Scott. "I warned you to stay away from her," he said softly.

"And I told you no. Besides I was invited." Scott brushed past him. "Jessie," he called as he walked through the home he'd spent many hours in while growing up.

"In the kitchen." She stood at the sink scrubbing a blackened pan. "You okay?"

"I'm fine, but our dinner isn't." Her gaze landed on the flowers, and her face softened. "Are those for me?"

"They're from my garden. Where would you like them?"

She turned the water off and reached out her hands for the flowers. "They're beautiful." She drew them close to her face and breathed in deeply. A smile touched her lips. "And they smell wonderful. I'd love to see your garden sometime."

"Yada yada," Brendon mocked from the doorway. "So he brought flowers. Big deal."

They both turned toward Brendon.

Jessie placed the flowers on the island countertop. "Why are you still here?"

"We aren't finished."

"Yes. We. Are." Her bare feet slapped the floor as she walked toward him. "I'll see you out."

Curious, Scott followed. He heard the low rumble of Brendon's voice but couldn't decipher what he was saying.

Jessie yanked open the door. Her body stood rigid as if she expected him to argue about leaving, but instead Brendon kissed her cheek then dashed out the door.

"Of all the . . ." Jessie slammed the door and whirled around. She gasped when she spotted Scott. "Oh. I didn't know you were standing there. I thought you were in the kitchen." She moved back into the kitchen with Scott trailing behind.

"Sorry. I didn't trust him and wanted to make sure he didn't bother you."

"He bothered me all right. I'm really sorry about dinner." She looked ready to cry, but Jessie never cried.

"I can fix this." He pulled out his phone. "Do you still like the works on your pizza?"

She nodded. "Easy on the sauce please."

He grinned. "I remember." He placed the order. "It'll be here in forty minutes." His stomach growled.

"I made a green salad. We could start with that."

"Sounds good." What had happened to cause Jessie to burn dinner, and why had Brendon been here?

Jessie stood at the open fridge door not moving.

"You okay?"

She pulled out a bowl and dressing and placed them on the counter. "Fine." She sighed.

"I know whatever is going on between you and Brendon is none of my business, but I'm a good listener and know how to keep my mouth shut if you need someone to talk to."

Jessie added green salad to two bowls and drizzled Ranch dressing over hers. He chose the Italian vinaigrette. "Brendon is . . . what I mean is he wants a second chance. Even after cheating on me."

"He cheated?" *What kind of person does that?*

"Yes."

"Hurting the woman you claim to love works every time when you want her back." He shook his head in disgust.

Jessie shot him a look that said his sarcasm wasn't appreciated.

"Sorry. I know I said I'm a good listener and normally I am, but Brendon . . ." He clenched his free hand. "The man is not good enough for you, and it's clear he can't be trusted."

"Agreed." She thrust a forkful of salad into her mouth and crunched the crisp greens. Swallowing, she waved her fork. "There is no way Brendon and I will ever get back together. I'm thankful he dumped me when he did."

Now there was a sentence he'd never heard anyone say. They ate in silence until the doorbell rang.

"That must be the pizza." Jessie pulled out her wallet.

"I've got this."

"Nope. This thank-you dinner is for you. I'm paying." She breezed past him disappearing around the corner. A moment later she returned holding a large pizza box. "It smells wonderful." She placed the box on the island, then went to the cupboard and pulled out two white ceramic plates before sitting on the bar stool beside him.

The yeasty smell of the crust washed over him. He grabbed a slice and brought it to his mouth. *Mmm.*

"I forgot how good this is." Jessie grinned.

"*Tony's* makes the best crust in town."

"This is so much better than what I was trying to make. I should have started with pizza."

"When do you think we'll hear from the contest committee?" he asked.

"It closed for entries last Saturday. So I suppose anytime. Do you think we have a chance? I'm sure hundreds of people entered."

He shrugged. "The show is narrowing down the entries and then letting the public vote."

She frowned. "I didn't realize that. I was so excited when I saw the info about the contest I didn't read the fine print."

"What's wrong?"

"I could be on TV."

He laughed. "Wasn't that the point of entering? The grand prize is a TV deal."

"I know, but I'm in it for the money. I doubt I'll come in first. Who am I kidding? I probably don't have a chance of coming anywhere near the top ten, much less win the prize money for placing first or second."

"Don't sell yourself short, Jessie. You have talent."

"Thanks. So do you, and as long as we are having a heart-to-heart, I'm a little jealous of you. When did you get so great at designing? I mean, you've always been good, but what you did at that new build was spectacular."

His ducked his chin as his face heated. "Thanks. I studied horticulture and design in college. Landscape design is a passion."

She rested her hand over his. "Good for you. I don't have the eye you have and much prefer to execute my ideas than come up with them."

Another reason they would have made a great team. It really was too bad they hadn't stuck to their original plan as teens and gone into business together. Then again, it wasn't too late. But if Jessie wanted to join forces she was going to have to be the one to bring it up.

His cell phone rang, and a second later Jessie's did too. They looked at each other and pulled out their phones.

CHAPTER EIGHT

JESSIE STOOD IN THE MIDDLE OF her mom's kitchen and squealed as she jumped up and down. "I made it! I made it!" She ran to Scott and hugged him. "I can't believe this. I have to call my mom."

Scott laughed. "You're not the only one."

"You're going to call and tell your mom I'm a semi-finalist?" She knew Scott supported her, but that was weird.

He grinned wide and tapped her nose. "You can be so into your own world sometimes. No. I'm going to call and tell her that her son is a semi-finalist in the *Fresh and Fantastic* contest and that my entry will be on Monday's live show."

Jessie's eyes widened. "We're *both* semi-finalists?" She squealed again. "I can't believe this!" She hugged him again. "Congratulations."

He didn't let go as she loosened her arms. "I'm proud of you, Jessie."

She titled her head back and looked into his clear blue eyes seeing the truth of his words and something else that shot tingles through her. "You realize this makes us competitors again?"

"Nothing new." He winked and released her. "I'd better go. Thanks for the pizza." He strode from the kitchen.

"Any time," she called after him. The door clicked closed. "What just happened?" Could Brendon have been right? Did Scott really have a thing for her? Her brain was in overload—she couldn't think straight. Maybe she had imagined the look in his eyes.

The door that led to the garage opened. Mom stepped inside holding a cloth grocery bag. She sniffed and looked around. "What burned and where's Scott? I saw his pickup out front."

"He left as you walked in, and our dinner burned."

"Oh. I'm sorry to hear that."

"It's okay. Everything turned out fine in the end. We ordered pizza."

"Sounds delicious. Any left overs?" Mom glanced her way then paused. "What's wrong? You're flushed." Mom placed a hand on her forehead. "I hope you're not getting sick. You feel warm."

Jessie grasped her mother's shoulders. "Stop," she said gently. "I'm fine. Better than that, but I'm in a bit of shock. I'm one of ten semi-finalists in the *Fresh and Fantastic* contest." She couldn't believe how calmly she said that considering her stomach was doing somersaults.

Mom's face lit. "Congratulations! So what's next?" Jessie told her about the live show and the voting. "I'm going to call everyone we know and ask them to vote for you."

"No. That wouldn't be fair."

Mom snickered. "I don't know *that* many people, and if you think everyone else won't do the same thing you're dreaming."

"Scott is also a semi-finalist," Jessie blurted.

Mom stilled and a hush came over the room. "I guess I won't be asking Beverly for her vote then." She chuckled. "I'm so proud of you both. We'll have a viewing party and invite everyone over."

"Even Scott's family?"

"Why not? It'll be fun."

"But he's the competition."

"So you keep saying." Mom winked. "Don't worry, sweetie. Competitors or not, you and Scott should celebrate this with your friends and family together. This is a big deal." Mom put the groceries away. "Be sure to give me a list of everyone you want invited. We need to get on this right away. Monday is only three days away!" She tapped her nails on the counter. "Hmm. That's not much time to pull this off. Maybe just invite your closest friends."

"Sure." That would be a cinch since Melissa, her hubby, and a few girls she'd kept in touch with from high school were the extent of her social circle in Silver Springs. She'd spent all her time since returning to town trying to build up her business, and it had left little time to make new friends or renew many old ones.

"I'm going out." Jessie grabbed a sweater from the hook beside the garage door.

"Will you be long? I need that guest list."

"I don't know, Mom. I'll invite my friends and let you know how many people to expect."

"Perfect. Have fun." Mom's eyes glowed.

Jessie wandered down the street on foot. Getting behind the wheel of a vehicle in this state of mind could lead to disaster. She passed long-time neighbors weeding their yard and waved.

A car pulled up along the curb beside her. She glanced at it and stopped. "Hey, girl. I was on my way to see you."

"Hop in," Melissa said. "I'll give you a ride."

Jessie scooted inside then buckled up.

"You look ready to burst." Melissa shot a glance her way then focused on the road.

"I'm a semi-finalist."

Melissa grinned. "I told you! Congratulations."

"Thanks. There's a viewing party at my house this coming Monday. You and Josh are both invited." She explained the details.

"This is so exciting. But do you think your mom's house is going to be big enough? Between you and Scott, there could be fifty people there."

Jessie frowned. "I suppose it will be tight."

Melissa laughed. "Tight is putting it nicely."

"My mom is great at organizing parties. I'm sure she'll get it all figured out." At least she hoped so.

MONDAY EVENING, JESSIE SAT shoulder to shoulder with Scott in the middle of the couch facing the television set with about twenty-five of her and Scott's closest friends and family.

Scott's warm breath tickled her ear. "Are you nervous?"

Jessie held up her shaking hand for him to see.

He grasped her cold hand and tucked it between his. "Me too, but no matter what happens, it's going to be okay."

His warmth penetrated the iciness of her hand, sending shivers through her body. She'd never been this nervous around him.

"It's on," someone shouted. "Shh."

The semi-finalist's faces appeared on the screen. Jessie gasped. "There's Brendon."

CHAPTER NINE

JESSIE STROLLED DOWN MAIN STREET. A little girl she recognized from church ran up to her.

"May I have your autograph, Miss Morgan?" the little blonde with pigtails asked.

Jessie squatted to the girl's level. "You want *my* autograph?"

She nodded. "My momma says you're the most famous person to ever come from this town except for . . ." she bit down on her lower lip then stage whispered to her mother. "Who, Momma?"

The woman she recognized but didn't know whispered into her daughter's ear.

"Mr. Jacobs and Mr. Meyers."

Brendon and Scott? She couldn't say no to such a cute kid. "What would you like me to sign?"

The child held out a notepad. "Momma bought me an autograph book." She grinned. "We voted for you. Momma says a girl needs to win."

Jessie chuckled as she signed the book and drew a flower beside her name. "Thanks for your vote." She looked to the child's mother as she stood. "I recognize you from church, but I'm sorry I don't know your name."

"I'm Tara."

She visited with the woman for a few minutes then continued down the street. A few more kids asked for her autograph before someone grabbed her arm and dragged her into an alcove. It happened so fast she had no reaction time.

"Brendon. What are you doing?"

"Saving you from your fans. You need a manager, and I'm it."

She ripped her arm from his grasp. "No." Why wouldn't Brendon leave her alone?

"I know what it's like to be a celebrity in a small town. I can help."

He had a point. But Brendon couldn't be trusted. She'd learned that lesson the hard way. "I appreciate that you are looking out for me, Brendon, but I can handle this. You did fine without a manager, and so will I. Besides it's a conflict of interest, considering we are both semi-finalists." She darted from the alcove, leaving him before he could respond.

Who would have thought an innocent entry into a long-shot-contest would lead to all of this?

Scott strode out of the hardware store wearing a frown. "Hey, Jessie."

"What's wrong?"

He held up a piece of paper. "Did you know the townspeople are taking bets on who is going to win the *Fresh and Fantastic* contest?"

She groaned. "This is ridiculous. What if none of us wins?"

"Then all the proceeds will go to improving the park."

Jessie rolled her eyes. Had all of Silver Springs gone mad? "You know what? It's not a big deal. Let them have their fun while we go about our business. There's nothing we can do to stop them, and frankly, I don't have the energy to try. It's taken me thirty minutes to walk two blocks. Kids keep stopping me for my autograph."

He chuckled. "You too, huh?"

She playfully slapped his arm. "It's not funny."

He raised a brow. "It kind of is. Almost no one knew I existed until this contest. And now people are buying me coffee and wanting me to re-design their yards. At this rate, I'll be able to hire my old crew back from Brendon."

Jessie grinned. "I've had more business too. I hadn't considered the positive to all of this. Thanks for pointing it out."

"Sure." He draped an arm across her back, resting his hand on her shoulder. "Where were you heading. I'll make sure you get there quickly."

"Ha. You're as much in demand as me. In fact, I can't believe we've been left alone for the past five minutes." She looked around and gasped. Lined up across the street people had their cell phones out presumably either recording them or taking their picture. "Oh boy. Look."

Scott waved to the crowd.

"You're loving this." She never would have imagined her old friend eating up the attention, but here he stood acting as if this was an everyday event. She shrugged and waved to the crowd. Why not enjoy it while it lasted? It was sure to come to an end soon.

Scott leaned close to her ear. "Meet you at our secret place in two hours?"

Her eyes widened. She hadn't been there since they were teens. Was their old clubhouse still standing? "Okay."

SCOTT FINISHED WASHING THE last window then looked around the ramshackle clubhouse from their childhood. He'd been cleaning for the past half-hour, and it looked pretty good. His dad and Jessie's had built it for them in the woods on his parents' property. He hadn't been here in years, but his dad assured him it was sound.

He rushed to his pickup and pulled out the small throw rug and a huge bag filled with oversized pillows. Now that the place was clean he intended to make it homey. The eight by ten structure was in great shape. His dad and Mr. Morgan had shingled the roof and added real glass windows to keep the elements out when he and Jessie were kids. They'd even sided and painted it.

He rolled out the fall-toned rug in one corner then dumped the bag of pillows out.

"Oh my goodness."

He jerked around. "You're early, Jessie." He'd wanted everything to be perfect before she got there. The small table and chairs he'd picked up at the thrift shop still waited in his truck bed.

"Sorry." She stepped inside leaving the door open. "Has your dad been taking care of this?"

"I think every now and then." The smile she wore made sprucing this place up worth every penny. "You want to give me a hand bringing in the table and chairs?"

"Sure."

Ten minutes later, their old hangout looked exactly how he imagined it should look when they were penniless kids. "What do you think?"

"It's perfect." Awe filled her voice. She turned to him. "Why'd you do this, Scott?"

"Our lives are about to become a little crazy, and I wanted a place we could escape to where no one, besides our parents, would know to look for us."

She chuckled. "You are the best friend a girl could ever ask for." She stepped close and wrapped her arms around his waist. "Thank you for this."

He held her for a moment before leaning back so he could see her face. "There's something I should have told you a very long time ago."

She looked at him with trusting eyes. Her cell phone ringing ruined the moment.

He sighed and released her. "You'd better get that." He sat at the table and pulled out the puzzle he'd picked up. They used to love doing puzzles together. This one was a landscape of a snowcapped mountain.

A minute later Jessie joined him. "Sorry about that. My mom said some reporters called. Apparently they want to interview me."

"See what I mean? Crazy."

"What did you want to tell me," she asked as she sorted through the puzzle pieces.

He took a deep breath then let it out slowly. Not knowing if they had a future was worse than knowing. "I love you, Jessie. I've loved you since we were fifteen." There he'd put it out there.

Jessie's stared at the table—silently.

"I know this comes as a shock. Especially since I went to such great lengths to avoid you for so long, but I need to know if there is any hope of more than friendship between us." His heart pounded so hard she could probably see his shirt moving with the pulses. Why wouldn't she say anything, or look at him? "Jessie? You're kind of killing me here."

She finally met his eyes—a shell-shocked look on her face. "I don't know what to say." She pressed her lips together for a moment. "Why are you telling me this now? Is it because of the TV show contest?"

"I don't know. I guess having you back in my life stirred up my feelings again, and I wanted to act on them before it was too late like last time."

"You mean Brendon?" she asked softly.

He nodded. "So . . ."

Jessie stood and bolted for the door.

"Wait!" He rushed after her and stopped her before she left.

She whirled around. "What?"

"You forgot this." He cradled her face in one hand and wrapped the other around her waist. She closed her eyes. He kissed her soft lips tenderly then stepped back.

She blinked with a dazed look on her face before leaving, taking his heart with her.

What had he done?

CHAPTER TEN

JESSIE'S HANDS SHOOK AS SHE REACHED for the coffee mug Melissa placed on her table at *Java Java*. Christian music played over the speakers.

Melissa moved a chair close and sat facing her. "What's going on? I've never seen you like this?"

"Scott kissed me," she said softly. And it was the best kiss she'd ever had. "What am I going to do?"

"Did you kiss him back?"

Jessie blinked and focused on her friend. "Excuse me?"

"Did you kiss him back?"

"I heard you the first time. And yes." What difference did that make?

Melissa squealed then slapped a hand over her mouth. "Sorry," she said softly. "I knew it."

Jessie shook her head. "What?"

"You have feelings for him."

"What makes you say that?" How could her friend know something like that when she didn't even know the way she felt?

"Simple. You kissed him back. You wouldn't have otherwise."

"He took me by surprise. It was instinct."

"Call it what you want. I say you have feelings for him. I told you there was a spark."

Jessie didn't know what to think. She didn't want to hurt Scott. She cared for him in spite of everything, but love? "He said he loves me. What am I going to do?"

"No way! This is so much better than the book I'm reading." She leaned closer. "What else?"

"Nothing. What am I going to do?"

"Did you tell him you love him too?"

"Of course not," she snapped. "He just came back into my life. I don't see how I could possibly love him. Besides, he's my competition."

Melissa frowned. "Scott is not standing between you and your dream. He'd probably hand you the prize money on the proverbial silver platter if he won and you didn't. The man loves you, Jessie. That is way more important that winning this contest."

The passion in her friend's voice made Jessie feel shallow, but she couldn't change how she felt. "I don't want charity. I want to earn my way in this world."

"I can respect that, but don't close your heart to him simply because you're in a competition against him. You need to pray about this."

"That's your answer to everything." Jessie rolled her eyes. She believed in the power of prayer, but it would be nice if her friend could give her some different advice once in awhile.

"Because prayer works, girl. What's wrong with you? Are you so full of yourself that you can't see how much the Lord loves you and wants to guide you?"

"It's not as easy as you make it sound. I've asked for guidance before and didn't get a response."

"Of course He answered. You weren't listening. I suggest you get out of your head and into the Word so you know when He has something to say to you. How do you expect to recognize His voice if you never listen to it?" Melissa stood. "I have to get back to work, but you know I'm here for you anytime. Right?"

Jessie nodded.

"Sorry for preaching." Melissa rested a hand on her shoulder.

"You're forgiven." Jessie gently squeezed her friend's hand. Alone with her thoughts, she sipped the now lukewarm coffee. Brendon had been right about Scott. Her mom had been too, in her own way.

Scott had always been there for her when she needed him, back when they were close. He was sweet, generous with his time, and he was a true friend. How could she not have seen his feelings?

She finished off the coffee, stood, and waved to Melissa before she left. One thing was certain—she refused to fall in love with a man who had the potential of putting her out of business. She'd made that mistake once already and would not do it again.

An hour later, she donned gloves and attacked the flowerbed in her mother's backyard. Ever since the contest had started she'd neglected the yard and weeds had crept in. She ripped a thistle from the soil and tossed it into a bucket.

"There you are."

Jessie looked over her shoulder. "Hi, Mom. Want to join me?" She looked around the bed she'd been working in for the past hour and smiled with satisfaction—much better.

"Sure. I thought I might do a little pruning." She headed for the Canadian White Bud.

"You really should wait until the fall to cut it back."

Mom shrugged. "This tree is hardy. It'll be fine."

She was right. The tree grew like a weed and could handle some pruning, even in the summer heat. Jessie reached for another weed and tugged.

"You're sure passionate about annihilating those dandelions. Everything okay?"

"Fine."

"Any word from the TV show?"

"Not yet." She wrapped both hands around a stem and pulled hard. The root yanked free of the soil, and Jessie landed on her rear end with a thud. "Ouch."

Mom chuckled. "Are you okay?"

"I'll live. But this weed won't." She added it to the bucket.

"I was visiting Beverly this afternoon when Scott popped in. He looked upset. Do you happen to know what's up with him?"

"Maybe." Her mom was fishing, but Jessie didn't want to have that conversation again. In fact, maybe it was time to take Melissa's advice and break out her Bible. She hadn't looked at it since church on Sunday, and although she didn't appreciate it at the time, her friend had given her some good advice. She brushed her hands together and picked up the bucket. "I'm finished for today."

"Okay." Mom looked at her with concern in her eyes. She never could fool her mother, but she still wasn't ready to fill her in.

Jessie stepped inside right as the doorbell rang. *Who could that be?* She rushed through the kitchen then into the entryway. She could see a woman through the window who looked a lot like a reporter from a Portland news station. A man holding a television camera stood behind her. She pulled open the door. "May I help you?"

"Hi, Jessie. I'm Clara Dempsey with—."

"I've seen you on TV. What can I do for you?" She thought to hide behind the door so the reporter and her cameraman couldn't see the dirt caked to her but figured it'd make her look wimpy.

"I spoke with your mom about an interview, and I was hoping now might be a good time."

Jessie looked down at her dirt-covered knees and could only imagine what the rest of her looked like. "I was working in the yard and am a mess."

"That's okay. Our viewers will understand." She thrust a microphone in Jessie's face. "There is a rumor that you and Scott Meyers are romantically involved."

Talk about being ambushed. She smiled sweetly. "That's news to me, Clara. Did you get to see *Fresh and Fantastic* on Monday? I'm thrilled to be a semi-finalist in the contest."

"I'm sure you are. This town has three semi-finalists. That's quite the feat. What can you tell us about your competitors?"

"They are both excellent at what they do." She smiled. This was not the way she wanted to be interviewed. "Perhaps you'd like to schedule a time to sit down with me and we can talk when I'm not covered in dirt."

"You look fine. I heard you and Scott tried to enter the contest together, but were disqualified."

Jessie held in a sigh. "You were misinformed. We considered it, but after having the fine print brought to our attention we decided to not send in a joint entry. It's been lovely talking with you, but I really need to get cleaned up." She started to close the door.

"Just one more question. How important is winning this competition to you?"

Jessie paused. "Very. Now if you will excuse me."

"Important enough to turn your back on love to pursue a career as a television host."

Jessie chuckled. "I think you're getting ahead of yourself, Clara." She closed the door and slid the lock into place. Where did that woman get her information?

Her cell phone rang—Melissa. "Now's not a good time, Melissa. May I call you back?"

"Don't hang up. I need to tell you something important, and you're not going to like it."

CHAPTER ELEVEN

JESSIE RACED UP THE stairs to her bedroom with her phone to her ear. "What's wrong, Melissa?"

"I messed up big time," Melissa said. "I was talking to someone in the coffee shop who'd overheard our conversation and well, a reporter from Portland was there and heard everything we said. I'm so sorry. The reporter was standing in the hall that leads to the restrooms, and I didn't realize she was there until she stepped out wearing a huge smirk."

Jessie pushed down frustration with her friend. It was clear from the tone of Melissa's voice how awful she felt. "It's okay. I never should have told you in a place where we could be overheard." She looked in the mirror and groaned. Not only did she have dirt on her nose, but a streak carved a path from her chin up to her cheek.

"I know it's awful. I feel so bad."

"It's not that. I just looked in the mirror. I was working in the yard and am wearing some dirt on my face. Which wouldn't be an issue if that reporter who overheard your conversation hadn't just been here with a camera man."

"Want me to come over tonight? Josh is working late. We could stuff ourselves with copious amounts of ice cream."

Jessie giggled. "No thanks." Her phone beeped indicating an incoming call. She checked the caller ID and noted it was the producer from the show. "I need to take another call, Melissa. Don't beat yourself up over the reporter. It was my fault. 'Bye." She accepted the other call. "This is Jessie."

"I have news. The Silver Springs mayor proposed an idea to me, and everyone here loves it. The town is going to hold a parade in honor of you, Scott, and Brendon. At the end of the parade will be a bandstand where we will announce which of you will be moving on in the competition and which won't. We'll incorporate the entire thing into the show."

Jessie sat on the edge of her bed. This was getting a lot bigger than she'd imagined. Unease gripped her. "Wow, that's really something." She tried to sound cheerful, but would rather skip the parade. That was not her idea of fun, at all. The producer outlined the details then disconnected the call. Everything was happening so fast. First Scott tells her he loves her, then a reporter ambushes her, then she finds out about the parade on Saturday.

What would be next?

MUSIC BLARED AS SCOTT waved from the backseat of a convertible and tossed candy to the people lined along Main Street. The high school marching band played a bandstand tune behind him, and Jessie followed in another convertible. Brendon led the tiny parade from his motorcycle.

The parade would finish at the end of the block. At least the town's people seemed to be having fun, even if this was the saddest excuse for a parade he'd ever seen. The convertible rolled to a stop, and he hopped out.

Never one comfortable at the center of attention, he wasn't certain his shaking legs would carry him onto the stage where the hosts of *Fresh and Fantastic* awaited their arrival. He squared his shoulders and plastered on a smile as he climbed the steps leading to the stage. Brendon was already seated. The band gathered around the stage and everyone else closed in the ranks.

"Excuse me," Jessie's voice rang out nearby.

Scott turned to find her in the crowd and spotted her near the stage, working her way to the stairs. At least people were letting her through. A minute later, she walked across the stage and took the seat beside him.

The host raised his arms for silence then explained how things would work and that everyone needed to be very quiet while they filmed.

Scott missed what happened, but the director must have said action or something because they were suddenly filming.

"Welcome to Silver Springs, Oregon, which three of our contestants call home. Due to this unique situation we here at *Fresh and Fantastic* decided to go on location and to announce who will be moving on as a finalist. Remember there will only be three finalists, and I can tell you now that at least one person sitting on this stage will be moving forward."

The crowd clapped and hooted.

The host egged them on even though he'd told them to be quiet earlier. Scott's stomach buzzed with excitement. One of them was moving on! No one had said what the outcome of this taping would be, and he was officially excited now.

The crowd noise dimmed and then hushed.

The host pulled an envelope out of his back pocket and slit the top. He slowly pulled out a sheet of paper.

Scott had to remind himself to breathe. He glanced over and saw the same excitement in Jessie's face. He grasped her cold hand and held tight.

The host's eyes grew big. "Folks this is a surprise! We have two finalists on this stage." He looked at each of them taking a grand pause. "The contestant who will *not* be moving on is Jessie Morgan. Congratulations, Brendon and Scott!"

The crowd erupted with applause and at the same time Jessie slipped her hand from his.

Jessie hugged him. "Congratulations, Scott. You deserve this. I hope you win."

He hugged her back, but too quickly she let go and left the stage. It wasn't supposed to happen like this. Jessie was supposed to be up here with him, not Brendon.

JESSIE SLIPPED THROUGH THE crowd, unnoticed, as they applauded the finalists. Her thick throat and burning eyes threatened to betray her. Finally free of the mass of bodies, she rushed to *Java Java*. The door was locked.

"Don't leave," Melissa called. She ran up behind her. "Sorry, I had a hard time working my way past a few strollers." She pulled out her keys then opened the door and locked it behind them. "Sit, I'll make you my new special coffee drink."

"I don't want anyone to see me." The dam broke, and tears streamed down Jessie's cheeks. She swiped at her face. "I hate this."

Melissa gently took her arm and guided her into the kitchen where a tiny table and two chairs were tucked into an out of the way corner. She handed her a handful of napkins. "Sit. I'll be right back."

Jessie needed to get control. She hadn't realized how much she wanted to win. Or maybe it was losing to Brendon that upset her so much. She'd caught his eye, and the smug look he sent her way before she left the stage.

"That was really something," Melissa said as she placed two cups on the table before sitting.

Jessie looked at her with what she was sure were red-rimmed eyes. "I'll survive." Her voice caught. "I hate feeling like such a loser."

"You will survive, and of course you feel disappointed. Anyone would be upset. Especially the way the show handled it. No one should have to go through that kind of humiliation."

Jessie nodded. She was right, but at the same time she had agreed to the publicity stunt. It was pride more than anything causing her tears. She took a deep breath and let it out slowly. "I'm okay." She told herself more than Melissa. "I'm happy for Scott, and I hope he wins."

Melissa grinned. "Me too. If Brendon's head gets any bigger it's sure to pop."

"You're a good friend." Jessie wiped her face on a napkin and sipped the coffee. "Mmm . . . this is even better than usual."

"Thanks, I added a little something extra that's been a hit."

"What?"

She pressed her lips together and shook her head. "It's a secret."

"I should go splash water on my face and touch up my makeup. I can't hide here all day."

"Good idea. I stashed your purse in that cupboard. I need to re-open the store too. You're going to be okay?"

"Yes. Thank you for being here with me, and thanks for suggesting I keep my purse tucked safely away here. I probably wouldn't have brought one otherwise, and then I wouldn't have had anything to fix my face with. You're the best."

"I know." Melissa shot her a cheeky grin before leaving the back room.

Jessie stood and went into the employee bathroom. Yep, her eyes were red, and her skin blotchy, but it was nothing a little water and makeup couldn't fix. Ten minutes later, she felt refreshed and ready to face the world again. She stepped out of the bathroom. Scott sat at the table she'd vacated. "What are you doing here?"

He stood and walked over to her. "I wanted to make sure you were okay."

"You're so sweet. I'm fine. You should be out celebrating."

"I will." He cradled her cheek in his hand. "I'm sorry about how things turned out."

"Don't be. The only reason I entered was to get money to help my business, but I have enough new clients to make up for not winning. It's all good."

He looked into her eyes as if he could see through to her soul. "Okay." He stepped back and sat again. "Join me? I have something to tell you."

Jessie sat. The excitement on his face stirred her curiosity.

"After you left, the host announced that each finalist must choose one person who didn't final to be his assistant. I chose you." He took her hand. "What do you say? Will you help me win this thing?"

Her stomach fluttered. "With pleasure." Her gaze landed on his mouth and her face heated with the memory of his kiss. A kiss she'd very much like to repeat right now.

He cleared his throat and stood. "I should be going, but we need to discuss the details soon."

Disappointment washed through her. Had she blown any future with Scott?

CHAPTER TWELVE

Scott whistled as he tromped through the woods on his parents' property. He needed thinking time away from people, and this had always been a good place to escape. Everything had happened so fast. He'd gone from not having enough work to having so much he needed to hire a two-person crew to handle maintenance jobs and run things while he and Jessie were filming in California next week.

The finalists were each assigned someone's backyard and given two days to make it over. Jessie, along with a crew of professionals, would assist him. He'd received photos of the yard in its current state, as well as the dimensions and a list of what the homeowners would like to see in their yard. Today he would draw up the design.

He broke through a stand of trees that ended at the clubhouse. He'd work here for now. He stepped inside and pulled up short. "Jessie?" She slept in the corner propped up by pillows.

Her eyes fluttered. "Hey, there. What are you doing here? I figured you'd be busy."

"I am, but my house has a constant barrage of well-wishers, and I needed a quiet place to think."

She stood. "I'll leave."

"Don't go. Why are you here?"

She looked to the floor then at him. "I needed a quiet place to be alone too."

"Is everything okay?"

"Sure." She stuffed her hands into her pocket and looked past him toward the door. "I don't want to keep you."

Something about the way she was behaving sent alarm bells ringing in his head. He stepped toward her. "I don't want you to leave. Since you're my assistant, will you stay and brainstorm a design with me?" He motioned toward the table.

"You're sure?" She looked skeptical.

"Very." He couldn't stop his thoughts from drifting to the last time they were here together. He was still waiting to hear how she felt about him, but with all that had happened, he didn't want to push her. Jessie had always been a person who needed time to digest things, and she seemed to need even more now than when they were younger.

"Okay." She pulled out a chair and sat at the table. "What do you know?"

He handed her his phone with the pictures and information regarding the yard. Her brow wrinkled. He wanted to reach out and smooth away the tension, but remained still. "They like to entertain. The pool is staying, but as you can see the yard is unusually large. We could easily add a cabana, outdoor kitchen, water feature, a few palm trees and the putting green they asked for."

"That's an ambitious project for only two days."

He nodded. "But we have professionals in each of these areas at our disposal. I only need to provide them with a plan." For the next hour, he took notes on his phone as they tossed around ideas. He leaned back in the chair. "This has been great. You've been a big help. I'm glad you were here."

"Me too." She grinned, and for the first time in a while, she looked completely relaxed. "I'm going to go now, but I want to thank you."

"There was no way I'd choose anyone but you to be on my team. And lucky for me I was given first pick."

"That's not what I was talking about, but thanks for that too."

He frowned. "Then what are you thanking me for?"

"For giving me time to consider my feelings for you."

"Oh." He snapped his mouth shut.

"I want you to know that I care about you a lot, but as far as love goes . . ." She shifted in the chair. "I'm not sure I'm capable of loving like that again."

He leaned forward. "What do you mean you're not capable?"

"I gave my heart to the wrong man, and he wounded it—badly. I'm not sure I can trust someone else with it."

"I'm not just anybody, Jessie. You know me, and that I would never hurt you. At least not intentionally."

She pointed to her head. "I know that in here, but it doesn't take the fear away."

"Hmm." He didn't know how to respond to that. At a loss, he stood. "I'll walk with you. Where'd you park?"

"I walked from home."

That shouldn't surprise him since she'd done it often when they were teens. They walked in silence through the woods. A squirrel scampered up a tree and chirped at them as if they'd done something wrong.

Jessie slipped her arm around his, sending his pulse skyrocketing. "I enjoyed brainstorming with you."

"Yeah. It was fun." As happy as he was about the good in his life right now, all he really wanted was Jessie's love. He had a strong feeling she loved him but didn't see it—yet. He'd have to pray the Lord would reveal her feelings to her—and that she'd realize she could trust him in all ways. And pray that He'd do it soon.

JESSIE WALKED BEHIND THE MOWER AT a client's home, her thoughts swirling. *Lord, please help me to know my heart. I'm afraid to love again, but Scott is a good man who loves You and would never do anything to hurt me. It's so difficult to trust again.*

She turned the mower and headed across the lawn diagonally. A pickup stopped on the curb. Her fists tightened around the mower's handle. *Brendon.* If he wanted to talk with her he could wait until she was finished. He got out of his truck and leaned against the side with his hands in his pockets, watching her.

As much as it unnerved her, she kept working. Finally the lawn was finished, and she killed the motor. Pushing the mower to her pickup, she then rolled it up the ramp she'd created. "What's up, Brendon?"

"Nothing. Just thought I'd stop and see how you're doing."

Why did everyone keep asking her that? "I'm fine. Why wouldn't

I be?"

He rubbed the back of his neck. "Look, I know I was a jerk, and I'm sorry."

She stopped and stared. Brendon *never* admitted fault or gave a real apology. She studied his face and saw sincerity.

He sighed. "Do you remember when you kept bugging me to go to church with you and I refused?"

"Yes."

"A buddy of mine here in town called me out on what I said to you that night about having multiple affairs. What he said really got to me so much so, I decided I needed help and started seeing a counselor. My buddy talked to me about God and invited me to his church. What I heard made sense." A slow smile crossed his face. "I became a Christian two nights ago."

Nothing could have shocked Jessie more. "Wow. That was a great decision."

"Thanks. I should've made it a long time ago."

She sat on the side of the truck bed, her feet dangling beside him.

"There's more. According to what I've read in the Bible I realized I needed to come clean with you. You need to know the truth."

Okay. He really had her attention now.

"I lied. There were no other women. I didn't leave you for anyone else. I was angry, and I wanted to hurt you. I knew saying I'd had multiple affairs would cut deep. I'm sorry. What I did to you by lying was bad, even for me. And for the record, I left because I didn't think I was good enough for you."

Shock reverberated through her. How could anyone be so cruel? Yet, he seemed sincere now. "You didn't think you were good enough for me?"

"I know. Crazy." He shot her a sheepish grin. "But, you're so amazing, and I'm a has-been. I lived in the past because that's all I had going for me."

"I don't understand. We had a great business, and we were happy."

"You were happy. I was living in the past. I missed my football days. Don't you see? You were part of my glory days. When I was with you, I was somebody."

"You're somebody now."

A sadness filled his eyes. "At your expense. I'm sorry for that too. Like I said, I've been a real jerk."

"Agreed. But thank you for apologizing and telling me the truth. So there really were no other women?"

He shook his head. "Will you forgive me, Jessie?" He turned to her and took her hand.

She slipped it away. "Yes. But I don't think we can be friends. You really hurt me, and what you did was messed up."

He looked down. "I know. My counselor has helped me see the damage I've caused. I feel really bad about everything, but I'm starting fresh. This is the new me."

She hopped off the side of the truck. "Good. I'm glad for you." She shot him a grin. "But don't expect Scott and me to give this competition anything less than our best."

"I won't." He started to turn away. "Oh, I almost forgot. I'm sure you figured out I was holding something over Ted and that's why he went along with everything I told him to do. If you still want to do landscapes for him, I'll tell him it's okay."

Whoa! She'd suspected it was something like that, but hadn't known for sure. "Thanks, but I'm not sure I care to do business with Ted anymore. I'm curious about one more thing."

He nodded for her to continue.

"Why did you really tell Scott to stay away from me in high school and then again at the nursery?"

He sighed. "This is embarrassing to admit and if someone told me a week ago, that I would be talking to you like this I wouldn't have believed it. But I'm not that person anymore. I had no idea I could feel so different, but I do."

Jessie could hardly fathom Brendon's words.

"I was jealous of your relationship with Scott. That guy is crazy about you, and whether you realize it or not, you feel the same. I'm really sorry I was so selfish and ruined things."

"It's hard to believe you."

"I know." He took a long look at her. "Are we good?"

"Yeah. We're good."

"Thanks." He sauntered to his pickup and drove off.

Knowing Brendon hadn't cheated on her and that she hadn't been blind to what was going on around her lifted a weight off her. Everything suddenly became clear in her mind, and she knew what she had to do.

CHAPTER THIRTEEN

California sunshine beat down on Scott's back. No wonder the homeowners requested palm trees for their backyard. The space had no shade and was *hot.* Good thing he'd chosen a species of palm that would help with that issue.

Jessie sidled up to him and nudged her shoulder against his. "How's it going?"

"Great. I finished digging the last hole, and the trees will be here any minute." He rested one hand on the shovel and ran his other arm across his sweaty brow. "I don't know about you, but I'm ready to call it a day."

"Me too. Are we still on for dinner tonight?"

"Yep. I'm looking forward to a juicy burger and fries."

"Me too."

He glanced toward a cameraman headed his way. It looked as though he wasn't going to be able to leave as quickly as he'd hoped.

"Hey, Scott. We need to get a shot of you guiding the trees into place."

"Okay." As much as he enjoyed creating the backyard oasis, he didn't like having to constantly stop what he was doing to play host for the camera to explain what he was doing. Did he really want to win this competition? Regardless, he'd give it his best. The homeowners were counting on him and so was Jessie. He spotted her laughing with one of the crewmembers. Not for the first time, he was pleased to have her here with him. It wouldn't have been any fun without her.

Jessie glanced his direction, catching his eye. She waved and his heart melted a bit. He loved her so much—If only *she* knew how she felt. He was happy to be with her like this, but he wanted more and prayed daily that the Lord would help her know her heart.

JESSIE KNOCKED ON SCOTT'S hotel room door. The day had been long and hot, and she was more than ready to sit in an air-conditioned restaurant and enjoy a tasty meal. His door opened, and she caught her breath. He wore jeans, a loose fitting blue and white plaid button up shirt with the sleeves rolled to his elbows, and he smelled fresh.

Like he'd recently stepped out of the shower. His damp hair confirmed that observation. "You ready?" Jessie asked.

"More than." He closed the door behind them and rested his hand on her back as they walked down the hall and into the lobby. "I hear the hotel's restaurant is great. Do you mind if we go there?"

"Not at all." She'd heard good things about the place and was going to suggest the same thing. "The yard turned out fantastic."

"Thanks. It was a team effort, and I couldn't have done it without you and everyone else."

"Agreed." She shot him a cheeky grin and received a poke in the rib. She bent away from him, chuckling. They climbed a few stairs to the restaurant.

The hostess greeted them with a smile. "Two for dinner?"

"Yes," Scott said.

She pulled menus out of a wooden slot. "Follow me, please." They sat at a window seat that looked onto the pool. Jessie recognized a few of the crewmembers from the show horsing around in the water.

Scott flipped over the menu and beamed a smile her way. "I'm having a chocolate shake and a cheese burger."

"Sounds perfect. I'll have the same." She had so much she wanted to say to him. Her heart was full with all the new feelings Brendon's confession had released. She opened her mouth to tell him right as their waiter approached and took their order.

After placing their order, Scott stared out the window and looked a million miles away in thought. Maybe tonight wasn't the best time to tell him. Tomorrow was a big day, and he probably didn't need anything more to process.

"I can't wait until after the show tomorrow, so all of this will be over." He leaned back and focused on her.

"It won't be over if you win."

"True. But not knowing what's going to happen is driving me nuts. I hate the unknown."

"I remember. I'll never forget how irritated you were when your parents threw you a surprise party on your thirteenth birthday."

He chuckled. "I was such a brat. I had to apologize to them for getting angry."

Her eyes widened. "You got mad at them? I don't remember that."

"I was smart enough to wait until everyone left to express my feelings about their surprise, but not smart enough to be grateful my parents wanted to give me a memorable thirteenth birthday. It didn't take me long to realize my error and apologize."

"Good. That was a fun party."

He grinned. "I suppose it was."

Their food arrived and they devoured it.

Scott leaned back and patted his stomach. "Do you mind calling it a night? We have to be at the studio early tomorrow."

"Not at all."

They paid and walked back to their rooms and came to stand outside their doors, which were side-by-side. On impulse she planted a kiss on his cheek.

His eyes widened. "What was that for?"

"Just because. See you in the morning." Not waiting for a response, she stepped into her room. Exhausted, but too excited to sleep. She flipped on the TV and noted a promo for the contest. Scott's face flashed across the screen followed by Brendon's.

She was a little surprised their paths hadn't crossed since being in Los Angeles, but maybe the show was keeping them apart on purpose. She yawned, suddenly ready for sleep.

Her stomach churned. She'd find out tomorrow if Scott would win and possibly leave her life for good since he'd be in California filming a television show, and she'd be in Oregon.

CHAPTER FOURTEEN

SCOTT STOOD BESIDE BRENDON AND THE other finalist in the TV studio. Hot lights shone down on them. He shifted from one foot to the other, anxious to get this over with. The show's theme music started to play.

A spotlight shone on the host. "Welcome back to *Fresh and Fantastic*. Today we reveal the winner of our search for the next great landscaper. The winner will receive a TV show development deal with the network as well as fifteen thousand dollars! The runner up will receive ten thousand dollars and the chance to pitch a television show idea to the network. For the past two days, these gentlemen, along with handy crews, have worked hard to implement each of their designs. Let's take a look."

The screen cut to footage from Brendon's project site along with a short interview, then cut to Scott's site and interview, and finally Trent, the other contestant.

The host flashed a million-dollar smile at the camera. "I don't know about you, but I'm ready to find out who the winner is, after a few words from our sponsors." During the commercial break he turned to them. "Those projects look great. I'm glad I wasn't a judge."

Scott nodded. He wouldn't have wanted to be a judge either. Brendon's project was as good as his, although he didn't care much for Trent's. It would come down to the judge's personal preferences.

"Welcome back." The host teased the audience a bit longer then pulled a card from the envelope containing the results. "Whoa." He looked to the other finalist. "I'm sorry, Trent, you will be going home empty handed. Thanks for all your hard work."

They shook hands, then Trent left the stage.

The host looked into the camera. "This was a close vote of five to four. Congratulations . . . Brendon Jacobs. You're the winner!"

Relief washed over Scott. This experience had taught him that he did *not* want to be in front of a camera all the time.

THE FOLLOWING EVENING JESSIE found Scott at their clubhouse sitting at the table with his laptop. "Hey there. Why didn't you respond to my texts? I've been looking all over for you."

His face brightened. "You found me." He closed the screen.

She sidled up to the table and sat. "We haven't really talked since before the show yesterday. I wish they would have let me stick around to run the press junket, but I guess assistants weren't important enough." She smiled to let him know she wasn't upset. "Are you okay about not winning?"

"It's been a whirlwind, but I'm better than okay. The only thing I felt when Brendon's name was announced was relief. I didn't want that life."

"Good. Because I like having you here." She reached across the table and grasped his hand.

He raised a brow and looked pointedly at their hands.

"This summer has been eye opening for me, and I've learned a lot about myself."

He ran his thumb back and forth over the top of her hand. "What'd you learn?"

"That I *can* love again. That you are an amazing man, that I don't ever want you out of my life again, and most important of all—I love you." Her heart pounded in her chest.

A slow grin spread across his face.

"Say something."

He stood, drawing her up with him then pulled her into his arms. "Those are the only words I've ever wanted to hear from you. What took you so long?"

"I was waiting for the right moment. I wanted to tell you at dinner that night in California, but you were so tired and had a lot going on. It didn't seem fair to add this to everything else."

"I wish you would have, but I'm glad you're here now." He lowered his head, and his warm lips captured hers.

Her insides melted as he deepened the kiss, pulling her closer. Her body tingled, and she leaned back to catch her breath. "Wow."

His eyes sparkled. "Will you marry me?"

She nodded. "Absolutely."

"Will you also partner with me to make us the most desired landscape design company in Oregon?"

"Mmm-hmm. I don't think that will be too difficult, considering you took second in a national televised competition."

He chuckled. "But what about your business?"

"We can come up with a snappy new name so people will know we've joined forces."

"I like that. Something like Mr. and Mrs. Landscaping and Design Services." He winked before his lips found hers, sealing the deal.

The End

HUNGRY HEARTS

By
Debby Mayne

CHAPTER ONE

"ARE YOU SERIOUS? CAMERON IS BACK?" Melissa's stomach lurched. She'd thought that once he left Hyacinth, she wouldn't ever have to face him again. Even though he came home to visit his family during the holidays, it didn't matter since they lived miles away from her.

Melissa's best friend Janice smiled and nodded. "As serious as I've ever been." She redirected her gaze to something behind Melissa. "Don't look now, but he's coming this way. He's about ten feet behind you."

"Tell me when he's gone."

Janice's eyes widened. "Um . . . too late now."

"Well, if it isn't Melissa Shaw. It's been a while."

Melissa glanced up and forced a smile. "It sure has been, hasn't it? What are you doing in town? I thought you'd moved on."

She was fully aware of how sarcastic she sounded, but she really didn't care. Cameron Prater had pursued her through high school and college, and when she finally gave in and agreed to date him, he showed his true colors. It didn't take him long to wring her heart dry as he moved on to the next girl who played hard-to-get.

"I did, but now I understand the old saying about the grass being greener elsewhere. I've decided to move back home to Hyacinth."

"That's nice." Melissa glanced at Janice who remained in the same spot, watching them banter, her head turning back and forth like a spectator at a tennis match. "Isn't it nice, Janice?"

"What? Oh . . . yeah. Very nice."

"Is this your place?" He pointed to the Spoons Diner.

She nodded. "Yes."

"So you finally made the jump, huh?"

"The jump?" She lifted an eyebrow as she tried hard to ignore that odd sensation in the pit of her stomach. That was what had gotten her into trouble in the first place.

"Yes, the jump into your lifelong dream. I remember you telling me you always wanted a little café."

"Oh . . . yes, I suppose you can say I *made the jump*."

He looked inside the window. "Looks like a success."

She lifted her chin and nodded. "I can't complain. I make a good living."

"That's good to hear because I'll be moving in a few doors down."

"Moving in?"

He smiled. "Yes, I'm opening *Chili and Chips*."

Now the feeling in her stomach had turned sour. "*Chili and Chips*, as in the food?"

"You nailed it. In case you don't remember, I've always made killer chili, and now I'm turning it into a business."

"Here?" Her voice squeaked, so she cleared her throat. "In downtown Hyacinth?"

"Yep. You'll have to come check it out sometime. It'll be a few weeks before I'm able to get the place up and running, but when I do, stop by for a complimentary bowl of chili and all the corn chips you can eat."

She snickered. "Sure, I'll do that."

Cameron narrowed his eyes and turned his head slightly to the side. "Are you still holding a grudge?"

"No, of course not." She wasn't able to look directly at him.

"Nothing has changed, has it?"

Before Melissa had a chance to respond, Janice nudged her. "Your delivery is here."

Melissa lifted her hand, wiggled her fingers in a mock wave, and gave Cameron a forced grin. "Sorry, but duty calls. Gotta get back to work."

As soon as Melissa and Janice went inside Spoons Diner, they looked at each other before Melissa allowed her shoulders to sag. She wasn't sure if what she felt was anger, fear, or a combination of both.

"I hope you're not mad I'm saying this," Janice said. "But Cameron's right. Nothing has changed between the two of you."

"I don't know what on earth you're talking about. I haven't seen him in ... in a long time."

Janice tilted her head forward and looked at Melissa from beneath her perfectly shaped eyebrows. "The very thing that attracted you to Cameron in the first place is the same thing that drove you apart. It's still there."

"I have no idea what you're talking about." Melissa took a deep breath and slowly blew it out.

"You know exactly what I'm talking about. Remember when you were both running for student council? I remember that election getting pretty ugly."

"I should have won." Melissa's mind flashed back to some of their old high school campaigns. "But he fought dirty."

Janice shrugged. "Y'all weren't all that different in your tactics, if I remember correctly. You asked the students if they thought being on the football team qualified him for student council, and he asked the same question about your being a cheerleader and on the homecoming court."

Melissa scowled at her friend. "Whose side are you on, anyway?"

"Yours, of course, but I shouldn't have to pick sides—especially now, ten years after high school. This whole thing should be over by now."

"It is." As soon as those words escaped Melissa's lips, she realized how clipped—and unconvincing—she sounded.

"Oh, really? It didn't look . . . or sound like it to me."

"That's because he's trying to put me out of business."

Janice let out a nervous laugh. "Like when he was trying to keep you out of college when you found out you were neck and neck for class Valedictorian?"

Melissa glared back at her lifelong best friend. "I won, remember?"

"Yes, of course I do. But you still would have gotten that scholarship to Clemson, even if you'd been Salutatorian." Janice sighed and shook her head. "I'm saying this because I truly care about you, Mel. You have to let go of this competition thing with Cameron, or you'll wind up making yourself crazy."

"Someone needs to tell him that." Melissa had to get the last word before turning her attention to the reason they went inside. "I thought you said the delivery was here."

"I thought it was." Janice glanced away momentarily. "I guess I was mistaken."

Melissa appreciated Janice's concern, but the frustration that welled inside her whenever Cameron was around had returned even stronger than before. She was well aware that her attraction was what made it worse than it should have been. In fact, if some total stranger had decided to open a chili restaurant a few doors down, she would have welcomed him and possibly even suggested some cooperative advertising.

But no way would she do that with Cameron. Based on experience, that would turn out to be a disaster—at least for her it would. Besides, why would Cameron think it was okay to open a restaurant a few doors down from hers? He obviously hadn't gotten over the need to compete.

At least she had her best friend to vent to. Melissa had no idea what she would have done without Janice by her side.

Janice had gotten married shortly after college, and they'd moved to Charlotte, North Carolina. Her husband Noah didn't like the company he worked for, so when his dad offered him a position as a general manager of his tire company in Hyacinth, South Carolina, they didn't hesitate to move back. Janice had her degree in library science, and there were no jobs available, so she agreed to work part-time for Melissa. It worked out well for both of them because Melissa trusted her best friend, and Janice was able to work around her husband's schedule.

Melissa had also hired Betty, a middle-aged woman who used to work in the school cafeteria when she was in high school. Betty was known as the "soup lady" at school, so she was a natural for a restaurant that specialized in soups.

"Hey, Melissa, do you want me to serve what's left of yesterday's special?" Betty asked. "We have enough for about a dozen customers."

"Sounds good."

Janice came out of the storage room and placed her hand on her hip. "Or we can deliver it to the shelter."

"I like that idea better," Melissa agreed. "Are you up to taking it over to them?"

"I thought you'd never ask." Janice headed back to the kitchen where Betty had already gone.

Melissa continued getting the dining area ready for customers. Since they were on Main Street, only a fraction of their business was dine-in. Many businesses around them called in their lunch orders to be picked up. She'd been open for two years, and she was just now getting comfortable with the routine.

Many people said she'd struggle, since she was only open six days a week and only for breakfast and lunch. But fortunately, that hadn't been the case. Monday through Friday, they had regulars, and on Saturday, quite a few of the people they saw were tourists on their way to Charleston. She'd left flyers at all of the hotels along the interstate with coupons for free desserts or muffins. What always made her smile was when those same tourists stopped by on their way back from Charleston to have lunch and get muffins to take home with them.

"If you keep going, you'll wind up wiping a hole into that table."

She glanced up and saw Cameron watching her from the front of the diner. "What are you doing here?"

"I'd like some lunch . . . unless you can't serve me for some reason." He held his hands out and glanced down at himself. "I have the required shirt and shoes, and I took a shower this morning."

"Sit anywhere you want. I'll get you a menu."

"Do you talk to all of your customers like that?"

"No," she said as she dropped a menu on the edge of his table. "Only the ones I think might want to put me out of business."

"Is that what you think I'm doing? Trying to put you out of business?"

She shrugged. "I can't think of any other reason you'd want to open your restaurant so close to mine."

He tightened his lips and glanced down at the menu. "Your menu is quite a bit more extensive than mine."

"Are you here to steal ideas?"

He dropped the menu, propped his elbows on the table, and looked directly at her. "Why would I do something like that?"

She shrugged. "Who knows why you do anything?"

"Look, Melissa. I don't know why you're acting this way. I really want us to be friends. I realize we parted ways on a bad note, but that's in the past. Can't we work through our differences and at least get along?"

"We're getting along just fine."

He shook his head. "Doesn't sound like it to me."

She swallowed hard. He was right. She was the hostile one. In fact, he hadn't said a single thing that was out of line since he'd been sitting here.

Finally, she lifted her chin and nodded. "Okay, you win. I'm sorry for acting so stupid."

"You're not acting stupid."

"However I'm acting, I'm sorry." She took a step toward him and extended her hand. "I mean it." She forced a smile. "Friends?"

He smiled at her, stood, and took her hand in both of his hands and held it for a few seconds, sending that familiar bolt of electricity up her arm and straight to her heart. The floor seemed to shift beneath her. At that moment, she knew that being *just friends* with Cameron would be nearly impossible.

"Are you okay?" He got closer and placed his arm around her shoulders. "You don't look so good."

She stiffened, pulled away, and shoved her hand in her jeans pocket. "I'm fine. Have you had a chance to look over the menu?"

"You just gave it to me, remember? Give me a few minutes."

"Okay." She backed toward the kitchen. "I'll bring your drink in a few minutes." Then she darted out of the dining room to get away from him before she made a fool of herself.

A few minutes later, after she had his drink ready and gave herself an extra minute to regain her composure, she brought out his drink and set it on the table in front of him. "Here ya go."

"I didn't order my drink yet," he reminded her.

Her eyes shot open wider. "You didn't?" She started to pick up the glass, but he grabbed her hand and pulled it away.

"But you brought exactly what I would have ordered. Ginger ale with a twist of lime." He smiled as he let go of her hand to take a sip.

"Perfect. I'm flattered that you remembered."

"I am so sorry. I guess old habits die hard."

He nodded. "Even old habits that you thought you'd gotten rid of a very long time ago." His expression changed, as though he'd thought of something that he didn't want to. "The beef and barley soup sounds good."

"It is. Remember Betty from the school cafeteria?"

His forehead crinkled. "The soup lady? What about her?"

"That's the one. I hired her to make all of our soups."

He leaned back in his chair and gave her a look of approval. "Now I'm impressed. It wouldn't have crossed my mind to recruit kitchen staff from the high school."

Melissa shrugged. "She's the best, and I only hire the best. I'll go give her your order. The soup's already done, so you'll have it in a few minutes." She started to take the menu, but he pulled it away.

"I'd like to see what all you have so I don't duplicate anything."

She gave him a long look before turning around and heading to the kitchen. She still didn't trust him completely, but there wasn't anything she could do at the moment without sounding angry.

"I recognize that look on your face, Melissa," Betty said as she gave her the order. "It's the same look you used to have every day at lunch when you stood next to Cameron in the lunch line."

"It is?" Melissa scrunched her face. "I'll try to be more careful with my expressions."

Betty laughed. "There are some things you can't hide, and being in love is one of them."

CHAPTER TWO

"You don't have to say it, sweetheart." Betty scooped the soup into the bowl and put a hunk of French bread on the plate. "Want me to fix you a plate so you can eat lunch with him?"

"No way . . . but thanks." She picked up the plate with the bowl on it. "Besides, until Janice gets back from the shelter, there's no one else to wait on tables."

Betty gave her a knowing smile but didn't say another word. Melissa carried the food out to the dining room and was relieved to see that a couple more customers had entered.

She placed the soup and bread in front of Cameron. "I'll check on you after I get everyone's order."

"That's fine." He took a bite of soup. "This is delicious."

She grinned. "I know."

As Melissa handed out menus and took orders, she was very aware of Cameron's presence. She had to focus really hard on what she was doing so she wouldn't mess up an order or stumble over her own feet.

He finally finished eating and stood. He reached into his wallet, pulled out a credit card, and tried to hand it to her.

"I run an old-fashioned diner. Come on up to the cash register, and I'll take your payment there."

"Looks like you're doing quite a business, so old-fashioned is obviously working well for you. The place filled up quickly. Have you thought about expanding?" He leaned on the counter as she processed his credit card. "I bet you could bring in twice as much if you added a few more tables."

"This is only a fraction of our business, since most of it is carryout and catering. We like it the way it is."

He looked surprised. "You cater?"

She nodded. "Yes, mostly business meetings and small . . . very small weddings."

"Weddings, huh?" He lifted an eyebrow and gave her a sarcastic grin.

"Yes, weddings." She glared at him.

His lips turned up at the corners, hinting of a grin. "Then who am I to argue with success?"

"I agree." She forced another smile and walked around from behind the counter. "I need to get to work. Thanks for stopping by Spoons."

He chuckled. "After I open my place, I'd like to have you as a guest. In fact, I'll probably invite all the downtown business owners for a preview chili tasting night."

"Sounds good."

She turned her back on him and tried to concentrate on the other customers. When she heard the bells on the door as he left, an odd sensation that bordered on sadness came over her. She couldn't figure out why he affected her this way after all this time, but she'd make sure she kept her distance—at least until she got used to the idea of having him back in town.

Janice must have come in through the rear entrance because she walked out of the kitchen, looking around. "Betty said Cameron came for lunch. Where is he?"

Melissa shrugged and attempted nonchalance. "He must have left." She tried to walk around Janice, but she was blocked. "What are you doing?"

"I want to hear all about it."

"All about what?"

"Come on, Melissa. I've known you a long time. I can tell when you have something on your mind, and I know for certain that Cameron showing up like he did really messed with your head."

"Okay, so I was surprised. But I'm over it."

"No, you're not. You and I both know that you have some unresolved issues."

Melissa laughed. "Don't try to psychoanalyze me. Cameron and I obviously have a past, and when he showed up, it surprised me. That's it."

"Okay, whatever. I'll take care of the customers out here while you go back to the kitchen and recover."

"There's nothing to recover from." As Melissa said those words, she knew there was no hiding the fact that Janice was right. After seeing Cameron, she was on the edge of her nerves ... and that was after nothing happened. If something had happened, she was pretty certain she'd be a mental case. "But I should go help Betty. She's been working by herself for a while now." She started for the kitchen but stopped. "How were the ladies at the shelter?"

Janice shook her head. "The two who have been there a while are fine, but there's a new woman with two kids. They're all shaken up. I really feel for the little girl. Apparently her daddy beat her up pretty bad." Janice's chin quivered, and she bit her lip. "She had a broken arm and a black eye."

Melissa gasped. "How old is she?"

"Three or four. She's little." Janice's gaze darted to something behind Melissa. "Let me go get some menus for the customers who just walked in. Wait here for a sec. I want to talk to you about something."

Melissa nodded as she thought about what Janice had told her. She couldn't even fathom a man breaking his little girl's arm. If she hadn't met a few of the women who'd come through the shelter she never would have believed some of the stories about what they'd endured. She and Janice had started the shelter ministry shortly after she opened the restaurant. The two of them had to go through extensive training before they could work directly with the women referred by the authorities.

Melissa straightened up the drink and condiments station while she waited for Janice to seat people and take their orders. As she worked, she thought about the mission and how she'd changed and grown after working with the battered women.

Melissa, Janice, and a couple of other women took turns driving the ladies from the shelter to church on Sunday. Afterward, they took them out to lunch. Once a month, Melissa opened Spoons for the women and children from the shelter. Betty always made extra batches of soup the week before, and she came in immediately after church to warm the food. Melissa and Janice handed everyone menus, including the children, and let them order whatever they wanted. It provided a sense of normalcy to the lives of people who had to hide away from their former spouses or boyfriends.

Now that Melissa thought about it, her feelings about Cameron were insignificant compared to what the women and children in the shelter had experienced. He'd never even come close to what the men in their lives had done. In fact, she remembered the one time a boy knocked his girlfriend against the locker in school. Cameron had gone after him fist first, and asked questions later. When Melissa asked him why the boy hit his girlfriend, Cameron had said it didn't matter. There was absolutely no excuse for a guy to physically abuse a girl, even if she did something horrible.

Janice grinned as she joined Melissa. "Everyone wants the same thing. Apparently, some guy has been going around raving about how delicious the beef and barley soup is." She gave a lopsided grin.

Melissa narrowed her eyes. "Don't tell me. Let me guess." She made an exaggerated gesture of tapping her index finger on her chin. "Is it Cameron?"

"It is. I asked the second group what the man looked like, and they described him very well."

"I wonder what he's up to."

Janice chuckled. "Don't be so suspicious. Maybe he's trying to make amends."

"Okay, so you wanted me to hang out here because you wanted to talk to me about something."

"That's right." Janice glanced around. "You know how you've been considering bringing someone else in part-time?"

Melissa nodded. "Yeah, I think we're ready for another person."

"So do I. That's why I believe you should consider training some of the women from the shelter."

"To work here?" Melissa thought for a moment. "Don't you think that would be dangerous?"

"Not if we give them low-profile jobs. They can work in the

kitchen or help clean up after hours. It would be a great way for them to make a little money and learn a new skill, and you'd have the help you need."

It actually sounded like a good idea, except for one thing. "How about their kids?"

"Well . . ." Janice gave her a sheepish grin. "I've sort of discussed it with them, and they have agreed to take turns watching each other's children."

Melissa gave Janice a mock scowl. "I think you forget who runs this place."

"I know." Janice tilted her head. "Sorry, but I got caught up in the moment when they were talking about what to do next and Rita said she didn't have any job skills, and Andrea said the only thing she knew how to do was illegal."

"I'll talk to Betty and see if she's up to teaching one or two of them how to make soup."

Janice nodded. "I've already talked to her. She said she'd love to do whatever she can to help give these women some independence."

"You are incorrigible."

"And that's why we're such good friends, right?"

Melissa nodded. "You got that right. Are you sure you have the front covered? I'd like to start working on a new bread recipe. We've had a lot of people ask for gluten-free lately, and I found an interesting recipe on the Internet."

"I'll be fine. If it gets crazy and I need you, I'll let you know."

"Thanks!"

As soon as Melissa walked into the kitchen, Betty pounced on her. "What do you think about Janice's idea?"

"Sounds good to me." Melissa paused. "The question is, what do *you* think?"

"I'm actually pretty excited about it. I've wanted to do something special for those ladies, but all I could think about was cooking for them. I guess I didn't realize a few of them didn't have any skills at all." She shook her head. "It breaks my heart to hear the stories of what they've been through."

"I know." Melissa went to the pantry and started pulling out some ingredients. "I need to order some quinoa flour."

"We have that," Betty said. "Look behind the wheat flour."

"Did you order this?"

Betty nodded. "I ordered it when you mentioned having some gluten-free bread. And I cleaned out the smaller oven so you can bake it separately."

"You are amazing, Soup Lady."

Betty grinned. "I know, Boss Woman."

As Melissa gathered the ingredients to make gluten-free bread, Betty anticipated what she needed. She finally finished getting everything she needed and laid it all out on the counter. She quickly fell into her baking groove that was always a comfort when she felt stressed.

Betty opened her mouth but clamped it shut when she glanced toward the door. Melissa glanced over her shoulder to see what had snagged her attention.

CHAPTER THREE

"Did you need something, Cameron?" Melissa asked.

He laughed and then smiled at Betty. "Hey soup lady. It's good to see you."

"Hi there, Cameron. You haven't changed a bit."

"If Melissa ever starts treating you bad, come talk to me."

"Hey," Melissa said. "Don't try to poach my employees. What do you want, Cameron?"

"I'd never do that." Cameron focused his attention on Melissa. "Can I talk to you for a few minutes?"

Melissa glanced at Betty who nodded. "Sure, but I don't have much time."

He looked around the kitchen. "I see that. Don't worry. This won't take long."

"Why don't we talk in my office?"

A goofy look came over him. "You have an office?"

"Yes, of course I do. I have to have a place to keep my files and conduct business." She laughed. "Don't tell me you don't have one in your restaurant."

"Now that you put it that way, I'll make sure I do." When they reached the tiny office, he waited for her to enter, and then he followed. "You haven't changed a bit, have you? Still as organized as ever?"

She scrunched her forehead. "Are you being sarcastic?" Her mother who was a neat freak to the nth degree had complained when she saw all of Melissa's exposed files, charts, and calendars.

"Not at all." He pointed to the calendar. "You have everything written down and at your fingertips. I bet you never miss a meeting or forget to do anything."

She relaxed a bit. "That's what I kept trying to tell Mama, but she thinks this place is a mess."

"Consider the source. I don't think I've ever been to a neater house than your parents'."

"I'm sure you didn't come here to discuss my neatness . . . or my parents. What did you want to talk about?"

"It looks like the codes department is going to fast track my restaurant, so I'll be opening a little sooner than expected."

She remembered that one of his football teammates now worked for the City of Hyacinth. "I'm not surprised."

He tightened his lips for a second but continued. "What I want to do is schedule a Grand Opening and maybe have other businesses participate. So many of the business people are new in town, and I can't seem to get through to any of them."

It took every bit of self-restraint for her not to gloat about the fact that his "golden-boy fame" as one of the best athletes that had ever graced the halls of Hyacinth High School wasn't immediately recognized by anyone new in this small town. "What do you want from me?"

"Could you talk to some of them for me?"

"Why do you think it would help for me to talk to anyone?"

He shrugged. "You've been here longer, and they know you."

Melissa leaned back in her chair as she arched her eyebrows. "Just so I have this straight in my mind ... You want me to make things easier for you by telling all the business people in downtown Hyacinth that you're the town hero?"

"I didn't say that." He steepled his fingers. "I think you need to let go of the past."

She sighed and gave him an apologetic look. "Yeah, you're right."

"I know it's hard, after how competitive we used to be."

"It is," she agreed.

"I understand. It's not easy for me either."

She swallowed hard. She'd have to work at getting over some of the things she felt years ago. "Have you tried using that charm you used to be so good at?"

He let out a snort. "I tried, but they were all too busy to talk to me."

"What makes you think they're not too busy to talk to me?"

Cameron dropped his gaze to the floor before looking into her eyes again. "You're not going to help me, are you?"

Another flicker of guilt washed over Melissa. "Tell you what, Cameron. There's a Chamber of Commerce meeting on Friday. Why don't you go as my guest, and I can introduce you to everyone? There will be more people that you know, and they'll probably sing your praises. I think that'll be much more effective than anything I can do."

He slowly nodded. "That sounds good. You know how much I hate groveling … or even asking a favor, for that matter."

"Yes, I do know."

"But this would be a huge help." He stood. "Tell me where to be and when to be there."

She gave him all the information he needed. After he left, she sat there and stared at the wall across from her. She knew that what she felt could seem petty, but Cameron's mere presence often brought out the worst in her. Her mother once commented that her feelings for Cameron were too strong, and it made her feel weak where he was concerned.

Melissa closed her eyes and said a prayer, asking for God's guidance and blessing. Relying on her own feelings would have her spinning in circles, since she wasn't sure whether she was coming or going whenever Cameron was around.

After she recovered, she went back to the kitchen. Everything was still laid out as she'd left it, and Betty was busy working on her soup.

"So how is Cameron coming along with his new place?" Betty asked.

Melissa shrugged. "He'll be able to open sooner than expected. Apparently, the codes department has put him high on their priority list."

Betty chuckled. "You don't sound all that happy about it."

"Oh, I am. I'm just thrilled about it."

Again, Betty laughed. "So have you got that gluten-free bread figured out?"

"I think so." Melissa stuck the bowl in the bread mixer and flipped the switch. "I'll let you know in a couple of hours."

CAMERON REALLY DID HATE asking her for anything. But when he'd walked up and down the street to meet the other merchants, he'd gotten a friendly but distant greeting, which surprised him. He'd always been well known and liked in Hyacinth, but so many of these people had no idea who he was. The old-timers knew him, but the newcomers weren't as trusting.

Looked like something Melissa had said years ago was spot on. She'd told him that he wouldn't be able to use his small-town stardom for the rest of his life, and he'd have to come up with more substance. He thought he had, but this wasn't the first time he'd hit a brick wall.

Throughout high school, he'd been intrigued by Melissa. When she finally agreed to date him during college, he realized she was not only intelligent and gorgeous she also had the ability to make him lose his swag and render him helpless. He didn't have the maturity to handle her at the time, so he came up with a lame excuse to break up.

After college, he moved to Charleston where he'd gotten a job managing several office buildings. After he proved himself there, the company promoted him to their corporate headquarters in Atlanta. The job bored him to tears, but he figured he'd pay his dues before moving up to the next position. A few years later, it became painfully obvious that he wasn't plugged into the network enough to meet his goals, so he tried other means to find a way in. None of his old tricks worked—not his skills, not his charm, and certainly not his athletic ability.

He'd decided to come back home to Hyacinth—the town he thought he'd outgrown, but now realized would always be home. Not only did he think he'd fare better here, his parents had retired and wanted to travel, and they liked the idea of having him close by to help watch the house when they were gone. His mother had added that if he ever settled down and had children, she'd be more than happy to babysit.

And he'd thought he was over Melissa. She was as beautiful as she was smart, but that wasn't the most important thing for him. Her faith in the Lord was steadfast—always was and would probably always be.

Melissa Shaw was the only girl who ever got the best of him. Back in high school, he'd been unable to keep his competitive nature off the court and field. They'd established early habits that were hard to break, and he said and did things that made him want to kick himself later.

He shouldn't have been surprised that she'd seen him as wanting to compete and put her out of business when he returned. And subconsciously he realized he might have wanted to one-up her . . . but not enough to hurt her business. He simply wanted to do a little bit better. Once he realized what he was subconsciously doing, he regretted it. Unfortunately, he'd already signed a five-year lease on the location, and when he tried to back out of it, he met with complete resistance. He considered having another type of business, but his contract stated that it had to be a restaurant. So he had no choice but to follow through with his plans.

He let himself into the restaurant from the backdoor into the kitchen area. The restaurant that had been here in the past hadn't succeeded because they tried to provide German cuisine, something that wasn't right for a small country town in South Carolina. People here liked down-home cooking and casual fun food. There was never any doubt in his mind that chili would go over big, and he didn't see it as competition for Melissa's soup restaurant. But he might have to rethink that if he wanted any hope for peace between them.

The sound of someone banging on the front door caught his attention. He got up to see who it was.

"Hey, Rocky." Cameron pulled the door all the way open and stepped back to let his former co-captain Rocky Jamison in. "Welcome to my chili shop ... or whatever I decide to serve here."

Rocky lifted an eyebrow as he glanced around. "It still smells like sauerkraut in here."

"I know, but I have a crew coming in to gut the place next week. After that, we'll add all new flooring, clean up the tables, chairs and booths, and paint. Are you interested in helping out?"

"I might help for food."

Cameron laughed. "Nothing much has changed with you."

"You got that right." He looked directly at Cameron. "Speaking of change, are you thinking about changing your plans for the restaurant?"

Cameron offered a clipped nod. "I'm afraid it might be too close ... too similar to something else on the street."

A smile slowly crept over Rocky's lips. "Are you talking about Spoons Diner?"

"The one and only."

"I wondered if she'd get to you again. Why would you let an old girlfriend dictate what you serve at your restaurant?"

Cameron bristled. "She's not just some old girlfriend."

"You still like her, don't you?" Rocky lifted an eyebrow and waited.

Cameron rubbed the back of his neck as he tried to decide whether to deny his feelings for her or swallow his pride with the one guy he made a point to see when he came back to Hyacinth. With Rocky's unblinking gaze focused on him, he finally decided to 'fess up.

"Yeah, I do, but that's beside the point. There's no point in trying to compete with someone who already has momentum and a strong clientele."

Rocky glanced around and nodded. "Yeah, I see what you're saying. What else do you have in mind?"

"That's the problem. I have no idea what else to do here. I know how to cook a lot of things, but chili has always been my specialty."

"Who says you have to be the cook?" Rocky countered. "You can bring in someone to handle that while you take care of the business."

"Got anyone in mind?" Cameron asked.

"I might. Remember Yubi Chou?"

Cameron narrowed his eyes as the image of a middle-aged Chinese woman crept into his mind. "Isn't that the name of your mother's housekeeper?"

Rocky nodded. "She left to help her cousin open a Chinese restaurant in Charleston, but when his family came from China, she was out of a job. Mama had already hired someone else, so now Yubi is out of a job."

"You think I should hire Yubi to work for me?"

"You could. She's an awesome cook. Remember those eggrolls she used to make?"

Cameron grinned. "Those were melt-in-your-mouth good."

"She made those from scratch."

It hadn't even dawned on Cameron to open a Chinese restaurant, but this did shed a different light on things. "I'll have to think about this."

"It's just a suggestion. You don't have to stick to Chinese food, though. You can have a variety and offer Japanese and Thai food too."

"Is Hyacinth ready for that? The German place didn't make it."

"I think so. Asian food is different. Have you been to that sushi restaurant by the Interstate?"

Cameron shook his head. "I didn't even know there was a sushi place anywhere around here."

"It's doing great."

"What else can Yubi cook?"

"From what I remember, almost anything ... including American food. Mama wasn't much of a cook, so that's always been required of anyone she hires to clean."

"Yes, I definitely do remember Yubi's cooking."

Cameron looked up to see Melissa standing in the doorway. He glanced over at Rocky who was trying his dead-level best not to laugh.

CHAPTER FOUR

"How long have you been standing there?" Cameron asked.

"Long enough to hear that Rocky wants you to hire Yubi." She gave him a jaunty head toss he always thought was so cute. "Let me know what you decide to do because if you don't hire her, I might."

"Oh, I'm planning to hire her." He had no such intention until now. No way could he let her get the best of him.

She folded her arms and narrowed her eyes. "When did you make that decision?"

Before he had a chance to blurt a comeback, Rocky held up his cell phone. "Why don't I give her a call and see if she can come talk to you?"

"Good idea," Cameron said.

"Tell her if it doesn't work out with Cameron, she can come talk to me." Melissa gave Cameron one of her fake smiles. "She made some pretty awesome soups from what I remember."

"Won't Miss Betty be upset if you bring someone else in?"

Melissa shook her head. "She said she'd like to train someone to help out in the kitchen."

Rocky glanced back and forth between Cameron and Melissa as they talked before he spoke up again. "Yubi will be thrilled to have these opportunities. I know she's been looking for work. She talked to the guy who has the sushi place, but she said he was a taskmaster and expected quite a bit of overtime."

"I'll give her whatever hours she wants." Cameron rubbed the back of his neck. "Of course, she'll have to work within the hours we're open."

"And what hours are those?" Melissa asked, still grinning. "I don't recall hearing when you plan to be open."

At that moment, Janice came running in. "Melissa, I've been

looking for you. Betty said you were here."

"Is there an emergency?"

Janice nodded. "We're getting slammed. Apparently, one of the hotels handed your flyers to a busload of people, and now they're all waiting in line."

Melissa waved as she left Cameron and Rocky. "Don't forget to let Yubi know she has a choice of working at an established restaurant with a guaranteed clientele or one that hasn't even opened yet." And then she was gone.

The silence in the semi-dark room rang in Cameron's ears. Finally, Rocky spoke up.

"Nothing has changed, has it?"

Cameron shook his head. "Afraid not. She can't seem to get past the competition."

Rocky belted out a hearty laugh. "You're kidding, right?"

Cameron shot his friend a curious look. "No, in fact, you said it yourself. Nothing has changed with her."

"And it clearly hasn't changed with you either."

"What are you talking about? I'm the one you were talking to about Yubi."

Rocky nodded. "I know, but until Melissa offered to hire her, you didn't make a commitment one way or the other."

"I didn't have a chance to." As soon as Cameron said those words, he realized that Rocky was right. If Melissa hadn't said anything, he wasn't sure he would have been so generous with a job before interviewing her.

"At least you know there's plenty of business out there." Rocky moved toward the front window that was partially blocked with old signage. "Yep. There's a line clear down the sidewalk. If you were open now, some of those hungry people could come here."

As Cameron thought about Rocky's words, he realized how upset he'd be if someone did that to him. He knew she'd worked really hard to build her business, and for him to waltz back into town and open shop a few doors down was like pulling the rug out from under her.

He let out a sigh of frustration and shook his head. "I can't do it."

Rocky frowned. "You can't do what?"

"I can't open a restaurant here."

"What? Are you kidding me?" Rocky glanced out the window again. "That's the most ridiculous thing I've ever heard. You'll make a killing in this location." He gestured toward the line. "I mean, look at all those folks."

"That's just it. It's not my killing to make." Cameron joined Rocky and looked at the people standing in line. "Melissa has obviously put a lot into this, and for me to follow through with my plans would be like mooching off of her."

He continued watching as Janice came outside with a try of samples. That wasn't something he would have thought of doing, but it was brilliant.

"You need to have your head examined, unless . . ." Rocky gave him a sly grin. "Unless you still carry a torch for that girl."

Carry a torch? Nah. He wouldn't go so far as to say that. But he had to admit, although only to himself, that he still felt something for Melissa—even after all this time.

"HERE YA GO." BETTY handed Melissa another plate of food to take to the people waiting in line. Fortunately, most of them were in a good mood, and they weren't demanding instant service like some people had in the past. "I don't know how we're going to get all these people fed, since they're all together."

Janice had just entered the kitchen, and she spoke up. "They know they'll have to eat in shifts. After the first group finishes, they'll walk around downtown and wait for everyone else."

Betty nodded. "Well, that's good. Too bad we don't have more help in the kitchen, though. At least I have experience feeding huge groups in a limited amount of time."

Melissa remembered how well she maintained her cool during the high school lunch period. In fact, she was always the one smiling behind the serving counter.

Janice took the plate from Melissa. "I'll bring this out to the line."

Her gaze darted to the kitchen door.

Melissa turned and saw Cameron standing there with his hands on his hips. "Can't you see we're busy?"

He nodded toward the plate. "Why don't you let me do that? You can stay in here and help Miss Betty."

Melissa started to tell him no, but Betty spoke up. "We really appreciate that, Cameron. Thanks." She stepped over to Janice whose mouth was hanging open, took the plate from her, and gave it to Cameron. "After that's empty, there'll be one more." Betty turned to Janice. "Why don't you go out to the dining room?"

Janice nodded and did what she was told. Before anyone had a chance to say another word, Cameron left the kitchen with the plate in hand. Melissa turned to Betty.

"Why did you do that?"

Betty shrugged. "We need help, and he offered. How could we not accept?"

"But—"

Betty tilted her head forward, looked at Melissa from beneath her salt-and-pepper eyebrows, and lowered her voice. "Look, Melissa, I know that you and Cameron have a history, and you seem to think he's back in town strictly to compete with you." She paused. "But you and I both know that he's a decent man, and he won't do anything underhanded."

Melissa sighed. Betty was right. As competitive as both she and Cameron were, deep down, she knew he was a good guy.

"Why don't you go take a look?" Betty said. "Check on him to ease your mind. And then come help Janice serve the customers."

"I don't need to check on him."

"But I'm asking you to," Betty said. "Please."

"Since you said 'please,' I will." Melissa glanced over her shoulder and smiled at Betty on her way out of the kitchen.

She walked past Janice and said she'd be right back. Janice was doing a great job of covering the small dining room, but she did need help.

All she had to do was open the door and glance at the group around Cameron to know he'd charmed the socks off the guests. The plate was empty, but the people didn't seem to mind. They were all riveted to whatever he was saying.

When she'd opened the door, her first thought was that he might be telling them about the restaurant he was about to open. But from the looks on their faces, that wasn't what was happening.

She approached Janice who leaned over and whispered, "I heard from one of the guys he was speaking to. He's telling them funny stories about the history of Hyacinth."

Melissa felt a combination of relief and confusion. She had no idea why he'd suddenly taken on a helpful role.

Over the next hour, they seated people, took orders, and served the remainder of the bus group. After the last people left, they all looked at each other and let out a collective deep breath. Cameron was right there with them.

"You did a great job," he said. "I'm really impressed with your success."

"Why are you doing all of this?" Melissa asked. "I totally don't get you, Cameron. One day I get the impression you're trying to put me out of business, and the next day you help me out."

He gave an exaggerated shrug. "I'm just a nice guy, I guess." Then he pursed his lips, closed his eyes, and hung his head for a few seconds. Finally, he looked at her. "I've been doing some thinking. In fact, I might not open the restaurant after all."

"What?" Melissa tilted her head. "Why not?"

"It doesn't seem fair to do that to you, after all you've done to get this place up and running. Why should I come in and take advantage of your success?"

"But I thought—" She stopped talking as she realized she was disappointed in his announcement. Shouldn't she be happy?

"Rocky and I were discussing the crowd waiting in line. I know they didn't just appear for no reason. You've done a tremendous amount of marketing ..." He looked over at Betty who stood by the kitchen door, listening and watching. "And you've hired the best soup lady in South Carolina. Who do I think I am to take advantage of all this?"

Betty raised her eyebrows and turned to Melissa. "Well, what do you have to say about that?"

Melissa shook her head and glanced down. "I-I'm not sure what to say. I have to admit I was pretty upset, but now I'm disappointed." She looked up at Cameron. "It's sort of weird, I know."

He looked confused. "So you're saying you want me to open a restaurant?"

She made a face and slowly nodded. "I think that's what I'm saying. Just not a soup restaurant." She paused. "But do you have to specialize in chili?"

"Of course he doesn't." Betty stepped forward. "Now come here, you two. It's time to make amends. Shake hands."

"We already shook hands," Melissa said.

"Not the way I'm talking about." Betty lifted her eyebrows as she glanced back and forth between them. "Shake like you mean it."

Melissa looked shyly at Cameron, and he slowly grinned. "Okay. I'll shake hands if she will."

She reached out and accepted his handshake. The second their skin touched, she regretted it. She jerked her hand back as soon as she could without appearing mad. But when she looked at him, she saw that he noticed something.

"All better." Betty turned her full attention to Cameron. "Now talk to Yubi and find out what all she can cook. I can help you out with the menu if you need me to."

Melissa shot her a look, but before she could say a word, Cameron spoke up. "Thanks, but I think I can handle the menu." He turned to Melissa. "But if you want to have final say, I'm willing to let you look at it before I print it."

She shook her head. "No, I don't think that'll be necessary."

Something odd was happening, and it made her extremely uncomfortable. Cameron was being more agreeable than ever—a very suspicious thing considering their past.

CHAPTER FIVE

CAMERON HATED THIS SIDE OF HIMSELF. Not that he disliked being agreeable. But Melissa kept shooting him suspicious glances. And no matter how much it bugged him, he liked it.

He left Spoons Diner with an odd sensation of having won something, but he knew in reality the only victory he could claim was that she'd softened somewhat. It was still all about the business, which disappointed him. He had an unexpected desire to make her happy on a more personal level.

He had to laugh at himself. He hadn't been this conflicted since the last time he saw Melissa. She kept him on his toes, which also had him teetering on the precipice of an emotional cliff.

After locking the door of the place he was starting to regret leasing, he went out to his truck. He was still in the parking lot behind the building when his cell phone rang. It was Rocky. He pulled over to the side and answered the phone.

"Dude, this is crazy." Rocky roared with laughter. "That girl still has a grip on your heart."

"Um . . . no." Cameron paused before correcting himself. "Maybe, but we're still talking about business. I have to do what's right for me."

"Then open that chili restaurant like you originally planned. I think it'll do great in that location."

"But Yubi—"

"I already talked to her, and she informed me that she can cook anything ... even chili."

"Well ..." Cameron didn't want to appear to completely cave in to Melissa, so he thought about another reason the chili restaurant wasn't such a good idea. "One of her soups is chili, and she already has an established clientele. So I thought it would be good to have something for folks who aren't in the mood for chili."

"Remember, she's not open for dinner, so you can serve whatever you want."

"True." Cameron had thought about that, but he kept coming back to the potential of a powerful feud between himself and Melissa—something he didn't want to go through again. Light banter was delightful, but a full-on war would make them both miserable. "I'll pray about it."

"Speaking of praying, are you planning to attend the Hyacinth Community Church now that you're back in town?"

"Probably." Cameron paused. "Do they still have two services?"

"Yep. One at 8:00 and one at 10:30."

"I'll be at the early one," Cameron said. "Which one do you go to?"

"Are you kidding? You know me."

Cameron laughed. "Yes, I'm afraid so. So I won't be seeing you at church then?"

"Maybe I can make myself get up in time to go to the Bible study between the two services."

After they hung up, Cameron went to the county administrative offices to get a list of restaurants in Hyacinth. Maybe he could figure out what to do based on what was needed.

Over the next several days, he worked with the crew to help clean out what was in the existing location. However, he didn't want to renovate until he knew what type of restaurant he'd be putting in.

On Sunday morning, he stood in front of his closet and finally pulled out something he hadn't worn in a while. Hyacinth Community Church had always been jeans casual, but he decided to dress a little nicer for his first day back.

As soon as he walked into the church, he took a long look around. He recognized a few people, but for the most part, he felt like a stranger in the church where he'd once known everyone who wasn't a visitor.

"Hi, I'm Brad. Welcome to Hyacinth Community Church. Are you new in town?"

Cameron turned to face a man who appeared to be about his age. "Not exactly new, but I've been gone for a while."

The man shook his hand. "If you have any questions about the church, please feel free to ask. We have—"

"Refreshments in the fellowship hall and a Bible study immediately afterward." As soon as Cameron finished his sentence, he felt like kicking himself for interrupting the man who was trying so hard to be nice.

Brad's expression instantly changed to one of confusion. "Have you been here before?"

Cameron smiled as he nodded, hoping to soften some of his rudeness. "I'm sorry I interrupted you. Yes, I used to attend here every Sunday before I went to college, and when I was home on break I never missed."

"Then you know what all we offer . . ." Brad paused. "But if there's anything you don't understand or want to know, please don't hesitate to ask me." He glanced around Cameron and nodded to someone. "I'll let you go find a seat now. Enjoy the service."

As Cameron walked to the pew where he used to sit—at times with Melissa—he thought about the times he stood at the door and greeted people. He doubted he would have handled someone coming across as abrupt as he had as well as Brad did.

He glanced around the half-filled sanctuary before sitting down. He hated to admit it even to himself that he'd hoped to see Melissa. But he didn't. All he saw were a few people he barely recognized sitting in the midst of strangers. At least the church appeared to be thriving.

The worship team found their place on the stage and began leading the congregation in music. The rest of the service was familiar. Gary Buchman was still the pastor, and he hadn't varied from the order of service that had worked so well since the beginning.

After the service was over, Cameron returned to the room where the Bible study had always been held. He let out a sigh of relief when he saw a few more people he recognized.

Before long, several of his old friends spotted him and pulled him into their group. He kept glancing toward the door.

"Looking for Melissa?"

Cameron turned around and saw Rocky. He nodded.

Rocky rubbed the back of his neck. "I forgot to tell you yesterday that she's speaking to the group this morning about one of our ministries."

"So she'll be here?"

Rocky nodded. "In fact, she's already here. I saw her out in the hallway talking to one of the women from the shelter."

"Shelter?"

"The women's shelter," Rocky explained. "Apparently, even in Hyacinth, there are some bad dudes who like to take their frustrations out on the women and children in their lives. We're supporting one of the shelters."

"Okay, now it all makes sense. I overheard something about this a few days ago."

Rocky tipped his head toward the door. "Here she comes now. Why don't you get coffee while I go find us a seat?"

Five minutes later, Cameron sat down next to Rocky, coffee in hand, waiting to hear what Melissa had to say. As she walked up to the podium in the front of the room, he felt that familiar quickening of his pulse.

At first, he couldn't help but think about how intelligently she spoke of this topic that she was obviously so passionate about. But after a few minutes, he was totally wrapped up in what she had to say. He knew that some men abused the women who loved them, but he didn't realize how bad the situation was . . . or how common. When she said that more than four million women were abused by their husbands or boyfriends each year, his hand clenched into a fist. If he ever saw a man strike a woman, he knew he'd see red.

"And that's why we appreciate all donations of money, clothing, food, or whatever else you can do for the shelter." Melissa smiled as she gestured toward someone in the back of the room. "One of the women we serve has graciously agreed to speak to you. Come on up, Rita."

Cameron took a long look at the woman walking toward Melissa. She appeared to be in her early twenties. Her blond ponytail swished as she walked, giving her more of a carefree look than the demeanor of someone who'd been beaten.

When Rita got to the podium, she looked around the room before speaking. "I've been at the shelter for three months, after a very long two years of dealing with the abuse of a man I loved. We had some good times, too, and I lived for those. But they didn't last long. If it weren't for my baby, I would probably still be with him … or dead. But when he shook my little girl for crying, I knew I had to get out of there."

Cameron's blood boiled at the very thought of any man hurting a child. He squirmed in his seat.

Rocky nudged him. "I know what you're thinking, Cam. It's rough."

"How can—" Cameron stopped when he saw that Rita was about to say more.

"I tried moving in with my parents, but he came after me. He begged me to move back in with him . . . so I did. And it happened again." She squeezed her eyes shut and shook her head. "I'm ashamed to admit that it took my husband breaking my little girl's arm to move out for good."

Melissa walked up to her, gently placed her arm around her shoulder, and whispered something in her ear. Rita nodded.

"Now that I'm at the shelter, I feel safe. He has no idea where I am or how to find me. Thanks to this church, I never have to worry about where my next meal will come from, and my baby is getting decent medical care." She glanced over at Melissa who nodded. "If you have any questions, I'll try to answer them."

A couple of people raised their hands and asked how they could help beyond what the church did. She explained that everything needed to go through the church because they had to maintain a certain amount of secrecy to protect all of the women in the shelter.

After she finished speaking, Melissa led the group in prayer before dismissing everyone. Cameron stood, sucked in a deep breath, and slowly blew it out.

"That was powerful," he said softly.

"I know." Rocky offered a sympathetic smile. "Ever since I found out about it, I've seen things differently.

"It makes me want to be a bodyguard for those women and children."

Rocky laughed. "Good luck with that. They won't let you anywhere near the shelter."

"Why not?"

"As it stands now, anyone who knows where it's located has to go through a very extensive background check."

"Okay," Cameron said. "I'm willing to do that."

"And be a woman." Again, Rocky smiled.

"Oh." Cameron raked his fingers through his hair. "I'm sure I can still help."

"You'll need to talk to Melissa about that. She's the coordinator. In fact, she and Janice are the people who started this whole ministry because someone we all know and love from high school was abused by a guy we thought we knew."

Cameron frowned. "People we knew?"

Rocky nodded. "Remember Jennifer Maxwell and Zach Hurley?"

"No way."

"Yeah, they were still on their honeymoon when he beat her senseless. She wound up in the hospital, almost dead. When Melissa found out, she and Janice went to see her. They promised her they'd do whatever they could to help her and anyone else in her position. That was when Melissa did some research and found a training program that she and Janice went through to start the program here."

"Where is Jennifer now?" Cameron asked.

Rocky shrugged. "No one knows."

"How about Zach?"

"We know where he is—serving a prison sentence at the state penitentiary." Rocky looked down for a second. "Unfortunately, he won't be there much longer."

"I never would have thought Zach was capable of something so horrible."

"Apparently, he grew up with it. His dad beat his mom, so he continued the pattern."

"Just goes to show that appearances can be deceiving." Cameron glanced up and made eye contact with Melissa. "Let me to talk to Melissa. Call me later, okay?"

CHAPTER SIX

"Well, what did you think?" Melissa asked before he had a chance to say a word.

"That was powerful . . . and surprising. I had no idea."

"I know, right? It shocked everyone when we started doing research on domestic abuse." A sad look came over her as she slowly shook her head. "It breaks my heart that we can't help more people, but at least we're doing something."

Cameron's heart melted as he studied Melissa's face. This was what he'd always loved about her—that her feelings ran so deep for others.

"I want to help," he said. "I'm pretty good with a hammer if they need anything fixed at the shelter. Or maybe I can sit outside the place and watch for bad guys."

She gave him a sympathetic smile. "Sorry, but no men allowed. I appreciate the thought, though."

"No men ever? What if something breaks?"

"That's already taken care of. But if you really want to help, maybe you can work with me on a fundraiser."

"Sure, that's fine." Cameron understood the premise of the policy, but Melissa had known him most of her life. Even though they'd always been fierce competitors, surely she knew he was trustworthy. At least he'd never given her any reason to think otherwise.

"Don't get your feelings hurt, Cameron. You're being too sensitive."

He scowled at her. "I am not sensitive."

"Sure you're not. Don't forget that these women have been abused by men, and having a man around might make them uncomfortable." She patted him on the arm and took a step toward the door. "Gotta run. I promised Rita I'd sit with her in church."

"Where's her baby?" Cameron asked.

"The church nursery." Melissa flashed a brief smile and then took off, leaving him standing there alone.

He stared at the wall for a few seconds before an overwhelming urge to see Rita's baby came over him. He headed straight for the nursery where there were several babies being cared for by the nursery workers.

"May I help you?" one of the older women asked. Then she blinked and grinned as she shifted the baby she was holding in her arms. "Why it's Cameron Prater. What are you doing here? I thought you'd moved on to seek your fame and fortune in a bigger city."

"Bigger cities are overrated," he said. "I recently moved back, and I'm here to stay."

"Did you need something?" she asked.

Cameron shook his head. "No, I just wanted to walk around and see if anything has changed. He glanced around the nursery over the bottom half of the door that remained closed. "I heard a powerful story about the shelter. Which one of these children belongs to Rita?"

"This one right here." She held the little girl up so he could see her. "Isn't she a doll?"

As soon as he smiled at the little girl with the elastic band sporting a big pink bow around her still nearly bald head, she grinned right back at him. His heart constricted. "She's precious."

"I would let you hold her, but we have policies, you know." The woman whose name he couldn't recall turned and glanced over her shoulder. "In fact, I don't think I'm supposed to be talking to you right now."

"Then I better leave. I don't want to get you in trouble."

"Good seeing you, Cameron."

After he walked away, he wondered about what kind of monster would dare to hurt such a sweet, innocent child. He knew right then that he had to do something to help the shelter, even if he couldn't go there in person.

Cameron left the church with a mission. He needed to figure out something he could do for the women and children at the shelter. The image of that sweet little baby girl remained etched in his mind. If he ever had a daughter—or a son, for that matter—he'd protect the child with his life.

Rocky caught up with him in the parking lot. "It's a tough pill to swallow, isn't it?"

"What?"

"The fact that any man can be so rotten."

Cameron pursed his lips and nodded. "It's worse than rotten. What kind of animal does that?"

"I know, right? The Lord wants men to protect their families. Until Melissa and Janice brought this information to the Bible study class, most of us had no idea how bad it was. All we knew about it was what we saw on the news . . . from other places."

Cameron stopped and turned around to face his buddy. "This is Hyacinth, South Carolina. It's a place where people live in harmony and raise their children to be kind to others. We're a bunch of law-abiding citizens who go to church." The truth had begun to seep into his mind—that no place could live up to the image he'd conjured.

"It's sin nature," Rocky reminded him. "We all have it."

"Not like that guy."

"Thank the Lord for that."

Cameron took a deep breath and puffed his cheeks as he slowly blew it out. "Amen. Now what are we going to do to help those women?"

"The Bible study group already donates money and has food drives to make sure their pantry is well stocked. We get diapers and formula from some of the stores."

"But I want to do more," Cameron said. "That's just maintaining people's existence. I want to help get to the heart of things and turn their lives around. Those children need to know that they have hope."

"They do. Janice picks the ones who are old enough to be without their mothers and takes them to the church for Bible studies and counseling. And they do fun stuff like go to the movies and roller-skating."

"How about the mothers? What are we doing to make sure they don't go back to those men who abuse them?"

Rocky placed his hand on Cameron's shoulder. "We can't make

them stay away from the men who hurt them. In fact, a couple of the women who used to be at the shelter have gone right back into their abusive situations."

"That's not acceptable," Cameron argued.

"I agree, but there is absolutely nothing we can do about it. They're grown women, and they are free to make their own decisions."

"Why would they do that, though? Don't they understand that they don't have to?"

"Who knows?" Rocky lifted his hands out to his sides, palms up. "I think some of them don't think they deserve any better."

"I bet there might be fear of being alone or financial worries too."

"Very well could be either . . . or both." Rocky gave him a look of understanding. "But like I said, there's nothing we can do to stop them."

Cameron nodded. "Okay, thanks for talking to me about it. I have a lot of things to think—and pray—about."

Rocky gave him an understanding grin. "I know how you feel, buddy. The first time I heard about this whole domestic abuse thing, I was on a personal mission to make it stop. Now I'm more realistic and do what I can to help out. Those women deserve respect, and their children need a warm, safe home." He paused. "At least they have that in the shelter."

After Cameron got in his truck, he shoved the key into the ignition, and paused to say a prayer for guidance. *Lord, You are the almighty. You see and know everything. Please show me how I can be the man You want me to be in this and in all other situations. I know I have failed You many times, and I pray for your forgiveness.*

He allowed his mind to relax before he said, "Amen," aloud. It pained him to know that such horrible things existed in Hyacinth.

On Monday morning, Melissa headed to the diner before the sun came up. She knew Betty would be there making biscuits, and she had something to discuss with her before anyone else arrived.

"Good morning, sunshine." Betty smiled under a layer of flour that always managed to smudge her cheerful face. "What brings you here so early? We don't open for another hour or so."

"I know, but I need to talk to you."

"Uh oh." Betty feigned a frown. "Sounds serious."

"It is, but it's a good kind of serious. I was thinking about Janice's idea to hire a few of the women from the shelter to work here. I'd like to go ahead and bring Rita in to help you in the kitchen and then eventually bring in others as the need arises . . . and when they're ready to handle additional responsibility."

Betty held the rolling pin still for a few seconds before nodding. "Yes, she's probably the closest to being ready."

"One of the issues is transportation. Rita has her license but no car. You have to be here so early, and the shelter is out of the way for you, so I can't expect you to pick her up."

"I'll do it if you can't find something else," Betty offered.

"I know you will. But there has to be another solution."

"There is."

The male voice from the doorway startled Melissa. "What are you doing here, Cameron? How did you get in?"

"The back door was wide open."

"Oh." Melissa knew the back door sometimes swung open if not closed all the way. "So what did you hear?"

"You need a car for one of the women to work here. Let me find her one."

Melissa met his gaze for a few seconds before she frowned. "It's not that easy."

"Nothing is easy. Tell me what the car needs, and I'll make that my mission."

Melissa ran through a list of everything she could think of, and Betty added more. Finally, she paused and sighed. "Don't forget that we have to protect those women."

"And their children," he reminded her. "I've already got a couple of car seats."

"Car seats?" Melissa looked at him with confusion. "Why would you get car seats when we don't even have cars to put them in?"

"Don't you take them places?"

She nodded. "We have car seats in the van."

"Now you have more car seats in varying sizes." He held out his hands. "And now it's time for me to find cars for them. How many do you need?"

Betty chuckled. "You make it sound easy."

"In case you've forgotten, I happen to know the Ford dealership owner's son."

Melissa remembered. "Didn't he play football for one of our rival's teams?"

"Yes, he played for Summerville. Anyway, we became friends after graduation, and I bought my truck from his dad. They're good people. I think they'll give me a good deal on a used car if I'm allowed to tell them what it's for."

"You've been working hard on this since yesterday," Melissa observed.

"Not so much hard work as thinking about what I can do to help. I wanted to go there, but since I'm not allowed, I had to get creative."

"How about hiring one of the women?" Betty asked.

Melissa spun around to face her. "I'm not sure—"

Betty cut her off with a glare. "You can't be the only business that hires them. We don't have enough of a need for every woman who wants a job."

"True." Melissa looked at Cameron. "But you're not even open yet, and from the looks of the place, it'll be a while."

"We'll get the inside whipped into shape pretty quickly once I figure out what kind of restaurant it'll be."

Betty stopped working again. "Don't you have it in your lease?"

He shook his head. "No, I was able to have it more open-ended because I know the owner . . . but it does have to be a restaurant."

"Oh, that's right," Betty said, rolling her eyes. "When you're the town's golden boy, you can pretty much call the shots." She laughed. "Just kidding."

"I don't know about golden boy. A lot of people have no idea who I am. It's weird being greeted and treated like a newcomer."

Melissa tossed him a jaunty look. "That's what you get for

leaving."

His reflective expression surprised her. "You're right."

"I was just kidding. Lighten up, former golden boy."

He laughed. "That coming from the queen of sensitivity?"

Betty stepped away from the counter and placed her hands on both of their shoulders. "Stop it, you two. You're about to become business neighbors, so isn't it about time you learned to get along?"

"I'm not doing anything—"

Betty cut her off with a look. "We're all going to work through this—whatever it is that's going on between y'all." She turned around to face Cameron, so Melissa stepped away.

"I'll be in the dining room setting up for breakfast if you need me."

As she walked away, she heard Betty discussing options for his restaurant. "And if you want to keep the chili theme, that's fine too. I don't think it'll hurt us in the least bit since you'll have other options that aren't anything like ours. Plus, you'll be open for dinner, while we close at 3:00."

Melissa didn't hear Cameron's response. But now that she thought about it, Betty was right. A chili restaurant wouldn't hurt Spoons Diner, unless she let the quality slip. And as long as she owned the place, that wouldn't happen.

CHAPTER SEVEN

Rather than let Betty have the last word with Cameron, Melissa decided to say something to him before he left Spoons. When he ducked his head into the dining room to let her know he was leaving, she motioned for him to wait.

"What?" he asked as he drew closer to her.

The intensity on his face nearly took her breath away. That had always been one of the things she loved about Cameron. When he had his mind focused, his face showed it, and that was when he was the most handsome. As irritating as he could be, she still found herself drawn to him in a way she almost couldn't resist. So she glanced away to keep him from seeing it.

"You wanted to talk to me?" he asked.

She nodded before venturing another glance in his direction. "I just wanted to say that I agree with Betty. Go ahead and open your chili restaurant."

"But I thought—"

"My first reaction was more surprise than anything else. Now that I think about it, a chili restaurant won't hurt my business, and I think it'll do well."

He gave her a dubious look. "Are you sure?"

Melissa tossed the towel she'd been holding onto the closest table and folded her arms as she spun around to face him. Huge mistake. The intensity of his gaze nearly undid her resolve to keep her distance.

She reached for the chair next to her, grabbed it, placed it between them, and held on tight. "Positive … and don't ask me that again."

He laughed. "I remember that about you. When I used to ask if you were sure, you got mad and told me you wouldn't have said it if you weren't."

"Okay then." She let go of the death grip on the chair and picked up the towel. "So it's settled now? You'll be opening a chili place?"

Cameron shrugged. "Maybe. Now that I've got Yubi committed, I'll want to consult with her. She might have some better ideas."

"When will you talk to her?"

He pulled his cell phone out of his pocket and glanced at it. "In about an hour. She wants to see the place."

Melissa made a face. "I hope it doesn't scare her away. It's still a mess in there."

"I know. But it'll look great once we finish with it." He glanced around the dining room. "As I'm sure you know."

"Yeah, this place has been everything from a ceramics shop to an ice cream parlor. I think either one of them would have done well with the right kind of marketing and management."

"And your business mind." He smiled. "You obviously know what you're doing, and you're doing an excellent job."

Melissa blinked. A compliment? Coming from Cameron? The only things he'd complimented her on in the past had been her looks and her ability to talk to strangers. It was almost as though he didn't want to acknowledge that she had brains.

"Don't look so surprised." He paused and looked directly at her. "I've always thought you were the most capable person in Hyacinth."

"Then why did you—?"

"Always try to one-up you?" he said.

She nodded. "Yeah."

"Maybe because you were so good at everything, and I always felt like I had to keep up."

That was exactly how she'd felt too. Perhaps that was what went wrong. They were too much alike.

He took a step back and paused. "I'd better run." As he walked toward the door, he added, "Thanks for permission to keep the chili theme."

"Permission?"

"Of course. I wouldn't do anything without getting your permission first." He feigned fear by holding his arms in front of his face. "Don't throw that salt shaker."

"Don't worry. I wouldn't want to waste perfectly good salt."

After he left, she chuckled and then sighed. Something had changed between them in the last few minutes, but even more importantly, some light had been shed on their relationship. The whole time she'd seen him as someone who could make her toes curl with a single look while at the same time infuriate her with whatever came out of his mouth. Was it possible that what she'd perceived as arrogance had actually been insecurity?

CAMERON WAITED BY THE door to watch for Yubi. She arrived about two minutes early, looking almost identical to how he remembered her, only with a few more laugh lines around her eyes and mouth.

"Good morning, Cameron. And welcome back to Hyacinth."

"Thanks. It's good to see you, Yubi." He held the door open as she walked inside. "Well? What do you think?"

"I hope you've hired a demolition crew. This place is one hot mess."

He laughed. "I agree, but you should have seen it a couple of weeks ago. The crew has already removed a lot of things. We're going to try to salvage some of it, but it was much worse than this."

She walked around, looked behind walls, and turned to face him. "Where's the kitchen?"

"Come on. I'll show you."

Yubi followed him around the wall and into the room that still housed oversized industrial appliances. She touched the stove and then quickly pulled her hand back as she made a face. "That's just gross."

"I know. After we finish gutting the place, I'm bringing in some Ninja cleaners."

She smiled. "That's definitely what this place needs." She walked out to the front area that would eventually be the dining room. "So what are your plans, and where do I fit in?"

He remembered Yubi's directness, and he appreciated it more than ever right now. "My original plan was to turn this into a chili restaurant that opens for lunch and dinner. Then I got some negative vibes from someone, so I thought about changing it."

"But now?" Yubi lifted an eyebrow. "What are you thinking now?"

He held out both hands, palms up. "I'm back to thinking chili."

Yubi's face was hard to read, but she eventually nodded. "I think that's probably a good idea. Sometimes you have to go with your gut, and most people in Hyacinth like that kind of food."

"Can you cook chili?" he asked.

She tilted her head back and let out a deep laugh. "Can I cook chili? Oh yeah. In fact, my chili is far better than any Chinese food I've ever cooked. You do realize I've been in the States longer than I lived in China, right?"

"Y-yes, of course." He hadn't actually thought about it, but it wasn't hard to do the math. He knew she wasn't very old when she went to work for Rocky's mom, back when he was a little boy.

"Not only can I cook chili, I can fry some of the best chicken you ever tasted." She made a funny face. "And I'm talking southern fried so light and crispy it'll make your eyes roll back in your head."

He laughed. "I'll have to try that sometime."

"Have you thought about making this a southern style restaurant?"

He shrugged. "I figured most people ate that kind of food at home."

"Maybe a long time ago, but people are getting so busy they don't have time to do it right."

"That's definitely an idea."

She gave him a clipped nod. "Think about it. From the looks of this place, you obviously still have time."

"So what do you think about working here?" he asked.

"Until Rocky told me it was you, I didn't think I'd want to do it." She cleared her throat. "But I always knew that you'd be someone important someday, and I've always liked being associated with success."

"Thank you, Yubi."

She shook her head. "You don't have to thank me. I'm simply speaking the truth. And that's another thing. You know I don't mince words, right?"

He nodded. "Yes, I remember that."

"So if I don't like something, you won't have to guess my thoughts. I'll let you know."

"I actually like that."

"Good, because that's what you're going to get from me." She grinned. "You asked me what I think about working here." Before he had a chance to answer, she continued. "I'll definitely work for you, Cameron."

"Aren't you going to ask about the salary?"

She shrugged. "I've never asked about money before, and I don't intend to ask now. If I trust you enough to work for you, I trust that you'll pay me a fair salary."

"Let me think about the southern food versus chili."

"Don't think too long. You'll need to know which one to go with before you start building it out, and I want to have input." She started toward the door. "I need to leave now. Let me know when you need me, okay?"

"Okay." He held the door. "Oh, before I forget. How are you at decorating?"

"Very good. In fact, I already have ideas for whatever you decide."

"Why am I not surprised?"

"Because you know me." She grinned and waved. "Bye for now, Cameron. See you soon."

He stood at the door and watched her disappear around the corner. Something about Yubi Chou gave him the feeling that all was well. Maybe it was her confidence, or perhaps it was her take-charge demeanor. Whatever the case, he had no doubt that whatever type of restaurant he chose would be successful with her working for him.

And now he had an overwhelming urge to discuss it with Melissa. He took a few steps toward her place and saw the breakfast crowd. This obviously wasn't a good time.

He went back to his place and called Rocky. "Thanks for sending Yubi. She's perfect."

"I knew she would be. Have you decided what kind of restaurant to open?"

"Melissa told me she thought the chili place would be good, but now Yubi has me thinking about downhome southern cooking."

Rocky laughed. "What's happening to you, man? You used to make decisions and act on them without consulting anyone. Where's your confidence?"

"I've actually found my confidence. Acting without thinking didn't always get the best results. Now I have the confidence to ask people who know what they're doing."

"Oh, that's deep."

Cameron laughed. "Not so deep as much as not wanting to lose my shirt on a business I didn't take the time to research."

"Good point." There was a brief pause before Rocky spoke again. "I wanted to let you know that I've gotten a few toy donations for the shelter, and I need help picking them up."

"When?"

"Now."

Cameron snorted. "What if I'm busy?"

"You're not. I happen to know that you can't do anything until you finish getting the restaurant cleaned up, and you've been standing there waiting for me to call."

"You're crazy, Rocky. But okay, I'll do it. Where do I need to go?"

CHAPTER EIGHT

MELISSA HAD BARELY FINISHED HELPING THE last of her lunch customers when she glanced out the large front window and spotted Cameron walking toward the diner with a look of determination on his face. What now?

He opened the door and took a long look around, and then his gaze settled on hers. He smiled.

She narrowed her eyes and mouthed, "What?"

He crooked his index finger and motioned for her to go outside. Before she had a chance to say no, Janice came up from behind.

"Go see what he wants."

Melissa didn't see that she had a choice, so without a word, she nodded and followed Cameron out the door to his truck. He reached up and pulled off a tarp, exposing an enormous number of toys.

"What's this all about?" she asked.

"Rocky's buddy is closing one of his stores, and he donated these things for the women's shelter."

Melissa couldn't help but laugh. "That's enough for ten shelters. We only have one."

He rubbed the back of his neck as his smile faded. "I know, but isn't there something we can do with them? I mean, they were a donation, and I thought—"

She didn't want to dampen his enthusiasm, so she nodded. "Of course. We can bring a few things over to the shelter and store the rest of them at the church. Toys don't last that long, so it'll be nice to have a selection to replace the old, broken, and misplaced ones."

"Good. Why don't we take some toys over to the shelter after you close?" He lifted the tarp to cover the toys before turning back to face her.

"Nice try, Cameron." She clasped her hands in front of her and grinned. "We can haul that stuff to the church and pick a few things and then Janice and I can take them to the shelter."

"I don't know why you won't let me at least drop stuff off. I don't even have to go inside."

"That's not the point, Cameron, and you know it. We have a very strict policy about not letting men—"

"Why *all* men?" he interrupted.

"Because if we let one man go, then all kinds of things can happen. First, we have a policy that as long as the women are at the shelter, they need to focus on getting their lives in order, and men can be a distraction. Second, some of the children—and women—are afraid of men after what happened to them. We want them to feel safe and secure, without distractions or setbacks."

Cameron hadn't thought about those angles. They actually made sense. "Okay, I understand. So when can you be at the church?"

"I can leave now. Janice and Betty can close the diner."

"Okay, I'll head on over there." Cameron stepped off the curb. "See you in a few minutes."

Melissa went back into the diner and told Janice and Betty what Cameron and Rocky had done. "You should see the mountain of toys. We won't have to buy any for at least the next year or two."

"That is so sweet," Janice said as her forehead crinkled.

Betty's face had lit up. "I'm not surprised. For all their exterior machismo, Cameron and Rocky are very sweet boys."

As Melissa grabbed her handbag and keys, Janice got to work cleaning the tables. "As soon as we lock up, I'll go straight to the church and help unload and sort things."

"Thanks!" Melissa left and headed toward her car.

Cameron and Rocky were in the church parking lot when she arrived. She exited her car and her cell phone rang. She thought about not answering, but when she saw that it was Rita from the shelter, she knew she had to.

"We have an emergency," Rita said, her voice rushed and tight. "Taylor's ex-boyfriend found her, and now he's threatening her and her kids."

"Did you call the police?" Melissa asked as she glanced over at Cameron who gave her a questioning look.

"I did, and they're sending someone over. But I'm afraid—" Her voice was interrupted by something crashing and people shouting. "I gotta go." *Click.*

"Sorry, Cameron, but I need to go to the shelter now. One of the women's boyfriends has found her, and it sounds like something terrible is about to happen."

Without another word, she hopped into her car and took off. She had to get there quickly, so she took a chance and sped the whole way. When she rounded the corner toward the house, her skin crawled with goose bumps. She sure hoped the other women remembered the emergency drill about protecting the children if something like this ever happened.

She parked at the edge of the driveway where an old, beat-up car sat, its engine still running. That must be the abusive boyfriend's, she figured.

Before she got out of her car, she saw that Cameron and Rocky were right behind her. She quickly cast a disapproving glance in their direction, but she didn't have time to let them have it. She turned back toward the house and ran up the sidewalk. While a man and woman screamed obscenities at each other, she thought about the children. Her heart ached through the fear that clenched her insides. All kinds of possibilities of what they might be dealing with flitted through her mind.

Rita ran toward her and shoved her into the hallway. Melissa looked the frightened woman in the eye. "Where are the police?" she whispered.

"I have no idea. I called them right before I called you."

Melissa took a deep breath and slowly let it out. She couldn't let her fear hamper judgment. "I'll go in the bathroom and call again," she said. "Where are the children?"

"Taylor's kids are locked in the bedroom. The rest are in the backyard."

Melissa nodded and slipped into the bathroom a few feet away to call the police. Immediately after hanging up, she heard the sound of

Cameron's voice, letting her know he was in the house.

Her heart hammered so hard it felt as though it might beat a hole in her chest, and she had to force herself to focus on maintaining her cool for the victims in the shelter. She managed to get out of the bathroom, work her way toward the kitchen, and out the backdoor without being noticed. Once outside, she spotted two of the women, Andrea and Bethany, with their children and Rita's little girl, all hovering in the corner of the yard beside a small storage shed. She ran over to them.

"What happened?" she asked the women.

The sound of police sirens silenced them for a few seconds. They all looked at each other with stony faces.

Andrea finally sniffled and wiped her nose with the back of her hand. "Taylor's boyfriend found out where she was. We're still not sure how. Anyway, he came to the door and tried to get in. When we wouldn't open it, he broke a window and climbed in. We were making cookies with the kids when he first stormed through the house, but Rita told us to turn off the oven and get the kids out of the house as quickly as possible. Taylor locked her kids in the bedroom, and she refused to let us take them with us."

"Did he hurt anyone?"

Andrea and Bethany glanced at each other and nodded. "He slugged Taylor," Bethany said. "She'll probably have all kinds of bruises later."

Melissa looked at both of them and saw the pain on their faces. These women knew exactly what Taylor was going through first hand. And their children. One look at them let her know that this was dredging up all kinds of horrible memories. Her heart ached, and helplessness swamped her at not being able to make the pain and heartache go away.

"Who are those guys who came with you?" Bethany asked.

"They didn't come with me," Melissa explained, "but they followed me here. They're good guys, though. You don't need to worry about them."

Silence fell over the backyard. The hollering inside the house had stopped, casting an eerie mood over the women and children all clustered together.

"What are they doing now?"

Melissa shook her head. She wished she knew what Cameron and Rocky were doing, but she didn't dare risk going back into the house to find out.

After what seemed like hours but was probably more like a few minutes, Cameron and one of the police officers walked out to the backyard. Melissa resisted the urge to run toward Cameron and throw herself into his arms.

"Everything is all right now," Cameron said, a shell-shocked expression belying the even tone of his voice.

Melissa took a step toward him. "Where is Rita?"

"She went to the hospital with Taylor. Her boyfriend hit her pretty hard, so she'll probably need stitches."

Melissa turned to the police officer. "And where is the boyfriend now?"

"On the way to the jail. He won't be around for a while. This isn't his first time behind bars."

Melissa shuddered as she thought about how bad things were but how much worse they could have been. She looked directly at Cameron. "What did you do in there?"

He shrugged and didn't say anything, but the police officer spoke up. "We didn't get the information we needed when that first lady called. She didn't stay on the phone long enough for us to get the location. By the time we got here, the boyfriend had broken the door down to the children's room. If it weren't for Cameron and Rocky, there's no telling what might have happened."

Melissa narrowed her gaze as she looked at Cameron. He shrugged. But Rocky came up from behind and slapped his pal on the back.

"I've known this guy practically all my life, but this was the first time I ever saw him deck someone."

"You hit him?" Melissa asked.

He nodded, rubbed his fist, and turned to the police officer. "I guess I'll probably get arrested now."

The officer grinned. "Bad guess. You had no choice but to use force to protect those children. But you will have to go in for questioning."

"That's fine." Cameron looked around at everyone in the yard and then settled his gaze on Melissa. "We need to talk soon."

"I know." She glanced down at her feet. "Thank you, Cameron. I appreciate what you've done."

The officer gestured toward the house. "Why don't you follow me to the police station?"

After they left, Melissa walked back to where Andrea and Bethany remained with the children. "Is that your boyfriend?" Andrea asked.

"No." The word came out so quickly Melissa realized she sounded defensive. "He used to be, but that was many years ago."

Bethany let out a sigh. "If I could find a guy like that, all my problems would be solved."

"No they wouldn't," Andrea argued. "Men can't solve your problems."

Bethany shrugged and bobbed her head. "Yeah, you're right. But I've never had a guy look at me the way he looked at Melissa."

Melissa didn't want to talk about Cameron right now—not the way he looked at her, not the relationship they once had, and certainly not the feelings she realized she still harbored for him. As much as she hated to admit it, even to herself, she had no doubt that she still loved him. But that wasn't something she needed to discuss now. Her main goal for the day had to be protecting these women.

"Looks like we're going to have to move the shelter," she said with a heavy heart. It had been rough finding a place to rent for these women—a safe place that allowed more than one family. She escorted the children back into the house and then called a window company to repair the damage.

Since she couldn't leave the women and kids alone until she was certain they'd be safe, she called the pastor of the church to let him know what had happened. He'd already heard from Cameron.

"I'm in the process of securing another location," he said.

"Do you have something in mind?"

"Yes. My father-in-law has a rental house that has recently been vacated. It's bigger than the one they're currently in, and he lives in the house next door."

She thought for a moment. It would be nice to have a decent male figure in these women and children's lives so they could see how a man was supposed to behave.

After she got off the phone, she told the women about the move. To her surprise, they were disappointed.

"This house was just starting to feel like home," Andrea said.

"I know." One of the other women looked at her children. "They'd finally gotten past their nightmares, and I've been getting some decent sleep."

"Remember that it's not the place that's home," Melissa reminded them. "It's the family you're with."

At that moment, they heard the sound of a truck pulling into the driveway. Melissa separated herself from the others and opened the front door to let Cameron and Rita in.

"They're keeping Taylor at the hospital overnight for observation," Rita said. "She has a concussion."

Cameron stood by the door with his arms folded. Andrea came up from behind Melissa and gave her a gentle shove toward him.

CHAPTER NINE

CAMERON SAW WHAT HAD HAPPENED. THE woman who pushed Melissa in his direction wore a smug smile, so he had no doubt she could read his mind. Now he knew that he wanted Melissa more than anything he'd ever desired.

Melissa stumbled for a second but quickly caught herself before she landed in his arms. She looked up at him. "Did you know they're moving?"

He nodded. "Yeah. Gary called and said his father-in-law has a place. His wife is getting it ready, so we should probably start loading up their stuff."

"They're moving today? But I thought—"

"They can't stay here anymore . . . not even another day. It's too dangerous." He looked over at the children. "Which ones are Taylor's?"

One of the women stepped forward with a baby. The sweet little face was so precious his heart melted, and he reached for her.

At first, the woman pulled back, but when she glanced at Melissa who nodded, she handed the baby over to him. "What's her name?"

"Angel."

He smiled down at the baby who appeared fascinated by his face. When he repeated her name, she gave him a big grin with only two bottom teeth showing. It was next to impossible to imagine any man even thinking about hurting something so small and helpless.

Melissa came up beside him and looked at Angel's face. "She's sweet, isn't she?"

He nodded. "Which one is Angel's sibling?"

The same woman who'd been holding Angel took a little boy by the hand and walked him toward Cameron. He should have known which child was the sibling. He looked like a male version of Angel.

Melissa took Angel from him, so he knelt down and smiled at the little boy. "And what's your name?"

"Adam."

Cameron reached out, took Adam's hand in his, and shook it. "It's so nice to meet you, Adam. I bet you're a very good big brother to little Angel."

Adam nodded. "I protect her from mean monsters."

It took everything Cameron had not to wince. The biggest monster either of these children had to face was their own father. He glanced up at Melissa and could tell she was thinking the same thing.

They spent the remainder of the day moving the women's belongings to the new place. Gary and his dad both came in and helped move things around to make the space work for the women and their kids. Janice and Betty arrived a little later to help get the kitchen set up.

"This place is so much nicer," Andrea said. "The other house was the nicest place I've ever lived . . ." She spread her arms wide. "Until this."

Mr. Buchman grinned. "I want y'all to have a comfortable home, so if there's anything I can do, let me know. Both my son Gary and I can fix just about anything that needs fixin', and my wife is a fabulous cook." He chuckled and rubbed his belly. "But I'm sure y'all probably already figured that out. Gary likes to come by every week, so you'll be seein' a lot of him, I reckon."

Cameron had liked Gary's dad since the first time he met him. The Buchman family wasn't from Hyacinth, but when Gary got the call to pastor the church, his parents had recently retired. So they sold their house and purchased this property, hoping Gary would want to live in one of the houses. However, Gary wanted to be closer to town, and he said he didn't need a house this big anyway. After looking around, Cameron understood why. It was humongous. It even had enough room for a couple more women.

Once they got all the furniture where the ladies said they wanted it, Cameron walked toward the door. "I'm only a phone call away if anyone needs me."

Melissa joined him. "I'll walk you to your truck." She remained quiet until they got outside, but then she started talking. "I hate that it had to happen this way, but I think this will be a much better place for the women and their children."

He looked around at the massive amount of land and nodded as his gaze met hers again. "They have plenty of places to play now. Mr. Buchman said he was excited about having the little ones around. He asked me to come back and help him build a play set."

Melissa smiled. She didn't appear to have anything else to say, so he turned around. Before he could take a step, she grabbed him by the arm. "Cameron?"

He spun around and faced her. "What?"

"Thank you so much for coming to the rescue. I don't know what we would have done without you."

"I didn't do anything."

"Oh yes you did. You showed these women how protective a man can and should be. I don't think any of them have been around a decent guy before."

He had to fight the grin that threatened. "So you're saying I'm a decent guy?"

She rolled her eyes and made a goofy face. "As much as I hate to admit it, yes, you are a very decent guy." She grimaced. "And even more than that, I appreciate you."

He feigned shock. "Have you taken a hit to the head, Melissa? Do I need to rush you to the emergency room?"

She gave him a playful swat. "You're being silly now. Seriously, Cameron, I've always known you were a good guy, but we've always been so competitive with each other it was hard for me to tell you." She cast her gaze downward before looking back up at him. "But the times we got along were some of the best times of my life."

He wanted to grab her and kiss her at that moment, but it didn't seem appropriate—not only because of their discussion but because there were a bunch of people standing on the porch watching them. "I agree."

"Do you mind if I call you later?" she asked. "I'd like to talk about . . . um . . . business."

"Sure. Or better yet, why don't I take you to dinner tomorrow night? We can drive into Charleston and go to the Hominy Grill. I recall that being one of your favorite restaurants."

Her eyes lit up. "You remember?"

"Of course I do. Exactly like I remember that peach and green are your favorite colors, and you like white roses and dark chocolate."

She pulled her lips between her teeth as her chin quivered. She sniffled and swallowed hard. "Cameron, I haven't exactly been fair to you since you've been back. You really are a terrific guy."

He reached out and touched the side of her face. "And you're pretty terrific yourself. Call me after you get home, and we can nail down the plans for dinner."

As difficult as it was to leave her, he needed to before he made a fool of himself in front of an audience. He wouldn't have minded for himself, but he didn't want to embarrass Melissa.

"THAT WAS SOME KIND of goodbye," Janice whispered as they walked back into the house behind the others. "I thought y'all were going to give us a real show with a really cool lip lock."

"Yeah, right."

"No, seriously, Melissa. When are you going to see what's so obvious? You and Cameron are in love . . . always have been, and I can't see that ever changing. Even when you bite each other's heads off, there's still that sizzling tension that is so evident. The two of you are made for each other."

Melissa opened her mouth to argue, but she decided against it. Janice was right. She was in love with Cameron, and she could tell he cared about her too. But she wasn't sure he was as smitten as she was. Some of the things he'd said a few minutes ago replayed in her mind, but she didn't want to hold him accountable for anything spoken during such an emotionally charged day.

As she helped put the finishing touches on the house, Rita, Andrea and Bethany each tried to bring up her relationship with Cameron. She had to put a stop to it before the conversation revealed how she really felt.

She finally left the house, confident that the women were in good hands with Mr. Buchman and his wife who promised to look in on them every day. They didn't have that kind of paternal care at the former house, and when she saw their jubilant expressions, she suspected none of them ever had it in their past.

Rita walked her to her car. "I can't believe how quickly everything happened." She opened her arms wide and gestured around the property. "And to think this was available at the perfect time."

Melissa nodded. "Yes, but remember it was God's timing." She paused to let it sink in. "And God's timing is always perfect."

"I can see that." Rita sighed. "Ya know, even though all of us were beaten by our husbands or boyfriends, I think God had a plan for us, and that was to meet you and all of your nice friends."

"He loves you, so He brought us together." Melissa opened her arms and hugged Rita. "Y'all have been a blessing to us as well."

All the way home, Melissa's mind drifted from one thought to another—all about what had transpired during the day. Her initial call from Rita seemed like eons ago, but it was merely a few hours earlier. She swung by the hospital to check on Taylor before going home. When she got to the hospital room, she saw that Cameron and Rocky had both had the same idea.

Rocky stood outside the door. "They're only letting one of us in at a time, and a hospital staff member has to be in the room when she has guests."

"That's understandable, after what she went through."

Cameron came out, looked at her, and blinked. "I didn't expect to see you here."

Although Rocky had gotten there before her, he motioned for her to go in next. "I'm sure she'd much rather see you than me."

When Melissa entered the room, she had to stifle a gasp. Taylor's face was covered in purple blotches, her arm was in a cast, and she had bandages all over her.

"Pretty bad, huh?" she mumbled. "How are my kids?"

"They're doing really well. Did Cameron tell you about the new digs?"

Taylor tried to nod, but she squeezed her eyes shut as she winced in pain. A few seconds later, she spoke. "He said it's a really nice house with a big yard for the kids to pay in. Adam will like that."

"I think you'll like it too."

"I'm sure I will. Do you know what they did with Jeremy?"

"He's in jail," Melissa said. "And I don't think he'll be getting out for a while."

"That's such a shame. I really do … I mean I did love him." She pursed her lips. "I bet you don't see what I saw in him."

She was right, but Melissa wasn't about to tell her that. "The only thing I care about right now is seeing you get better and going back to your kids. Any idea when you'll get out?"

"I could have gone back today if that doctor didn't insist on keeping me overnight for observation."

"You need to get some rest." Melissa backed toward the door.

"Oh, there's one more thing I need to tell you," Taylor said softly.

Melissa stepped closer to Taylor's bed. "What's that?"

"Cameron is madly in love with you. He's such a sweet guy, I think you need to listen to what he has to say."

CHAPTER TEN

TAYLOR COULD HAVE KNOCKED MELISSA OVER with a feather. "What? Where did that come from?"

"Well, maybe no one has come right out and asked him before, but I did."

"Asked him what?" Melissa leaned forward. "When?"

"I asked him if he was in love with you, and he said he very much was."

Melissa straightened her back. "Let's concentrate on getting you well and home with your kids."

In spite of her condition, Taylor laughed. "I get it. You don't want to discuss your feelings. And trust me, I understand. But one of these days you'll have to face it." She winced in pain again but continued. "You are so lucky to have someone like Cameron. I can kind of tell you have feelings for him too."

And that was one of the things she'd wanted to avoid. Her feelings had always gotten her into trouble in the past—particularly when it came to Cameron. As soon as she let her guard down, he zapped her with one-upmanship.

"I'll see you tomorrow when I stop by to take you home."

"That's not necessary," Taylor said. "Pastor Buchman said his mom and dad would come and get me."

"Are you sure?"

"Positive. They said you have a business to run, and all they have to do is stare at each other." Taylor laughed again before making another pained face. "Must be nice to have someone who loves you enough to want to stare at you."

"Okay, then. I'll see you soon."

When Melissa left the room, she didn't see Cameron or Rocky.

One of the nurses stopped. "Are you Melissa Shaw?"

She nodded. "Yes, why?"

"Your boyfriend said he'd see you tomorrow, and his friend got a call and had to leave."

Rather than correct the nurse, Melissa gave her a smile and thanked her. When she got to her car, she sat and stared out the window for a moment. Something odd was happening for everyone to assume Cameron was her boyfriend. But what bugged her the most was that she actually liked it.

Most of the next day she dodged conversation with Janice and Betty so she wouldn't have to discuss Cameron and their date that night. But then he decided to show up right before closing time.

Janice grinned at her but darted out of the dining room as soon as he walked in. She turned to him and waited for him to say something.

"The catfish creole at the Hominy Grill is calling your name. What time can you be ready to go?"

She glanced at the clock on the wall. "I'll have to go home and change, but since it'll take us about an hour to get to Charleston and find parking, how about 5:00?"

"Sounds good. I'll call for reservations. Wear comfortable shoes. I thought we could walk around while we're in the city."

She smiled and nodded. "Okay."

He gave her a curious glance before backing toward the door. "See you at 5:00."

The instant the door closed behind him, Janice came running out of the kitchen. "Why didn't you tell me you had a date with Cameron?"

"Why would I tell you?"

"Come on, Melissa. You know I care about you, and I want you to be happy. Don't get so testy."

Before she had a chance to respond, Betty joined them. "Janice is right. Don't you think it's time to relax and stop being so defensive?" She glanced over at Janice, who nodded her agreement. "And enjoy knowing that the two of you are meant for each other?"

"I think—"

Betty held up her hand. "And that's the problem. You think too much. Let it happen. Everyone else can see the sparks flying between you two. Stay still long enough to see if a fire ignites." She grinned. "That's what happened between Hugh and me. Once we let go of our silly little worries, we have had the most romantic life together."

Both Melissa and Janice spun around to face her. Melissa hadn't even thought about Betty's romantic life. "Y'all have been married a very long time."

"We sure have." Betty grinned. "And let me tell you, sweetie, it's a romance better than any you can read about in a romance novel. I still melt when he gives me one of those looks."

Melissa looked at Betty looked at Melissa. "That's what I want."

"Then you better start looking. Based on what I've seen, the pickings get mighty slim as you get older."

"Are you saying I'm an old maid?"

"Of course not," Betty said. "You have a few years before I would even think about calling you that." She burst into a belly laugh. "I'm kidding. You're doing fine. All I'm saying is that when Cupid pulls back his bow, pay attention."

Janice nudged Melissa. "Did you hear that?"

"Of course I did." Melissa took off her apron and hung it on the wall. "I'd better get on home and get ready."

CAMERON WAS AS NERVOUS as he was before his and Melissa's first date in high school. The odd thing about tonight was he wasn't even sure she'd consider this a date.

He took a deep breath, gave himself another once-over in front of the mirror then headed out to pick her up. He wanted more than anything for this to go well. He'd given up thinking he and Melissa could go on being "just friends". They were more than that. He now realized that their constant sniping at each other was the result of unacknowledged feelings that they'd both buried and refused to let out.

She flung open her door the second he knocked. He gave her an appreciative glance. "You look nice."

"Thanks. So do you." She reached for her handbag and stepped outside, pulling the door to. "I hope the traffic isn't bad. You know how it can get during rush hour."

This stilted conversation had to stop, or the entire night would wind up being awkward. He helped her into the truck, went around to the driver's side, and got in. But he didn't put the key in the ignition right away.

"What?" she asked as he sat there staring at her.

"We need to talk, but I'm not sure where to begin." He closed his eyes momentarily. When he opened them, she gave him one of her goofy grins.

"That's a first. Just spit it out."

"Okay." He turned his entire body around to face her.

Her eyes widened. "This must be serious."

"It is." He sucked in another breath and slowly let it out. "This is really hard for me . . . you know, after years of never coming to terms with my feelings."

"Feelings? Is that what this is all about?" She paused. "Look, Cameron, I don't expect our old feelings to have anything to do with—"

He reached out and lightly placed his fingertips on her lips to shush her. She blinked in apparent surprise.

"Melissa, I love you. With all my heart. I can't keep pretending not to."

Her chin dropped, but she didn't say anything. Now that he'd started, he couldn't take any of it back, and he had to continue, or he might lose his nerve.

"I don't know what I expected when I saw you again, but the second I looked at you, it was as though nothing and no one else existed. You were the only person who mattered at that moment, and now . . ." He took one of her hands in his. "Now I know the reason."

She withdrew her hand from his and pinched the bridge of her nose with her fingertips. Her silence caused an ache to form in the pit of his stomach, but he didn't regret saying what needed to be said.

"If you change your mind about going out tonight, I'll understand."

She shook her head as a smile slowly formed on her lips. "You might have decided that you love me, but you sure don't read me very well."

"What are you talking about?"

"I love you too. The difference is, I've known for a while." She let out a soft chuckle. "I figured it out before you did."

"Oh, so we're going to compete on this too, huh?" Her admission gave him the strength to jump back into the game. "You're on, baby."

"Huh?" She gave him a curious look.

"I'll have you know that I never stopped loving you."

She tilted her head forward and looked at him from beneath her gorgeous eyebrows. "Then why is it taking you so long to kiss me?"

"I-I don't know."

Before he had a chance to act on her challenge, she'd scooted closer to him and had her hands behind his head. In one quick motion, he took over, pulling her into his arms and kissing her the way he'd wanted to for years.

When they finally broke apart, she whispered, "You won that one." Then she scooted back into her place in the passenger seat. "If we're going to make out, let's find a better place than your truck. We're not teenagers anymore."

Cameron laughed as he started the engine. "Let's save that for later. I have reservations at the Hominy Grill, and I don't want to miss out on seeing your eyes roll back in your head from the delicious catfish creole."

"Now that's the most romantic thing you've ever said to me."

"Just wait. There's more."

"Be still my heart."

They bantered for the remainder of the evening. After dinner, they walked around Downtown Charleston and talked about everything, including all the changes that had taken place in this waterfront town.

Finally, he stopped her, turned her around to face him, and tilted her chin up to face him. "So what now? I'd like to make this permanent, but I don't want to scare you away with too much too fast."

"You're the one who's scared," she whispered.

"Is that a challenge?"

She nodded. "Yep."

Without waiting for more doubt to creep in, he dropped to one knee, looked directly into her eyes, and grinned. "You know how I am with challenges."

Again, her chin dropped. She started to say something, but only a squeak came out. Perfect. She was speechless, which made this the ideal time to do what he should have done years ago.

"Melissa Shaw, how do you feel about joining forces and forming a Hyacinth restaurant empire?"

Her eyebrows slammed together in a questioning look. "Say what?"

"I'm asking you to marry me in my own awkward way. So how about it? Will you?"

She rolled her eyes at first, but then she dropped to her knees and kissed him. "Yes, of course I will."

"No more challenges?"

"I didn't say that."

"That's fine," he said. "But the challenges have to change. After all, I've heard that we're not supposed to go to sleep at night when we're mad at each other."

"Okay, it's a deal."

An elderly couple had to sidestep to get around them on the sidewalk. "Sorry, but I proposed, and she said yes."

The elderly man chuckled. "Young people certainly do things different these days."

"No they don't," his wife argued. "You just forgot what it was like."

After the elderly couple got out of hearing range, Cameron and Melissa cracked up. "They sound like us."

She nodded. "I know, and they look happy too."

He stood and pulled her to her feet. They walked half a block before she spoke again.

"Do you think they look happy?"

"Yup." He stopped and pulled her into his arms. "Whose turn is it to start the kiss this time?"

"Yours."

EPILOGUE

BETTY CAREFULLY PLACED THE CAKE ON the table, while Janice arranged the forks, plates, and napkins. "I still don't see why you had to have your reception here."

"It's the perfect place," Melissa argued. "The food is good, and the price is right."

"True." Betty glanced over at Rita and Taylor. "Are y'all ready to help me with the rest of the food?"

After they nodded, Bethany and Andrea left to help Yubi at Cameron's restaurant. Both kitchens buzzed with activity getting ready for the reception after the wedding.

Betty made a shooing motion. "You need to go get ready for your big day. We'll see you at the church."

As Melissa left, butterflies fluttered in her abdomen. It had been six months since Cameron proposed, and a lot had changed since then. Not only had he opened his restaurant, they'd both hired women who lived at the shelter. All but Taylor now planned to make food service their careers. She decided she liked childcare more, but she was helping out until she finished her counseling sessions.

An hour and a half later, Melissa stood in the tiny bridal room at the back of the church, surrounded by her friends who were all giggly and excited. She felt an amazing sense of calm as she waited for the music to walk toward the man she'd loved since she was a teenager.

Betty gave her a hug before going into the sanctuary to find her seat. Her mother and Janice stayed by her side, until the usher came for her mother. Then it was only her and Janice.

"Are you sure you want to do this?" Janice asked.

"You're kidding, right?"

"Of course I am. Let's go."

Janice walked in time to the music toward the front of the church, glancing over her shoulder a couple of times to grin at Melissa who watched through the tiny square window pane in the top of the door. Once Janice got to the front, the music changed, signaling that it was time for Melissa and her dad.

He extended his elbow. "Ready, sweetheart?"

She nodded. The ushers held the double doors open to let them through. As she floated toward Cameron, she couldn't take her eyes off him.

Her dad handed her off to him, and he squeezed her hand. "I love you," Cameron whispered before turning to face Pastor Gary.

The ceremony went by in a blur. After Gary told them to kiss, the music changed again. Everyone applauded, and someone shouted, "It's about time."

After she changed into a regular dress, Rocky drove them to Main Street and let them off in front of Spoons Diner. They went inside, spoke to everyone at Spoons, and then they headed over to Downhome in Hyacinth, Cameron's southern-style diner where Yubi had a special table set up. They had to open both places to have room for everyone.

"I'm sure you two aren't that hungry, but you have to eat something before you leave." Yubi grinned at Melissa. "I got the catfish creole recipe from the Hominy Grill. I hope you like it."

After Melissa took a bite, she gave Yubi a thumbs-up. "Delicious."

People kept stopping by their table, making it difficult to eat. Yubi walked over, leaned down, and whispered, "I understand if you can't clean your plate. I'll make this dish again after you come back from your honeymoon. Then you'll be able to relax and enjoy it without the distractions."

"Thanks, Yubi." Melissa and Cameron each ate a few bites before he nodded toward the door. "Ready to go?"

"Absolutely!"

Once they got in his truck, Cameron turned to her. "I still can't believe it."

"Can't believe what? That we're married?"

"No. I can't believe you haven't challenged me once today in the whole two hours we've been together."

"Oh, trust me, it's coming."
He leaned over and kissed her. "That's what I'm talkin' about."

The End

MORE THAN MEETS THE EYE

By
Trish Perry

CHAPTER ONE

"OH, NO. NOW WHAT?" THE SOFT spot in Jensy St. Martin's heart was instantly touched when she came upon her best friend, Rebecca, crying again.

Jensy had come to work this morning as excited as a kid before summer vacation. After dedicating herself like a fanatic the past two years at The Summers Group—one of Washington D.C.'s top advertising agencies—she had finally been promoted to the position of Graphic Designer.

She was going to be introduced as such at the Monday meeting, and she had taken pains to look especially chic. Her latest fashion find, a believable knockoff of a Valentino black knit dress, looked perfect with her very smart, stiletto pumps. She had walked from the Metro with such pep, her long, dark hair had bounced around her shoulders as if she were in a shampoo commercial.

But the moment she rounded the corner to her desk, her happy buzz died. Rebecca huddled behind her own desk, next to Jensy's, and clearly struggled to keep her tears from drawing attention.

"Becks, what's happened?" She didn't even bother to sit down but dumped her purse and rested a comforting hand on Rebecca's shoulder.

Rebecca shook her head. "I don't want to talk about it. You need to focus on your big meeting. But my weekend was the worst."

"I thought you had such great plans with that Kenneth guy."

"Don't mind me, Jensy, really. You go get ready to dazzle 'em. You look great. And Kenneth was a total jerk." She pointed at her cell phone. "He just texted 'thanks but no thanks.'" She held up her hand and drew her thumb and index finger together for emphasis. "He came this close to telling me I was fat."

"He didn't! You're kidding me. What did he say?"

Jensy had worried about this. Rebecca was lovely, both inside and out. A curvy, voluptuous blonde. Maybe a tiny bit too voluptuous, but not obese. And none of that really mattered. Still, she posted about herself on dating sites and used filters and editing programs to make herself look "better." Jensy worried the alterations might cause problems if Rebecca's dates were shallow and communicating with her based solely on her looks.

"I don't want to talk about it." Rebecca sniffed. "But he insinuated I had fooled him into the date. But he fooled me, too! I mean, yes, he looked like his picture, but he came across as such a nice guy when we texted. And he was all about—" She opened her hands on either side of her figure, presenting it as evidence. "He was only interested in this. Just not so *much* of this."

Jensy sighed. "Rebecca, you're right. He's a jerk. Don't let him get to you. You're a fantastic young woman, and the right guy is out there." She drew in a deep breath. "But, I'm telling you, I think my plan is the smarter one."

"Your plan." Rebecca rolled her eyes. "I might as well enter a nunnery. Your plan is to go through life without any romance at all."

"No it isn't." Jensy chuckled and packed her purse away in her desk drawer. "But we're both so young. Twenty-eight is still really young. We should focus more on reaching our professional goals and making sure we're independent before looking for love, don't you think? It's certainly worked for me so far."

Rebecca glanced toward the conference room, and Jensy followed her gaze. People were starting to gather for the meeting.

"Well, you have a point there, I guess. You are reaching your goals here." Rebecca paused before adding, "Sister Jensy."

Jensy smacked her on the arm.

"But, really, Jen, when was the last time you even kissed a guy? High school?"

"Don't be mean, now." Jensy straightened the skirt of her dress. "Dan and I broke up after my first month here. So that was . . ."

Rebecca was shaking her head, her arms crossed. "You've been here two years, you loon. You're avoiding men, that's all. I think you're scared. I say it's better to have loved and lost than to have turned into a pruny old lady before your twenty-ninth birthday."

Jensy's boss walked past them and gave her a smile. "Ready?"

"I'll be right there!" She arched her brow and whispered to Rebecca. "I am neither pruny nor old, missy. And I'm not scared. I'm . . . focused."

"Mmm hmm. Go make a splash in there." Rebecca dabbed a tissue under her eyes. "And thanks for listening."

Jensy grabbed a notepad and pen. She winked at Rebecca as she passed her again. Rebecca looked sufficiently recovered.

"Knock 'em dead, Sistah Jensy."

Jensy was still smiling when she walked into the conference room. It had become fairly crowded, which was usually the case. She was used to attending the Monday meeting, but she had never had a place at the table before today. Her place had always been in the chairs at the periphery of the table, along with the interns and other assistant designers. As she entered the room, everything felt different. She approached the credenza at the side of the room, where hot coffee, breakfast pastries, and fresh fruit awaited her. Today she would have a place at the table. She had always shied away from balancing breakfast on her lap when she only had a chair, but she was hitting the big time now.

And she saw there were tablets and pens positioned for each person at the table. She felt a little foolish for bringing her own paper and pen. She glanced around to see if she could nonchalantly dump what she had carried in. She had been here for two years. Couldn't she have figured things out by now?

"For the love of Mike, will you relax?"

She started at the voice so close to her ear, and she turned to face one of her favorite people at the agency. She spoke under her breath.

"What are you talking about, Alfie?"

Alfie pushed his glasses up to the bridge of his nose and gave her a friendly smirk. As usual, his hair was a mess and his shirt collar was askew. "Give me that stuff, you nerd." He took her pad and pen. "And relax. You're only getting introduced. They're not going to make you tap dance on the table."

She laughed. "Just wait 'til it's your turn. You'll see."

"Not a chance." He shook his head. "You're putting too much store into the moment. Enjoy. Eat some melon. Grab a Danish. Get crumbs all over your chin."

"Oh, thanks. As if I needed something else to be self-conscious about."

"Stop. Everyone loves you. This isn't that much different from before your promotion. Just a title and a little more money. And responsibility. And deadlines."

"Will you go away?" But he had actually helped her relax. As he headed toward the chairs along the wall, Jensy's boss came up to her.

"So, I'll open the meeting and then I'll announce your promotion." He patted her on the back. "I'm so proud of how hard you've worked for this. And I'm looking forward to seeing your future work."

She smiled at him. "Thanks, Mr. Summers."

"Call me David."

"David." He had never corrected her about that before. Despite what Alfie said, this was definitely different from before her promotion.

She turned to put a little food on one of the china plates on the credenza, and David continued talking to her as he did the same.

"Also, I'll be announcing our newest member to the graphic design team."

She glanced at him. "Oh? I didn't realize anyone else had been promoted."

David shook his head. "No, this is a new hire, actually. Very impressive guy. I'll find him and introduce you."

She nodded and grabbed a napkin and fork. She carried everything over to the table and was about to sit down beside one of the well-established graphic designers when she glanced up and saw David approaching her with the new hire.

Her first thought was that he was very, very good looking. So much so that she immediately went into a full-on hot blush while standing there. Maybe Rebecca was right, and it *had* been too long.

But then recognition descended upon her. She hadn't quite set her plate on the table, and apparently she released it too soon, because it clattered loudly to the table as if she were making some kind of statement.

And she was. This wasn't a thought-out reaction. This was more an animal, gut-instinct moment.

The new hire—every blue-eyed, sandy-haired, athletically built inch of him—was none other than Phil Quinn, the one guy from high school she'd specifically prayed she'd never have to see again for as long as she lived.

CHAPTER TWO

Phil Quinn. What a nightmare. This was going to be horribly awkward, and she would have to explain to David about why she knew Phil without making it obvious she couldn't stand him. She tried to subdue the cringe brought on when David reminded Phil of her name.

"Jensy St. Martin," David said, "meet Phil Quinn. Phil's our new Graphic Designer, so you two will be working together quite a bit. Phil, Jensy has been promoted to Graphic Designer, but she's been with us for a few years now, so she can show you the ropes, as it were."

Phil put out his hand. She forced herself to look him in the eye, ready for him to say something cocky and embarrassing. But she could tell the moment she met his eye that he had absolutely no idea who she was. He gave her the friendly smile of a total stranger and warmly shook her hand.

"Looking forward to it, Jensy! And congratulations on your first day in the position as well."

She was dumbstruck. She stared at him as she tried to focus on giving him a strong handshake. But she couldn't believe he didn't remember her.

"You all right?" David chuckled at her reaction.

"Uh, yeah. Yes. Sorry. Nice to meet you, Phil. Welcome to Summers."

"Well." David checked his watch. "I'm going to get this thing started. I'll be introducing you both in a minute or two."

"Sounds great." Phil gave one quick nod to David and flashed another friendly smile at Jensy. "Mind if I take this seat?"

She looked at the chair next to hers as if it held a solution to her confusion. Phil cleared his throat.

"Yes. I mean, no. I don't mind. Feel free. Sit where you like." She suddenly felt prim and proper around him. That wasn't her usual behavior. But she couldn't seem to recover her usual behavior at the moment. She straightened up the area where she had dropped her plate.

They sat down as David started to encourage everyone else to do the same. Jensy was glad to be able to turn her back on Phil and face the head of the table.

Just before David opened the meeting, Phil leaned a little closer to her and whispered, "So are we going to keep on pretending we don't know each other?"

She jerked her head to look into his smirking face. So he *had* recognized her, and he had clearly enjoyed the fact that he threw her off her game when they met. Well, two could play that game.

"I beg your pardon?"

He chuckled. "Come on. I could tell you recognized me the second our eyes met."

Ugh. He said it as if it were a romantic moment or something.

"I did no such thing. Absolutely nothing of the sort."

He smiled at her as if she were the cutest little thing. "Nothing of the sort, huh? When did you become so Victorian?"

He was completely ruining her big day. She turned her back to him again. Phil spoke quietly. He was close enough that she felt his breath behind her ear.

"T. C. Williams High School. Your boyfriend, Mike Pierpont, and I were friends. You and I were in some class together, maybe Chemistry? I dated Emily Blanton."

She scowled at him over her shoulder. "Nice of you to remember she was your girlfriend."

"There you go." His laugh was soft behind her. "I knew you remembered. This will be fun, working together."

She turned around to look directly at him, because she wasn't sure what he meant by that. He gave her that sly, friendly smile and then looked at David, who called the meeting to order.

"First things first. Please join me in congratulating our own Jensy St. Martin as she steps up to the position of Graphic Designer here at

Summers."

Everyone in the room clapped and cheered for her. She appreciated them drawing her attention to the positive.

David continued. "I'm sure everyone here joins me in saying it couldn't have happened to a more hard-working colleague. And I want to take this opportunity to introduce the newest addition to our team, who is also joining us as a Graphic Designer, having recently relocated from Manhattan. Please welcome Phil Quinn."

Jensy got childish pleasure out of the less family-like, polite reception given Phil. Friendly smiles and nods from everyone, but he was obviously not as fully accepted as she was.

"Thanks." Phil raised a hand and nodded his head humbly. "Very happy to be here."

David grinned. "We'll see if you still feel that way after the next week or so."

Everyone chuckled, but Jensy didn't quite understand that comment. The firm had never treated her in a way that made her question whether or not she truly wanted to be here.

"What I have in mind is this," David said. "Many of you already know that we've landed a nice little contract with Chrysalis Regional Air. You're all familiar with them, right?"

A few positive murmurs waved around the table.

"I've flown them before," Phil piped in. "They fly out of Manhattan."

"Right." David pointed at Phil, and Jensy had to keep her annoyance private. David looked away from Phil to address the group again. "But they're based right here in the Washington area, flying point-to-point to some of the major and smaller airports on the east coast. And they'd like to raise their name recognition through our efforts."

David looked at Jensy, Phil, and the other Graphic Designers at the table. "So what I'd like to try over the next week is a little competition among our designers. I want each of you to come up with an idea for an ad for Chrysalis to air regionally and stream online. We'll regroup next Monday and hear each other's ideas. I'd like to hope we'll find a winner amongst the group, and then we'll talk budget. But do keep budget in mind as you create."

The rest of the meeting carried on from David's announcement, addressing matters that had far less to do with Jensy. Or Phil.

As the meeting adjourned and Jensy gathered the notes she had taken, Phil made a point of leaning forward to get her attention.

"This will be fun, don't you think?"

She frowned at him. "Sure."

He chuckled. "No, really. I was looking forward to working with you, but I think this will be a much more entertaining way to start off the job here at Summers. Healthy competition never hurt anyone. It brings out the best and the worst of a person. Helps break down barriers."

Jensy simply pursed her lips, which only seemed to fuel him on.

"And I can easily see, you've built up a few barriers since I last knew you."

She narrowed her eyes at him. "You've never known me. And I'd just as soon keep it that way." She held her notebook against her chest. "The only barrier I have up is against you. Anyway, I don't need to know more about you. I already know the worst."

He was unfazed. A twinkle glinted in his eyes, matching the humor in his smile. "Oh, I doubt that." Again, he leaned toward her, and he spoke more softly. "I'm much worse than you think I am."

She turned and started to leave, but not without glancing over her shoulder at him. She fixed the most disdainful expression she could muster. "That's not possible."

Even though she felt she had bested him or at least matched him in ill manners, he still managed to unnerve her as she walked out. His chuckle didn't sound mean or villainous. She didn't know how he did it, but he chuckled as if she had shared a wonderful joke with him. The one word that came to mind was appreciation. He sounded as if he appreciated her.

How had he managed to come off so much more maturely than she had?

In the back of her mind, she sensed that dealing with Phil Quinn was going to trouble her in ways she didn't yet understand.

CHAPTER THREE

THE FOLLOWING AFTERNOON JENSY MANAGED TO get the lunchroom to herself, since she was taking an early break.

Her friend, Alfie, passed her on his way out. "Why so early for lunch? You skipping breakfast again?"

"No, I have a few ideas for the Chrysalis ad, and once I start sketching them out, I know I'm not going to want to stop to eat."

"Well, I'm rooting for you. Let me know if you want to bounce ideas off me. I won't tell anyone I'm the creative genius behind your success, I promise."

"Thank you. I know my secret is safe with you."

She unpacked the salad and apple she brought and sat down with the novel she started before bed last night. She always felt more creative after reading fiction. But she read only the first two lines before both Valerie Leighton and Phil walked in, laughing about something together. They behaved as if they had known each other for ages, rather than a single day. Jensy quickly returned to her book.

"Oh, hey, Jensy!" Valerie was acting more girly than she usually did, which was clearly for Phil's benefit. She tilted her head just so and moved in a self-consciously provocative flow from the doorway to the coffee brewer. Jensy had to catch herself before judging Valerie too harshly. So what if she was flirting with him? What business was it of hers?

"Hey, Valerie. What's up?" She tried to avoid looking directly at Phil. But she was going to have to adjust to his being here, or this would be constantly throwing her off. "Hello, Phil."

He gave her a genuine smile. He actually looked pleased that she acknowledged him.

Valerie fixed herself a cup of coffee, talking over her shoulder to

Jensy. "You should have joined us last night after work. A group of us got together down the street at Max's Grill. You were missed." She glanced at Phil and gave him a conspiratorial smile. "Mr. Newbie here went, didn't you, Mr. Newbie?"

Phil retrieved a bottle of water from the vending machine. "I did! It was great getting to know some of the Summers people better. Valerie's right. You should have come."

Ugh. As if she needed him to invite her. It was because he was going that she didn't want to go. It had been stressful enough going through the workday with him settling in so comfortably at his desk, not all that far from hers.

"I had other plans. Couldn't break 'em."

Rebecca rushed in at that moment, flustered and talking as if she were an auctioneer. "Oh, my goodness, what a morning I've had, with walking out from my apartment to a flat tire and waiting for my insurance company to get someone out there to fix it and Mr. Farrow expecting me to have those images for him first thing and my computer locking up on me for I don't know *what* reason and now waiting for the IT guy to get up here before I lose my job—hi, Valerie. Hi, oh! Who are you? Are you the new guy?"

Phil laughed. "I am." He shook her hand. "Phil Quinn."

"Rebecca Little." She smiled—she looked suddenly girly as well—and shook his hand. She turned her back for a moment and faced Jensy. "Hi, Jensy." She widened her eyes and raised her brows in an obvious effort to express appreciation for Phil's looks before she looked at him again. "Well, welcome, Phil."

"Thanks."

Valerie said her goodbyes before sashaying out of the kitchen, and Rebecca resumed her slap-dash soliloquy. "So, Jen, it's so good I didn't come to your place last night to watch *Roman Holiday*. I mean, I love it and all, but my gosh, can you imagine if I had gotten that flat tire driving home from your place last night? What a pain!"

Jensy couldn't speak. She was too busy trying comfortably to avoid looking at Phil. Once again. She was reviewing the excuse she gave for not joining the group last night. And now he knew her "other plans" involved watching a simple movie at home. Alone. She felt like an eighty-year-old woman. She even knew eighty-year-old women who would have gone to Max's with the gang rather than staying home alone with a DVD.

"Anyway." Rebecca spoke into the silence. "I've got to get back to my desk." She put a lunchbox in the refrigerator and smoothed her skirt before she turned around. "Hopefully the IT guy has unlocked me by now. Later, Jen. Nice meeting you, Phil!"

"Yes, good meeting you too." His smile was all charm. To his credit he kept it plastered on after Rebecca left. He opened his water bottle and took a long drink before looking at Jensy.

She wanted to kick herself for just staring at him like she did. She quickly looked down at her novel, but she spoke to him. "Making quite a splash with the female employees, I see."

"Some of them, at least."

She looked up to find him smiling at her. She let her eyes roll a little before she looked back down at her book. She had read the same three words about five times now, and she probably couldn't recite them to anyone if she tried. She heard him walk toward the door.

"I'm only being friendly, Jen. You might try it."

One, she was irked that he used the shortened, more familiar version of her name. Two, just . . . ugh! She frowned at him.

"I am absolutely friendly. But I'm not so indiscriminate that I'm friendly to people who take advantage of nice people."

His calm in the face of her attacks was enough to make her spit. He was nearly out the door but he took the time to speak as if he were her therapist or something.

"Including all of your co-workers last night? They seemed nice enough. But you chose a fantasy story on a plastic disk over interaction with actual people. Maybe you're trying a little too hard to avoid emotional involvement."

She gasped audibly and was about to respond, but he was already too far gone.

Jensy realized she was gripping her novel, her palms sweating, as if she were on the Titanic clutching a floatation device. Ridiculous to be this tense. She had to collect herself. She took several deep breaths and waited for her heartbeat to slow.

While she stabbed at her salad and devoured her apple, she managed to think about what had just happened. This workplace conflict was only two days old, and she was letting it completely alter her experience here at Summers. Childish. The tension couldn't go on, and it was feeding off of her own attitude. So that was what she needed to change.

A few more calming breaths. Okay, so Phil had been a jerk in high school, but he had never actually done anything to *her*. And she was acting almost afraid he might hurt her emotionally. Really, who knew where his "victim" was now and what she was doing? For all Jensy knew, she—what was her name again? Emily. For all Jensy knew, Emily had totally forgotten about Phil and was living a happy life with a loving husband. Maybe kids. If that were the case, she was probably happier than Jensy was.

She caught herself there. Talk about a fantasy story. Jensy didn't want to concoct a happily ever after to covet. She was on track to do very well here at Summers, and she would think about love later. It clearly wasn't in God's plan for her right now, so she would carry on professionally and do the best she could with the blessings she was experiencing today.

And she would disregard Phil as someone from the past. The next time he rubbed her the wrong way, she would silently utter a little prayer. Maybe she'd even pray for *him*.

Or not.

CHAPTER FOUR

JENSY WAS EARLY TO WORK THE following Monday, because she wanted to be as fresh and prepared as possible for the weekly meeting. She was giving a final once-over to her digital storyboards when Rebecca arrived at her desk.

"Well, look at you, all eager beaver with your presentation." Rebecca shot a supportive smile her way as she stored her purse in her desk drawer. "I know you're going to win this competition, Jen. You're so creative."

"We'll see. I appreciate the vote of confidence." Jensy actually felt both calm and at peace with whatever the outcome would be. If her idea didn't fly this time, maybe the next effort would. She had done her best, and that was all she could do. "You seem upbeat. Good weekend?"

Rebecca gave her a secretive smile. "Maybe. I went to one of those meet-ups Saturday night. Met a guy who's a little different from what I usually like."

"How so?"

"Oh, I don't know." She shrugged. "Not necessarily the professional type. Maybe a little more artsy. A bit of a nonconformist."

"Hmm. What does he do?"

"Well, that's the thing. I'm not absolutely sure. He says he's between projects but he creates content for . . . like, websites. And video games. Stuff like that. At least he *mentioned* video games, so I think he was talking about creating them, not just playing them."

Jensy let her new mantra run through her mind. *I will not judge, I will not judge.* "Well, it will be interesting to hear what you learn about him."

"Yep. Seeing him tonight, so I'll let you know."

They both turned their heads at the sound farther down the hall. Phil had arrived at his desk and appeared to be reviewing his storyboards on his laptop, as Jensy had done.

Rebecca spoke to Jensy as if she were telling a secret. "He's such a cutie. And I hear he's single. Valerie's campaigning big-time for the position of Girlfriend Number One. But personally I think the two of you would make a terrific—"

Jensy's hand went up immediately. "Uh, no. Don't say it. Not the two of us. Not now. Not ever. Believe me."

Rebecca plopped into her chair. "I don't get it. What's with you? The guy's only been here a week, and already you've written him off? I know you're all wrapped up in being a professional and all, but who says you can't have both—a professional life and a *life* life? Especially if it's a co-worker. You could kill two birds with one relationship."

"I just know, okay? Not him."

"Wow, you don't know anything about him. Aren't you the tiniest bit curious?"

"Oh, I know, Rebecca. I know about him."

Rebecca went silent for a moment, and Jensy could practically see the gears grinding. Finally Rebecca's eyes brightened, and she spoke even more quietly. She leaned in toward Jensy.

"Oh my gosh, you dated him already?"

"No!" Jensy shook her head. She had managed to keep her mouth shut for an entire week. But she didn't like the direction Rebecca's imagination was headed. "Look, we both went to the same high school. I knew him then."

"Oooooh. Okay. And you dated him then?"

Jensy shook her head. "Never dated him." She glanced at her watch and then back into Rebecca's expectant expression. "All right, please don't share this with anyone else, okay? Promise?"

Rebecca held up the Boy Scout salute. "On my honor."

"So during my senior year, I dated a guy named Michael. A really good guy. He happened to be friends with our own Mr. Quinn, there."

They both gave Phil a quick glance. He was oblivious to them and walked toward the kitchen.

"And Phil had been dating a girl named . . . Emily. Yeah, Emily. I never knew her really well, but she seemed sweet. She was part of the drama club clique, so we didn't seem to end up in the same classes or places, you know?"

"Right."

"So near the end of the school year, suddenly Michael makes a point of telling me to steer clear of both of them—Phil and Emily, because that was a really messed up situation."

"Messed up?"

"I mean, it was high school drama, so I guess I shouldn't still put too much store in it, but it goes to a person's character."

"What does?" Rebecca glanced over her shoulder towards Phil's desk, which was still unoccupied.

"Michael told me Phil was a real run-around and had broken Emily's heart. She thought they were going to get engaged and the whole marriage thing, but then she found out Phil had been cheating on her all along. And he dumped her. I mean, it obviously wouldn't have lasted anyway, since he was unfaithful, but *he* was the one who dumped *her*. After what he did to her. Insult to injury."

Rebecca's curled lip rivaled Elvis Presley's. "Ew. What a cad. And what a waste of so much . . . pretty."

"Yeah," Jensy nodded. "She was pretty *and* sweet."

"No, I meant him!" She hooked her thumb toward Phil's desk.

Jensy rolled her eyes. "You're ridiculous."

"Ladies." Phil breezed past them, startling them both.

Jensy barely grunted a response.

Rebecca gave a girly wave and smile to him. "Hi, Phil!"

Phil was soon out of earshot as he headed toward the meeting room.

"Really, Becks?" Jensy shook her head. "Hi, Phil? Did you hear a word I said?"

"I'm sorry." Rebecca cringed and lifted her shoulders. "He caught me off guard. It's a habit around cute guys. Anyway, we all work here. I can't exactly throw my coffee in his face."

Jensy sighed. "You're right. I have to reign in my feelings and act more professionally." She gathered up her laptop and notes. "Say a prayer for me, will you? I think I'm going to need it."

DAVID SUMMERS CALLED THE meeting to order shortly after Jensy seated herself at the table.

"All right, everyone, I want you all to give your first impressions of each of our graphic designers' presentations for the Chrysalis account. First impressions are what viewers will have, so that's what we're considering today. The client will be here this afternoon, and I plan to present the idea or ideas I consider best. Jensy, you're up."

So sudden! She didn't have a chance to fret and sweat, so she supposed this was a blessing, going first. Still, her heart felt as if it were pounding visibly against her chest. She had the forethought to think a quick prayer as she carried her laptop to the front of the room and set it up to project her storyboards on the flat screen.

"Okay, so what I was thinking—"

"Nope," David barked. "Our commercial won't have any preamble before it airs. Show us what the viewer will see and tell us what the viewer will hear. Nothing more."

Cold water in the face. All right. All right. She could do this. She spoke as if she were a narrator while she drew everyone's attention to the first board.

"How do you envision flying?" Her first few boards showed people with stressed expressions, running to flights, standing in line, going through security checkpoints.

"Chrysalis is about change." Her next board showed a butterfly emerging from its chrysalis form. "Flying doesn't have to be stressful--" Her next board showed the butterfly flying through the airport. It was followed by a board with the butterfly fluttering at the gate, where a friendly flight attendant efficiently welcomed passengers. "—if your airline really cares about you, the passenger."

The next boards showed the butterfly flying through the airplane, making people smile and sigh with relaxation. Her narration promised efficiency that would keep the flight worry free. The final board showed a happy little girl in her seat, a butterfly landing on her outstretched palm.

"Let us change the way you think about flying. Chrysalis." Her last board showed the airline's logo, a simple line drawing depicting a butterfly as it leaves its cocoon behind.

The meeting attendees applauded Jensy's presentation. Now that it was over, she felt relief. She could relax and enjoy everyone else's ideas.

Three more people made their presentations after Jensy. She tried to judge fairly, and one of the ideas impressed her with its unorthodox simplicity, but when she allowed herself a quick glance at David, she didn't see much of a spark of interest on his face. Of course, she hadn't seen his face during her own presentation. Maybe he kept his expression stony on purpose, to avoid influencing the reactions of others.

When Phil's turn came up, she struggled to give him a fair audience. She had to admit, though, that she actually did like what he suggested. His idea was quite different from hers, very modern and focusing most acutely on the speed and efficiency of the airline. He proposed a purely computer graphic design, without any people at all. Sharp lines, intense color, the suggestion of quick flights, and a dependence on energetic music, from what Phil said. The effect was visually striking but somewhat devoid of an intimate touch.

Still, she had to applaud his unique approach.

"Feedback?" David stood at the front of the room. He hadn't asked for feedback between any of the other presentations, so Jensy assumed he was looking for first impressions on all of the proposals, as he had originally stated.

"I liked Jensy's a lot," Alfie said. "It was warm, but it also promised efficiency."

"It was a little frou-frou," quipped someone else. "Are they going to provide a happy little butterfly for *every* passenger?"

Jensy couldn't keep her face from flushing, especially when she heard a couple quiet snickers in response.

"Well, I really liked the idea."

It was Phil.

"I'm not frou-frou." He glanced around the room. "At least I don't *think* I am."

A couple women in the room responded with a laugh or almost guttural assurance that he most certainly was not frou-frou.

He continued. "But envisioning what Jensy described made me feel very relaxed about trusting the airline. I think that's a pretty good thing to feel these days when one gets on a flight."

Jensy had to make a deliberate effort to keep her jaw from dropping open. When he turned and looked at her, she couldn't help but look away. She spoke, but not directly at him.

"Thank you."

Comments continued for a short time longer. Jensy felt she owed it to Phil to make a positive comment about his presentation, especially because she liked it. But she overthought it and lost the chance. She wasn't sure what kept her silent—whether it was a grasp on the past that she couldn't release or the fear that her comments would simply sound like a payback for his compliment. She should have just opened her mouth and spoken, as she normally would have.

"All right," David said. "I'll report to you all in a couple of hours. I want to talk with the other departments about your ideas and their likely budgets. Once I have the client's feedback, we'll know where we go from here. Dismissed."

Everyone stood and departed the room quickly, all talking at once. Even though she and Alfie walked out together, Jensy was aware of where Phil was as they departed. But she acted as if she were oblivious to him. She had to shake her head at her own self-absorption as she headed to her desk. When she was able to sneak a look at him, he was flanked by two of the women from the meeting who were clearly charmed by either his presentation or his mere existence.

The last thing Phil Quinn needed from her was encouragement. Or anything else, for that matter.

CHAPTER FIVE

Later that afternoon Jensy sat next to Phil in David Summers' spacious office. His assistant had summoned both of them without explanation.

David hadn't yet returned from walking Teodore Ruis, the Chrysalis CEO, to the elevators. Mr. Ruis had a small entourage with him, and Jensy had heard them all talking simultaneously as they left, but she had no idea how well they received any of the team's presentations.

"So I guess they liked ours the most, don't you think?" Phil relaxed in his chair.

Jensy shrugged. "I can't imagine any other reason we'd be the only ones called in."

Phil tilted his head and raised an eyebrow at her. "Unfortunately for you, I understand David decides these close calls with a good old fashioned cage fight." He flexed his bicep and ran his hand over it. "And I've been practicing."

She barely rolled her eyes at him, even though she did find his ludicrous comment amusing. "That *would* be unfortunate. *I* can only hope he puts more store in brains than in brawn."

Phil's laugh was genuine and very disarming. She looked away and out the door, wishing David would hurry up and interrupt their little bout of verbal sparring. It felt too close to flirting for her taste, and she was afraid she might get desperate and bring up his checkered past to shut him up.

As if in answer to prayer, David walked briskly into his office. "Right!" He sat at his desk and did a two-handed point at them. "You two. You're the ones. I'll announce it to the rest of the team before everyone heads out for the night, but I wanted to congratulate you two personally first."

"We two?" Jensy glanced at Phil and then back at David. "You mean they want two commercials from The Summers Group?"

David shook his head. "No, just the one. But they liked the whimsy of yours, and they liked the impact of Phil's." He smiled at Phil, who returned the gesture but appeared as confused as Jensy.

"So . . . what are we—?"

"Combine them. Give me something by tomorrow afternoon that incorporates the warm fuzzy with the energy." He stood abruptly, which prompted both Jensy and Phil to stand as well, clearly dismissed. "I know you can do it. Work together and give me something excellent tomorrow afternoon, say, three o'clock." He called out the door. "Monica, I'm here tomorrow at three, right?"

Monica scooted her chair to his doorway. "Yep. You're here until four."

"Right! Dismissed!"

And he strolled out of his office ahead of them.

Jensy turned to Phil and saw him waiting for her. She sighed, not sure what to say.

"Hmm," he said. "Well, I hope you didn't have big plans for this evening."

"This evening?"

"Yeah." He drew his hand down the light stubble on his jawline. "If he wants our finished presentation by three tomorrow—"

"Oh." She nodded. "We'd better get it together tonight."

He walked ahead of her out of David's office, stopping at Monica's desk. "Say, Monica, Jensy and I need to work together on this presentation for David. Is there somewhere available where we can spread out? Maybe a small conference room?"

She gave him a warm smile which she then turned on Jensy. "He's leaving for the day in about half an hour. You can use his little war room back there if you promise to tidy up after yourselves. Good sized table in there. Quiet."

Phil's eyes sparkled at her. "You're the best!"

"Yes. Yes, I am." She chuckled. "Hey, congratulations, you two. Knock 'em dead. I'll call you both when David leaves."

THEY WORKED WELL INTO the evening. They stopped for a brief time when carryout arrived from Hunan Delight, but other than that, they bounced ideas off one another as they sought the blend the client requested.

Despite her discomfort with Phil, Jensy had to admit he was accommodating and open to her ideas. Their presentations differed substantially, but they were able to find the strengths the client liked in each and envision how the two approaches could work together.

"So what do you think?" Phil, standing, leaned forward and showed her a storyboard on his laptop. "We take the butterfly at this point and make it kind of streamline into the speedier, hard-edged graphic. Like that."

Jensy smiled. "Yeah. I like it. I think that's exactly what they meant by combining the two. And that could morph into their logo really smoothly."

"It could!" Phil nodded and looked at her, pleased with their apparent success.

It was the first time they had shared genuine pleasure with each other, and Jensy suddenly felt exposed in a way she both enjoyed and hated. She didn't want to like Phil. But she saw beyond his charm and into his own vulnerable desire for approval and camaraderie.

A knock at the office door made them both jump. Valerie, the woman vying for a spot on Phil's dance card, stood there, dressed in a black leather dress, every bit of her groomed as if she were camera ready.

Jensy caught herself as she tucked her hair behind her ear and inwardly cringed at how disheveled she must look after such a long workday.

"Well, hey, you!" Valerie looked at Phil directly, and then glanced at Jensy and gave her a friendly grin. "Hi, Jensy."

"Hi, Valerie."

"You're here late," Phil said, his smile as attractive as always.

"Ditto!" Valerie stepped in and looked at their laptops. "Good for you two, working so hard." She winked at Phil. "Had I known how late a workday you had in store, I wouldn't have kept you out so late last night."

Jensy didn't mean to stand up as abruptly as she did. "'scuse me a minute. I need to make a little trip to the ladies' room."

She grabbed her purse and left the room. Why she felt ruffled, she didn't know. So they were dating. Who cared? She wasn't surprised, and she certainly wasn't interested in Phil. Still, she felt a bit like a third wheel in there, and she hoped Valerie would leave by the time she returned to David's "little war room."

And that was the case. Fortunately, Phil had dispatched his groupie quickly. He acted as if they hadn't been interrupted.

"So, what do you think? Do you want me to handle the graphics here, on these last few boards?"

Despite her attempt at nonchalance, Jensy heard an edge to her voice. "No, I think we should get it done together. Unless you're in a hurry to leave, of course. In that case, I can finish up."

He straightened up and studied her. "No, we can work on them together. You okay?"

"I'm great." She sniffed. "Okay, so let's get these hammered out. I want to get out of here."

He paused, still looking at her as if he could force her to divulge her every thought if he waited long enough. She acted as if she didn't notice.

"Do you have plans tonight? A boyfriend?"

She looked at him and couldn't stand that she probably had a snooty look on her face—one she didn't seem able to shake off. "Not that it's any of your business, but no. I think we've spent far more time in each other's company than either of us needs."

He chuckled. "You're not very fond of me, are you?"

She struggled to give him as casual a smile as possible. "I don't really have an opinion of you, Phil. Good or bad."

"Oh, I doubt that."

She looked at the storyboards and spoke to the laptop, rather than to him. "Let's get these done, okay?"

"Sure. I'm wondering, though."

And that was all he said. Ugh, he was infuriating.

"What? What are you wondering?"

He shrugged. "I'm not sure what happened in our past that you think was a slight against you."

"Huh." She shut her eyes briefly before answering. "Your behavior of the past had nothing to do with me."

"Ah!" He looked as if he had a new burst of energy. "So it *was* something from the past that you're still judging me about today."

"Maybe you're just feeling guilty, Phil. I'm not judging you."

He nodded and looked at her as if he knew something she didn't. "Good. I'm glad to hear that." He folded his arms across his chest and leaned against the table. He stood far too close to where she sat for her comfort. "So, why did you and Michael break up?"

The question was so out of left field, she felt as if she had fallen out of her chair.

"What? Michael?"

"Yeah. Obviously you two broke up or you'd be together today. So what happened? Does it bother you to tell me?"

Now she crossed her arms over *her* chest. "No, it doesn't bother me. But, again, it's not really your business."

He said nothing, but his smirk made her blood boil.

"We grew apart, that's all, if you really need to know. We were going off to separate colleges, and it made sense to start fresh."

"Ah. You grew apart."

Ugh, his superciliousness made her glad she didn't have something worth throwing in her hand. A mean-spirited thought erupted in her mind and flew right out of her mouth.

"And how about you and Emily? What broke *you* up, if you don't mind my asking?"

She actually got no pleasure in watching his expression fall. She wasn't good at this spiteful bantering.

He nodded. "Oh. Yeah, Emily. That was unfortunate." He collected himself and gave Jensy another of his smiles, but this one was less genuine. "Like you two, I guess. We grew apart. There's always a lot of that when high school sweethearts move on to college life."

Jensy didn't know what to make of the expression in his eyes. If she didn't know him better, she'd think he was sad. But she was certain it was guilt. She wanted to give him credit for feeling guilt over what he had done to Emily. Maybe then she could give him credit for becoming a better person now.

"Say," he said, closing his laptop. "Really. Let me finish off these two storyboards tonight and early tomorrow. I promise I'll have something you and I can polish well in advance of David's three o'clock deadline. Sound good?"

She was out of energy. Sparring with him, along with trying to pour creativity out of one's brain, could be very draining.

"Okay." She grabbed her purse and laptop. She didn't want to ride the elevator down with him. "Thanks. But call me if you need to." She pulled one of her cards out of her purse and handed it to him.

He was fully back in charm mode. He looked at the card and gave her a rakish smile. "I'll try to refrain from harassing you until tomorrow."

She shook her head at him and walked out.

"Don't you want me to walk you to your car?" He quickly grabbed his security access card.

"No need. The security guard will do that. See you tomorrow."

As she rode the elevator down to her car, she tried to figure out exactly what emotions she was feeling. They weren't good. Was she feeling jealousy over the Valerie interruption? Disdain over the Emily history? Or her own brand of guilt for being a cold, stuck-up snob when he made the effort—however calculated—at being friendly with her? Maybe it wasn't any of those things. But she wasn't terribly fond of herself at the moment. She was going to have to spend a bit of time in prayer tonight. She needed clarity about how she could better represent a considerate but savvy woman toward Phil. And Valerie. And anyone else at Summers who might be looking to her for an example of what Christian kindness looks like.

CHAPTER SIX

THE FOLLOWING WEEKEND JENSY ARRIVED AT her parents' home in Alexandria just as her younger brother, CJ, and his wife, Donita, pulled up.

"Perfect timing!" Donita waddled toward Jensy with a good-natured smile on her face. She seemed to have been pregnant forever.

The two women hugged each other as best they could, considering Donita's girth and the casserole dish Jensy carried.

CJ approached them and gave Jensy a hug. He took the casserole from her and glanced down at the foil cover. "Are these your world-famous scalloped potatoes?"

"'Fraid not." Jensy sighed. "It's been a busy week at work, so I cheated. That's a broccoli-cheese thingy from the deli counter at the grocery store. Maybe next time."

"Sounds good to me," Donita said. "Of course, these days most food sounds good to me." She cocked her head toward the other dish CJ carried. "That apple pie had nothing to do with either CJ's or my efforts, either, so no judging here."

Jensy's mother was in the middle of a full-on laugh when the three "kids" walked into the house. She hugged them all. "Your father. I'm telling you. Men and women absolutely do not think the same." She pointed at the dining room table. "Does anything need reheating? Or do you just want to put everything out? We're starving."

Jensy gave her dad a quick kiss on the cheek. "Hi, Dad. Yeah, Mom, I need to reheat this a little."

Once they all gathered at the table, there were several conversations going on at once, which was always their style. But at one point, as Jensy told her mother and Donita about the competition she and Phil were working on together at Summers, she stopped herself to interrupt the discussion CJ and her father were having.

"Hey CJ, did you ever know Phil Quinn when we were in high school?"

CJ frowned as he thought. "Phil Quinn. Doesn't ring a bell. But I'm like you—I'm pretty bad about staying in touch with high school people. My class?"

"Mine." She looked at her mother again and continued.

But CJ had been hooked. "Wait," he said. "So who's Phil Quinn?"

Jensy shook her head. "He's working at Summers with me now."

"They're competing against each other," Donita told CJ.

"Well, we were. But we kind of co-won, so—"

Her father interrupted. "Co-won what? That's great, honey. What was the competition?"

Now she had the entire floor. "Chrysalis Airlines, this small regional company, wanted a new ad. Phil and I and the other graphic designers competed for the job, and the customer liked both Phil's and my designs, but wanted us to combine them. We've been submitting ideas to David Summers all week, tweaking it and stuff."

CJ squinted and put his finger up as if he were testing for wind. "I had a Samantha Quinn in my class. I think that was his little sister, right?"

Jensy shrugged. "I don't know. Maybe."

"Yeah." CJ nodded, as if memory flooded into his brain with each nod. "That's right, Samantha. Nice girl. But something . . . something bad. I remember . . ." He shook his head. "I don't know. I feel like there was something not so good there."

"I'm not surprised." Jensy helped herself to more of the roast beef her mother had made. "Phil wasn't the most noble guy in the world, from what Michael told me. Maybe his sister had issues too."

Her mother smiled. "Michael. Have you ever heard from him since high school?"

"Nope." Jensy took a small bite. "I'm sure he's done well. But once we split up, we never talked again."

"Oh!" Her mother jumped up from the table. "That reminds me, speaking of the past. You have mail from the high school."

"From Williams?" Why in the world would her high school send mail to her this long after graduation?

Her mother dashed into and out of the kitchen, an envelope in hand. She looked at it before handing it to Jensy. "Alumni Committee, T. C. Williams High School."

"Wow." CJ smiled as he rubbed his wife's back. "That sounds like a reunion invitation. Has it been ten years for you already?"

Their father reached for the broccoli casserole. "That's about right. You're turning twenty-eight in a couple of months, aren't you, sweetie?"

"Ugh. Don't remind me. I already feel so old and short on prospects."

"Prospects?" Donita looked at her, eyes wide. "*You're* short on prospects? Romantic, you mean? Seems like you've turned away someone new every time I've talked with you."

"That's not true." Jensy was shocked by the impression she had given Donita. "I just haven't come across anyone I've wanted a second date with, that's all. If there's no spark, there's no spark. I don't see the point in dragging it out."

"God will bring the right person along," her mother said. "But maybe the right person won't ignite a spark right off the bat. Your father and I were friends—and *only* friends—for quite awhile before we started dating."

Her dad winked at her. "But I felt that spark right away, sweetie. So I understand what you mean."

Her mother harrumphed and put her hand on her hip, even as she sat at the table. She couldn't suppress her smile. "Don't talk her out of every man who comes her way, Ted. It's not like that for every couple."

Jensy opened the mail. "Yeah. It's about my ten-year reunion." All of this talk about spark and prospects bothered her on the heels of discussing high school and reuniting and Phil. It was one thing to work with him at Summers. It seemed far more personal to consider that they both would likely be at that reunion. And so might Emily, Phil's discarded girlfriend. And so might Michael, which did rather cheer her up, although she figured he was probably married by now. Lots of her old classmates would be married by now. And she was so obviously *not.*

She should be more mature and self-confident. She shouldn't care about such things, but she found she did. It was one of her more annoying failings—worrying too much about how others viewed her, even people she hadn't seen in ten years.

"You all right, honey?"

She looked up at her mother and then saw they were all looking at her.

"Oh, sure. Fine." She shrugged, feigning indifference. "It's weird to remember all that stuff from back then. It feels like it was so long ago."

"But it seems like yesterday, too, right?" CJ looked at her, resting his chin in his hand. "It does to me, anyway. I can't believe that by the time Donita and I go to my reunion, we'll have a two-year-old daughter. At least. But I know my reunion is going to come quickly too."

"Yeah. That's the way it feels." Jensy nodded at him. "I feel like I've gone on with my life and become an adult, and all that. But just reading this invitation brings back so many memories. I feel like a teenager again, kind of."

"High school is funny that way." Her mother stood and reached for Jensy's empty plate. "You're going to go, aren't you?"

"I'll clear, Mom. You relax." Jensy pushed away from the table and gathered several dishes. "Yeah, as long as I don't have to work that night, I'll go. There are a lot of people I want to touch base with."

She hoped reuniting with former classmates would incite more pleasant feelings than had running into Phil when he joined Summers. She still got a vaguely sick feeling in her stomach when she thought about his being the same person who had shown such loser character traits ten years ago. And she felt worse still when she teetered between liking him and loathing him. The indecision made her feel like a foolish young girl. But she simply wasn't confident about her discernment in either direction.

CHAPTER SEVEN

Jensy and Alfie walked into the office kitchen for coffee the next morning. Their friend Rebecca was deep into an animated discussion with Valerie, the office vamp with eyes for Phil.

"Hey, guys," Jensy said. "You have a good weekend?"

Both women chuckled. Rebecca moved away from the coffee brewer and handed Jensy and Alfie Styrofoam cups. "Maybe not. I went out again with Kenneth, that video game guy I met at the meet-up last week."

"And?" Jensy chose a dark roast coffee pod and started the machine. "Me first, Alfie." She said. "I need the caffeine more than you do."

"Agreed." He pushed his glasses up on the bridge of his nose. "I slept the sleep of the innocents last night."

He actually looked as if he had slept in his clothes. Jensy loved him dearly, but she didn't know why he couldn't manage to get to work in a less disheveled state once in awhile. Always clean, but a wrinkled, ruffled mess. He looked at Rebecca. "Sorry, Becks. The video game guy? Report, please."

Rebecca and Valerie gave each other wry smiles. Valerie said, "Now she's thinking maybe he's being secretive with her about himself because he's not exactly what he pretends to be."

"Single, you mean?" Jensy asked. "You think he's married? Or already involved with someone?"

Rebecca sighed. "You might say that. Not married—no way. But I think maybe he's living in his mom's basement. I'm not sure he's actually even employed. And he's worn the exact same shirt all three times I've seen him, at the meet-up and on our two dates."

Jensy grimaced. "Well, maybe he doesn't have much money. Or a sense of variety in his clothing choices."

Rebecca shook her head. "But there was this, this stain—no, not a stain. A blob. A tomatoey blob on his sleeve at the first meet-up. I assumed it was from whatever he had for dinner right beforehand. But that same blob was there Monday night, and then Friday night, too. I mean, I'm not sure he's even washing *himself*, let alone his clothing."

"Wow." Jensy added cream to her coffee and gave it a sip. "You think he's homeless?"

Alfie laughed. "Well, that's a bit of a stretch. Even I can be a little crumpled sometimes, but I'm completely solvent and have a perfectly nice apartment and job. And a girlfriend, for that matter."

All three women looked at him for a moment and then moved on as if he hadn't said a word.

Valerie cocked her thumb at Rebecca. "She says he has a cell phone, which would be weird for a homeless guy, don't you think? And his mom has called him a couple of times when Rebecca has been with him. It sounds like he's a guy who'll always be a big kid."

"Don't you ladies realize we're always big kids?" Alfie walked to the door, coffee in hand. "Gotta go. But, Becks, if your big kid can't pay his way or do his laundry or be honest with you, he's worse than a big kid. You're too good for him by half." He left them with a wave.

"Each time." Again, Rebecca sighed. "Each time I went out with this guy, he wore that same dirty shirt and had these angry little phone arguments with his mother. I don't seem to be able to pin him down about his circumstances, either. He just says he doesn't want to talk about it—it 'bums him out.'"

Jensy laughed softly. "This guy must be gorgeous. *Way* too many red flags for me. The secretive thing would be enough to turn me off. Life is too short to mess with that."

Valerie pointed at her. "You are *so* right. Men! I don't think I'm going to keep trying with—" she looked at the door to the kitchen and lowered her voice. "—With Phil. He's playing so hard to get. I don't need that." Valerie grabbed her coffee cup and turned away. "But I *do* need to get back to work. Later, girls."

Once Rebecca and Jensy returned to their desks, Rebecca spoke again, quietly. "I don't think Phil is playing hard to get with Valerie. I think he doesn't want to *get* got by her."

Jensy laughed. "Okay."

"No, really. I think this is all her, not him at all."

"He went out with her, Rebecca. There was *some* of him in it."

"No, there was *not*." She turned her chair to face Jensy and scooted closer. "Valerie told me the only reason she had dinner with him last week is because she walked in on him in the restaurant before he had ordered, and she kind of muscled in on him."

"Huh. That's quite a coincidence, their both being in the same restaurant at the same time. You sure he wasn't just trying to be discreet?"

Rebecca quietly snorted. "Yeah. A coincidence. That's what all the stalkers say."

Jensy's brows lifted. "Are you saying she followed him?"

"I'm not saying that. Valerie came right out and said it. She said it was the only way she seemed to be able to get his attention."

Jensy remembered the tight black leather dress and realized getting Phil's attention had been quite a project for Valerie. Still, he hadn't looked uncomfortable with her efforts. She realized Rebecca was still talking, still supplying her with details.

"She said he was polite and even entertaining, and he paid for her dinner and gave her a ride home, but then nothing. Not a goodbye kiss at the door, not even a handshake. Only a charming smile. And no calls afterward."

Jensy opened her laptop and brought up the Chrysalis project.

"Well, it's none of my business. This is all too gossipy, and I need to fine tune the stuff . . . um, the stuff Phil and I have been working on."

"Mmm-hmm."

Jensy took her time looking back at Rebecca, who was smiling conspiratorially.

"What?"

"Come on, Jensy. You can't tell me you don't think he's just the slightest bit dreamy."

If Jensy was honest with herself, she had to admit she found Phil's handling of Valerie's stalking to be classy and yes, slightly dreamy in its kindness and sense of responsibility.

"Whether he's dreamy or not doesn't matter, Becks. He and I need to focus on getting a professional product together for David to show Chrysalis."

"And after that?"

Jensy chuckled. "What do you mean, after that?"

"There's no rule here about not dating co-workers. I think when you finish Chrysalis, you should go for it." She gave her fist a little shake to emphasis her argument. "It's kind of mysterious, the fact that he isn't involved with anyone."

"Why is that mysterious? *I'm* not involved with anyone."

Rebecca gave her a soft shove on the arm. "Oh, go on. You? You're the queen of uninvolvement. Of course you're not involved. You work hard at that. But you're not normal."

"Well. Thank you very much."

Rebecca laughed, which made Jensy laugh.

"Now leave me alone and let me get back to what's important before I lose my job. I don't want to have to move in with my parents and walk around with tomato sauce on my clothes. And date weirdos from meet-ups."

She got another shove for that one.

But when Phil walked past the two of them moments later, deep in conversation with a male co-worker, Jensy was glad Rebecca wasn't facing him. She didn't want any more baiting about the "mystery" that was Phil. Was he single because he was a player, as he had been in high school? Or was there more there than met the eye? She tried to shake off her curiosity and do what she said she wanted to do—get back to what was important. Thanks to Rebecca's nonsense, she was starting to question what, exactly, that was.

CHAPTER EIGHT

PHIL SIGHED DEEPLY AND SCRATCHED THE crown of his head. "Well, David Summers is no pushover, that's for sure. I thought we'd be farther along with this project by now."

He and Jensy walked side-by-side across Farragut Park, several blocks from the Summers offices. They had worked steadily all day and had hit a creative wall. Phil had rubbed his bleary eyes and suggested they get some fresh air and take a walk. "It might clear our minds."

Now they stopped at a food truck for ice cream. The early evening air was clear, and Jensy relaxed when the soft breeze passed over her.

"I think David's reflecting the client," she said. She took the fudgesicle Phil handed to her. "Thanks. Chrysalis has had that same tired campaign going for so long, I think they really want this new branding to be extra different and extra special."

"It's hard to see how else we can blend our two styles." He led her to a bench in front of them and pulled his laptop from its case. "I mean, look at this."

She sat next to him and watched as he moved from one storyboard to the next on his laptop.

"I think it looks great," he said. "What do you think?"

"Hmm." She reached over and flipped back to the beginning of the ad. "How about, instead of this abrupt cut here, when we go from the stressed out people to the smiley, happy Chrysalis environment? How about we have the two scenes kind of blend there, and have the Chrysalis logo on the wall sharpen into focus behind the people as that blend happens. Kind of fade from stressed to happy as the logo sharpens. A smoother transaction, instead of an abrupt cut."

Phil bit into his ice cream as he studied the screen. He nodded. "Mmm hmm, that works." And then, as if a light had been turned on, he sat up straight and raised his eyebrows. "How about the stressed-out part in black and white, and we fade the color in as the logo gains focus and the people become pleased?"

"Oh, I like that." Jensy smiled. "And we could fade in with soft colors, and then as we get to your more streamlined effect with the butterfly, the colors could intensify. Adds punch to the end and to the logo, don't you think?"

"I *do* think!" Phil grinned. "And that was one of the things David wanted, increased intensity in the logo." He turned his smile on Jensy. "We're geniuses!"

She couldn't help but laugh. She had to admit, he was easy to work with.

He frowned and glanced at her blouse. "Um, you have . . ." He pointed at her chest.

She glanced down and saw she had dripped fudgesicle down the front of her blouse. When she looked up, he already had a napkin raised toward her. She thought he was going to wipe up the ice cream himself, so she grabbed the napkin from him.

He huffed. "I wasn't going to, you know —"

"Right. Never mind. Of course you weren't. I'm being ridiculous." But she wasn't exactly sure she had misread him. He was, after all, a former cad, if not a current one. Then she saw embarrassment in his expression and knew she was being unfair. "We should probably return to the office."

He nodded and gave her a polite smile.

They walked a short distance in silence until she couldn't let it go.

"I'm sorry, Phil. I really *was* being ridiculous."

His smile relaxed into something more genuine. "No problem. Let's just get back and finish this up for the night."

After another hour's work at the office, they checked the full effect. When they came to the end, Phil simply turned to her and put up his hand for a high five. Jensy complied.

"Okay, Jensy, if David doesn't like this one, he's going to have to be more specific. Because this is awesome."

She lowered her head and massaged her neck with both hands. The relief she felt brought about a wash of good will toward Phil.

"Agreed." She relaxed into her chair. "I might actually be able to visit my family this weekend. Oh, hey, I think my brother and your sister were in the same class at Williams together. Umm, Samantha? Is that your sister?"

A brief cloud passed over Phil's expression before his features became more neutral. "Yeah. Sam's my sister. What was your brother's name?"

There was almost a defensive tone to his voice.

"Everyone calls him CJ. His name is Chuck. Charles. But he's always gone by CJ."

He nodded. "I don't think I've ever heard Sam mention him."

"Oh, right, that doesn't surprise me. I don't think they knew each other well."

Now she remembered CJ's comment about something bad in Samantha's past. She hoped she hadn't put her foot in her mouth, but it wasn't as if she had said anything monumental. Still, Phil's change in demeanor was plain awkward. She couldn't pretend she didn't notice it.

"I'm sorry if I said something wrong. Is Sam all right?"

He stood and began to pack his things together. "Yeah, she's fine." Then he stopped and turned to face Jensy. He rested against the edge of the table. "She just . . ."

Oddly, he seemed to be studying Jensy as if he were trying to figure *her* out. Maybe he wasn't sure he could trust her with personal information.

"She just . . .?"

He nodded, some kind of decision made. "Sam had kind of a rough time in high school. Pretty early on. She made some bad decisions, some people might say. You know how it is. Some of us sailed through the rough waters of high school, and others got pulled down by them."

"Is she all right now, though?"

He shrugged. "She's better. Some mistakes have more serious repercussions, that's all. Sam still struggles with that."

They had both gathered their things and headed to the elevators.

"Is it too nosy of me to ask what repercussions still linger after all these years?" She shook her head. "No, I'm sorry. That is too nosy. I shouldn't—"

"You're not being too nosy. I'm sure you're concerned. But it's not my right to talk more frankly about it. It's Sam's business, not mine."

They rode down to the parking lot.

"The good thing about Sam's high school troubles was they eventually led to her going to church with one of her friends. That pretty much turned her life around. She's a Christian now. She still has her moments, but I think her faith helps."

His comment shocked Jensy. Phil's sister? A Christian? Was the whole family Christian, then? Was Phil?

"I'm . . . that's so good to hear." Should she ask him? If he wasn't, it could sound like she was judging him, and she'd already done plenty of that. Maybe he would volunteer the information if she kept her mouth shut.

But they reached her Honda, and Phil opened the driver's side door for her. He looked directly into her eyes, and she felt an involuntary rush of heat up her neck. Those were some intense eyes.

He spoke softly, "So, we'll show our revisions to David in the morning, and maybe we can move on, right?"

Oh. So that was the end of that. She had liked the more personal direction their conversation had taken and was disappointed it was over. "Sounds great." She leaned into her car, put her things in the passenger seat, and stood upright. Phil still held her door open and had rested his other hand on the top of the car. He had her encircled. She liked it. Oddly, it felt as if he were about to kiss her goodnight.

And then he did.

And to her surprise, she kissed him right back.

When he put his arms around her, she found herself doing the same thing to him. A little voice in her head rambled on about the shock of this development. Her—Jensy St. Martin—avowed single, career-focused woman, in a full-on lip lock with Phil Quinn, handsome, two-timing bad boy from high school—

Which was when the magic immediately died. What in the world was she doing? She pushed herself away from him so abruptly that she saw embarrassment wash over his face.

They both apologized at the same time.

"It's from working together so much, that's all," she said.

He nodded and stepped back several steps. He ran his hand through his blond hair. "Exactly. Again, I'm sorry."

She put up her hand. "No problem. Really." But she was sweating as if she had just competed in a Scottish caber toss. She got into her car and pulled the door closed before he could close it for her. She quickly opened her window a few inches. "I'll see you tomorrow. I mean here. Not here in the parking lot. Here in the office. Upstairs."

"Got it." He stepped away from her and finally turned around and made his way to his car.

She would have laid her head against the steering wheel to wait to calm down, but she wanted to get away quickly. She drove out of the lot, blasting the air conditioning and letting that voice in her head lecture her all the way home. Of all people to get romantically entangled with, she had almost done so with the only person her old beau, Michael, had ever warned her against. There were millions of other guys out there, none of whom had ever cheated on anyone. She didn't need to confuse her life with someone like Phil.

No matter how nice those lips felt. And no matter how protective those arms felt.

Nope. Not her. Not him.

CHAPTER NINE

JENSY WALKED INTO THE OFFICE THE next morning, as bright and perky as a newly groomed poodle. She would carry herself this way all day, even if it killed her. The last thing she wanted was to show how confused and insecure she felt. When had she become such an indecisive, overemotional wimp? She was a newly promoted graphic designer in one of the most prestigious ad firms in Washington, not a silly school girl crushing on the class bad boy.

But the moment she saw Phil walking in her direction, she turned around and headed straight for the ladies' room. If he had seen her, he didn't let on.

Rebecca was at the bathroom sink, wiping tears away.

"Becks, what's wrong?" Jensy put her arm across Rebecca's back. "You feeling sick?"

"You bet. Sick of men, yeah." Rebecca straightened up and pursed her lips. "Jensy, what exactly is *wrong* with me, can you tell me that?"

Jensy sighed. "Now what? This isn't about that sloppy mess of a man who's mooching off his mother, is it?"

Rebecca went silent.

"Aw, Rebecca, come on. That guy sounds *so* bad. Please break that relationship off."

"No need. He's already done that." She wiped the last tear away.

Jensy couldn't help it. A laugh burst out before she could stop herself. "I'm sorry, Becks. I'm not laughing at you. I'm laughing at the arrogance of the guy. He broke off from you? Okay, let me ask you—was it in person? Was he wearing the same shirt he's worn every other time you've seen him? The dirty one with the glob of sauce on it, proclaiming him to be a slob and a certified loser?"

"He actually had a different shirt on this time."

"Ah. Well. A major loss for you, then."

"Don't joke. It's not funny."

"I know. But, Becks, there are better men out there. God blessed you with this break."

Rebecca rolled her eyes. "God's not listening to me. He doesn't care about me."

"Oh, that's not true, and you know it. He does care about you. And, even though you don't need a sermon right now, *you* might try listening to *Him*. Between the two of you, I can guarantee He knows what's better for you, and I have a hunch He didn't send this particular gem to you. Even if what's-his-name did finally put on a clean shirt."

She saw the slightest hint of a smile tweak in the corner of Rebecca's lips. "I didn't say he wore a clean shirt. Just a different one."

Jensy laughed. "More sauce?"

"No. I think it might have been . . . cheese."

"Ew. Okay, yes, the Lord wants to save you in more ways than one. You should see this as a good thing."

Rebecca sighed. "You're right. It's so hard, trying to find a good man out there. We can't all be focused on our careers like you are."

Jensy shut her mouth and entered one of the stalls. "Yes, well, I'll see you at our desks. Chin up, okay? You're terrific. Don't forget that."

When she returned to her desk, David Summers' secretary had left a note on her desk to join him and Phil as soon as she could. Her heart began to hammer against her chest, and she had to stop for a moment and take her own advice.

Lord, I know I need to lean on You, and I'm asking You to please help me to be mature and professional in this meeting. Please help me to not make a fool of myself or develop flop sweats of stress in front of David and Phil. Amen.

She definitely did lean on God's strength when she entered David's office. Phil stood when she entered the room, like an old-court gent, and it was all she could do to not sigh at the gallantry of the gesture. Instead, she gave him a quick, polite smile, which she then turned on David.

"Jensy!" David said, his enthusiasm blessing her with distraction and encouragement. "I love what you two did last night!"

She shot a shocked look at Phil, who gave a subtle shake of the head before she realized that, of course, David was referring to their revision of the ad campaign, not the passionate embrace at her car.

Her face was aflame.

"I'm . . . so glad. Do you think the client will like it?"

David nodded. "I feel very good about this. I think you two are a red hot duo, I have to say."

Bless me, Lord, for I am in desperate need of mature, calm thought here. Red hot duo? Really?

"Thanks so much." She hoped her voice didn't sound as weak as it felt coming out of her mouth.

Phil finally spoke up. "So, Jensy, David is going to arrange for us to do a presentation for Chrysalis next week. We have to get it fluid and closer to what the full production will look like, okay?"

She nodded. "Sounds great."

"Excellent!" David came around the desk and vigorously shook their hands. "So proud of you two. My newest designers, and really top-notch stuff. You let me or Monica out there know if there's anything you need."

They walked out together. Once they were alone, Phil spoke to her quietly.

"I'm really sorry about how uncomfortable that was. I never meant to make you uncomfortable here. I know you've worked hard to get where you are at Summers."

"No problem. I'm still very comfortable here." But she was barely able to get those words out of her tightly pursed lips. "I'm perfectly fine."

He nodded. "Good. Good."

She suddenly turned from him and stepped smartly back to her desk. Rebecca looked up at her when she arrived.

"What was that all about?"

"Oh, David wanted to talk about the Chrysalis campaign."

"No, not that." She tilted her head towards Phil's desk, where he had returned and proceeded to make himself busy. "That. You two look as rigid as a couple of Spanx models."

Jensy didn't follow Rebecca's gaze. She knew where she was

looking.

"I don't know what you're talking about."

Rebecca gasped, and Jensy jerked her head up. "What?"

"Oh, my goodness, you little stinker! You're into him, aren't you?" Her face lit up like Christmas. "I *knew* it! You're perfect for each other! What's happened? Tell me."

Jensy frowned so hard her eyebrows hurt. "*Please* don't be so infantile, Becks." But even she heard how formal and Jane Austen-ish that sounded. Her voice lowered to a whisper. "Please stop, Becks. This is really uncomfortable. And wrong."

"But why? He's a total dish, and he seems really sweet. And not a single blob of sauce or cheese about him. And he pays his own way and is smart enough to avoid Valerie—"

Jensy firmly placed her hands on her desk. "I just need to do a good job, okay? I don't want to be flip and foolish about what's important. Ultimately, he's bad news, and I'll get beyond this . . . whatever this is. A crush or something."

Rebecca nearly spun her chair around like a carousel ride. "Oh, this is so good! Okay, I'll chill. But don't write him off, Jensy. I feel like there's a good guy there. I know my judgment isn't the best for myself, but the Force is strong with me when it comes to others."

Jensy laughed. "Okay, crazy. Please, can we get some work done now?"

THAT EVENING JENSY AND Phil were both able to leave the office when most of their co-workers did. They had finally overcome their awkwardness from the night before and worked well all day, making excellent progress.

Although they hadn't planned it, they entered the same elevator with a few other people but were suddenly joined by a large group who pushed the limits of the elevator's capacity. Jensy and Phil were forced to stand tightly against each other, and neither of them dared so much as glance at the other. His arm was pressed against hers, and she was reminded of their embrace at her car. She could smell his soap or cologne or whatever he was wearing. It was the same scent he wore last night. She heard him expel breath as if he were exerting effort in some regard.

Everyone rushed out of the elevator at the main floor level, and Jensy and Phil were left alone to ride to the garage, below. As he moved slightly away from her, a tingle spread over her arm where he had been.

"Jensy."

Do not *look at him. Do* not *make eye contact.*

"Jensy." His voice was soft and full of . . . apology? Need? She wasn't quite sure. But when she lifted her face to him, she moved toward him as quickly as he did toward her.

Why was she kissing him? She was stronger than this. Stronger than blithely giving in to animal instincts. Wasn't that all this was? Just an incredibly charismatic guy with beautiful features and amazing lips, a man whose crystal blue eyes seemed so full of life and compassion? But she had to remember who he was. What he did.

Again, she mustered up the ability to push away from him. She actually shook her head to clear her thoughts.

"I don't want to do this. Please don't do that again."

He rubbed his face in both hands, clearly as frustrated as she was. "I'm sorry. You're right."

She pursed her lips, absolutely furious with herself. "You bet I'm right. I know better than this. I know who you are." The elevator doors opened, and they walked out.

But he hesitated, a frown on his face. "Who I am?"

She nodded quickly. "Yes. I know what you did. Back in school. Michael told me all about you." She even wagged her finger at him.

His features flattened. "I see."

"He told me to stay away from you. That you really let Emily down. You acted like you planned to marry her and then messed around on her *and* dumped her. I mean, he said you broke her heart."

He looked her in the eyes and said nothing.

She had to look away from him. She straightened her jacket and spoke to the ground. "So please let's not let this happen again, all right?

I don't plan to throw away my life over a handsome face. I'm smarter than that."

When she lifted her gaze, he gave her a slight nod. "Understood."

She started to walk away from him.

"And I agree," he said.

She stopped and faced him again.

He said, "You're smarter than that." And he pointed at her, as if he were pointing to the words that had come out of her mouth moments before. He looked at her a moment longer before giving her a sad smile. "See you next week."

He turned and walked to his car.

She furrowed her brows and walked to her own car. She wondered how anyone could say so much with so few words. The guy was clever. She felt completely uncertain, which was probably what he wanted. She stood more stiffly. He wasn't going to get under her skin.

The only problem was that she started her car, watched him drive away, and realized he *had* gotten to her, and far more than skin deep.

CHAPTER TEN

That weekend Jensy's co-worker Alfie joined her and her brother and sister-in-law on a casual visit to Mount Vernon, George Washington's historic home.

"We couldn't have picked a prettier weekend," Jensy said to all three of them. "Beautiful weather, and not that many crowds. Thanks for joining us, Alfie."

"Sarah really wanted to come, too," Alfie said. "She's lived in D.C. for ten years and has yet to see Mount Vernon. But they needed her at work today."

Donita sounded slightly winded as she spoke, resting her hand on her very pregnant tummy. "She can come with us next time. I wanted to walk a lot today to encourage this little one to get cracking. We're due soon, and I'm eager. I'm glad you didn't cancel."

"Oh, I wouldn't do that." Alfie hooked his arm through Jensy's. "Jensy and I never seem to have time for each other anymore, do we? Even at work."

"Yeah, between your love life and my ad campaign, it's hard to schedule," Jensy said. "I love my job, but I miss the old days a little."

They neared the building that had been used as the kitchen in Washington's time. Jensy led the way in. "I read the kitchen was built away from the mansion to keep the house from getting too hot."

"Or even catching on fire," Donita said.

Alfie smiled. "I'll bet they were happy about that on cabbage day, too. It's cool that they have it stocked with tables and cookware. You think they're original?"

"I kind of doubt they'd have it out in the open like this if it was," Jensy said, "not with renegades like you running loose."

"See, that's the kind of moral support I miss at work now. I hope

Summers will promote me soon. I'd love to work on a project with you. Why should pretty boy Quinn have all the fun?"

CJ was the last to enter the kitchen. "Oh, that reminds me." He handed Donita her water bottle. "Here you go, sweetie. It's still pretty cold. Hey Jen, about your local airline ad project—"

"Oh, right!" Donita cut into CJ's sentence. "CJ and I came across some of his old high school friends a few days ago, and they joined us for dinner. CJ asked, and they remembered Samantha Quinn, the sister of that guy you work with." She pointed at Alfie. "Pretty boy Quinn."

"Phil Quinn?" Alfie looked at Jensy. "You knew him before he joined Summers?"

For some reason a bit of dread began to seep into Jensy's veins. "I didn't really know him, no. But we were both in the same class in high school. Small world, huh?"

"Not really," CJ said. "I mean, you're both locals. You never left, and he returned home from New York, right? Didn't you say that before?"

Donita rested against the wall and took a sip of water. "But the big news is we figured out the 'something bad' that CJ forgot. Remember? At your mom's dinner?"

Neither CJ nor Donita seemed to notice Jensy's subtle shake of the head. This wasn't appropriate information to discuss in front of a fellow Summers employee, no matter how good a friend he was.

CJ carried on, unaware. "Turns out some guy sweet-talked her into . . . well right into getting herself pregnant."

"CJ!"

All three of the others stopped and stared at Jensy for her outburst.

"Sorry. It's just not our business, is it?" She was distracted as she registered that this was why Phil seemed so protective of Samantha's history. She made bad choices, yes, but it sounded as if some jerk took advantage of her youthful ignorance.

But Alfie pressed. "These days getting pregnant outside of marriage is hardly worthy of a blink, but that was still a big deal when we were all teens, wasn't it? So did they know who the father was?"

"I don't want to know, CJ." Jensy shot out the comment as quickly as she could. "Really, stop."

"No one knows, anyway. But that's not all of it," Donita said. "Her brother, your Phil—"

"He's not my Phil." Jensy felt her face blush with heat.

Donita smiled. "I was talking to both of you. You and Alfie. Your co-worker, Phil, okay?"

"What about him?" Alfie was shamelessly relishing this information. "High school shenanigans! Good grief."

CJ rested his hand on Donita's arm as he took over. "Anyway, Phil was furious with Samantha."

Without thought, Jensy huffed and spoke under her breath. "Pot, meet kettle."

Once again, they all looked at her. She shook her head and waved them off. "Sorry. Ignore me."

"So he was furious with Samantha, but even worse, his own girlfriend messed around with Samantha's guy, too. She two-timed Phil. While she was still dating him. Both girls, same guy. His sister *and* his girlfriend, can you imagine?"

"No." Now she had to set the record straight, for Emily's sake. "It wasn't Emily who messed around on Phil. It was the other way around. You're not being fair to Emily. Your so-called source has their information all wrong. That's what's messed up about gossip. It gets all twisted, and people keep passing it on."

"Really?" CJ frowned. "Huh. These people sounded so sure."

"That's what people do. They embrace their own versions and spread them, and it's not fair. Can we stop talking about it, please?"

They finally looked sheepish.

"Okay." CJ turned to take in their surroundings. "Sorry. Let's forget about high school nonsense and focus on history that matters."

Alfie raised his hand, feigning a timidity Jensy knew to be completely false. "Just one more thing?"

Jensy sighed, which he took as approval, apparently.

"What happened to the baby?"

Donita glanced at her stomach. "Given up for adoption. Really sad. But that was when Samantha was a sophomore. There's no way she could have raised a child."

No wonder Phil still seemed serious about his sister and the consequences of her choices. That baby would have been a part of his family, too. Even if he was making his own bad choices at the time, seeing this happen to his sister and niece or nephew? That had to be rough.

She wondered if Samantha's pregnancy and the loss of the child had caused Phil to change his stripes. He definitely seemed less slick than she pictured him, based on what he had done when they were all younger.

Although she hadn't behaved with as much abandon in her teen years, she had made mistakes, too. Maybe she wasn't being fair to Phil.

She forced herself to drop the entire matter from her thoughts as she spent the rest of the day sightseeing and dining with Alfie, CJ, and Donita. But as she drove home that evening, thoughts of Phil wafted through her mind. She was determined to let the past go. She would treat Phil as someone she never knew in high school. After all, that was the truth. She knew of him, and if she was honest with herself, she always thought he was kind of attractive before she learned of his shady behavior. But she didn't really know him.

So this week she would be gracious and open minded, and she would treat him as she did everyone else she worked with.

But truthfully, two levels of thought flitted through her mind simultaneously. On the surface, she tried to picture Phil as a new person, with no history as far as she was concerned. He was someone she would refrain from assessing other than what he showed her about himself and his ethics *now*.

Underneath that level of thought, though, was the realization that she was already drawn to what she saw in Phil. Of course she was, she kissed him, didn't she? Since his first day at Summers, he had been a little cocky, yes, but he had been good natured, easy to work with, kind, and even charming. This was the layer of thought that troubled Jensy. What, exactly, was she talking herself into?

CHAPTER ELEVEN

THAT EVENING, JENSY OPENED HER DOOR to an extremely cheery Rebecca, who held DVDs in one hand and a full plastic grocery bag in the other.

Rebecca struck a model's pose, her arms outstretched and her sturdy legs poised in a coquettish, sideways curtsy. "Rom-coms and Haagen-Dazs, baby! It's a night to celebrate!"

Jensy laughed and stepped aside for Rebecca to enter. "What are we celebrating?"

"Freedom!" Rebecca rushed into the kitchen. "Let me get these ice cream cartons into your freezer. I hate sloppy Dulce de Leche! And Cherry Vanilla. And Chocolate Chip Cookie Dough!"

"Are we expecting company?" Jensy took the DVDs. "That's a lot of caloric celebration you have planned there."

"Naw, that's so we can partake of multiple flavors at once. And if we happen to finish them off, no one need know but *toi et moi.*"

"And which freedom are we celebrating?

Rebecca turned to her from the freezer door. "I finally got it, Jen. I finally agree with you. No. More. Men. I'm going to focus on working my way up in the firm. I'm going to see if Mr. Summers would be willing to let me kind of apprentice under you and the other designers. Shoot, I'll even go to school at night, if I have to. I am so over the whole looking-for-some-man-to-fulfill-me thing. Like you, I'm swearing off men."

They walked into Jen's living room and Rebecca flopped onto the couch. Jensy sat in the armchair next to her.

"Well, that's great, Becks. I mean, the part about working your way up. I've always thought you were sharp and had great ideas and creativity that were being wasted with your Admin job."

"Oh, Jen, thank you." Rebecca sat forward to give her a big hug.

"You always know the right thing to say."

That made Jensy laugh. "Hardly. And I never meant to influence you to completely swear off men forever."

"Good golly, who said anything about forever? I'm not insane! I *love* men. But I can see how they distract me, and it's not as if the only thing God put me on earth for was to be some guy's wife, right? I mean, that would be great, but He gave me a brain. And like you say, creativity." She stood and again struck that ridiculous model's pose. "Not just this rockin' bod." Rebecca knew she was a little overweight and that Jen knew her insecurity about it, so the gesture was both humorous and vulnerable. And so endearing.

"I love you, Becks. And some guy will too. Some guy will appreciate all of the above. Now sit down and let's decide what to watch first. What do you have here?"

As Jensy spread the movies across the coffee table, Rebecca picked up the envelope on the small pile of mail in the corner of the table. "And what do *you* have *here*?"

It was the invitation to the high school reunion.

"Oh, right. My high school reunion is coming up." Jensy took the invitation from her, glanced at it, and handed it back. "It's been ten years. Can you believe it?"

"Time flies when you're trying to forget horrible decisions and near-fatal accidents in Shop class. You going?" Rebecca reclined on the couch.

"Yeah, I'll go. I'm terrible about keeping in touch with people, though. I don't really know anyone from school anymore. It's going to be a little uncomfortable at first."

"*Au contraire, ma cherie.* You are very much in touch with *one* person from high school, right?"

Jensy sighed. "Phil. I wonder if he's going. That might be more uncomfortable than meeting up with people I haven't seen in ten years."

"But why? I got the impression you two were warming up to each other, getting along really well."

Jensy studied Rebecca, trying to decide how much to tell her.

But she hadn't been joking about Rebecca being sharp. Rebecca sat up from the couch and pointed at Jensy.

"You haven't told me stuff, have you, you dawg? What's going on with you two? And don't even try to tell me nothing. You're absolutely terrible at the whole poker face thing."

Jensy got up and headed toward the kitchen. "I'm getting us some ice cream."

Rebecca followed her, the invitation still in hand. She took two bowls down from the cabinet. "Come on, tell me what's going on, Jen. You know I won't say anything to anyone."

Jensy sighed while she scooped ice cream into their bowls. "Okay, so we kissed."

"What?!" Becks stomped a foot and shook her head as if someone had kicked her. "You kissed him and didn't tell me? When was this?"

It was impossible not to smile at her reaction. "Well the first time—"

"The *first* time? How have you kept quiet about this? Are you telling someone else? My gosh, this is juicy. Give me more of that one-- the Cherry Vanilla."

Jensy obeyed. "So the first time was at my car. It was a night we worked on the project together, and it just kind of happened. But I put a stop to it right away, because . . . well, you know. The whole bad-boy thing."

Rebecca shook her head. "You are so boring."

"I am not!" But Jensy was laughing. "I'm rational. I'm not about to let some handsome jerk ruin my life."

"So. There were other times? Other kisses?"

"One other time. We met with David about our latest presentation, and he told us he was going to have us do a dog-and-pony show for Chrysalis. At their D.C. offices. And once we were alone we got talking about . . . some family things. His sister, well, she was badly treated by some creep in high school. I didn't know the full story until CJ and his wife happened to find out more information. But their information was flawed, so I'm not sure exactly what happened."

"What did they tell you?"

Jensy shook her head and handed a full bowl to Rebecca. "Nope, not going there. I don't know what's true and what isn't, so let's leave it at that."

"But what about the kiss?"

"Oh. Yeah. I was feeling kind of squishy towards him after what he told me about his sister. It was so caring and protective, you know? So that was in the elevator, on the way downstairs."

Rebecca's eyes widened. "The elevator? Well, honey, we don't even need those rom-coms tonight! You're living one!"

"Not quite. I see nothing comedic about it, and it's barely romantic."

"Right. I wish my life wasn't romantic like that."

They returned to the living room, and Rebecca studied the invitation more closely.

"Hey, is your computer on?"

"Always," Jensy said. "Why?"

Rebecca walked over to the desk and refreshed the computer screen. "Come on, let's see if Phil is going to the reunion."

"How are we going to find that out?" She watched the screen over Rebecca's shoulder.

"Look at the invitation. Don't you read your mail? It says they've made a special page on Facebook for responding. We should get you RSVP'd on there. It will help you to not feel like a stranger when you message back and forth with your old friends beforehand."

Becks brought up the page and scrolled the list at the top of the screen. "Phil Quinn. Quinn, Quinn, Quinn, yep! There he is. He's already listed as going. Look, people are already listing stuff about what their current status is. Okay for me to list you as going?"

Jensy shrugged. "I guess so. Hey, I want to see if my old boyfriend is going."

"Hang on, let me get you on there. You can fill in your info later."

Moments later, she glanced up at Jensy, ready to investigate. "Okay, what was the flame's name again? Mike, wasn't it?"

"Yeah. Mike Pierpont."

Rebecca scrolled and eventually shook her head. "No. I mean, his name is on the list, but he hasn't RSVP'd. Only Emily Pierpont has."

The name made something flip in Jensy's stomach. "What? Emily?" She leaned down to look more closely at the screen.

Rebecca read aloud and touched the entry on the screen. "Emily Blanton Pierpont. Her name is here, but she's not going. She entered some of her info here, though. A relation of Mike's?"

A light veil of sweat erupted along Jensy's upper lip. Now she read aloud. "'Divorced. Nine-year-old son.' What in the world?" Jensy straightened abruptly. "Oh my gosh. Oh my gosh."

"What?" Rebecca turned to face her. "What's going on?"

Jensy pointed at the screen. "Uh, Emily. Emily Blanton. She's, I mean, she was Phil's girlfriend. She . . . she married Mike."

Rebecca frowned. "Your Mike?"

Jensy merely nodded.

"So . . . do you think the nine-year-old son—?"

"He's Mike's. It was Mike. Oh, Becks, it wasn't Phil at all. That pig!"

"Phil?"

"Mike! Phil didn't cheat on Emily, which is what Mike told me, remember? I told you before. Mike, *my boyfriend*, told me to stay away from Emily and Phil. He said Phil was two-timing Emily and broke up with her—that it was all getting really ugly. But Mike didn't want me to find out that Emily cheated on Phil. With *my boyfriend*. Mike was the creep, not Phil."

"Wow." Rebecca scratched her head. "So that means Phil—"

"Was innocent in this. Becks, I've been so mean to him. I even accused him of all of that unfaithful stuff, and *Mike* was the one who did that to *him*. And he didn't defend himself. Not at all."

Rebecca spoke softly, with reverence. "It's like Darcy!"

"I . . . what? Darcy?"

"Phil let you think poorly of him, rather than speaking ill of his cheating hag of a girlfriend."

Another thought dawned on Jensy, and she gasped. "Becks! That also means that Mike was the one who . . . who got Phil's sister Samantha pregnant and left her in the lurch! CJ said both Emily and Samantha were involved with the same jerk. That was *my* jerk!"

Rebecca grabbed her bowl of ice cream and jammed a big spoonful of it into her mouth in a completely mindless gesture, as if the bowl were full of gossip. "Wait a minute. What? Phil's sister is pregnant?"

"No, not now. She was pregnant back then. In high school. She was only a high school sophomore. She gave the baby up for adoption. Stupid Mike—I told him I wasn't going to get intimate with him, so he went crazy on other girls instead. And it sounds like—"

"He got both of them pregnant?" Rebecca swallowed deeply. "Is that what you're saying?"

Now Jensy grabbed her bowl of ice cream and slumped onto the couch. "That's what I'm saying. I'm telling you, Becks, Mike always seemed like such a good guy. My parents even loved him. But he was so . . . deceitful."

"That's an understatement," Rebecca said.

"And this means Phil knew my boyfriend had done both of these despicable things and didn't say anything, let me go on thinking and saying that *he* was the awful one—"

"He was saving you from being hurt, since your boyfriend went full-on Tiger Woods on you." Becks swallowed another bite, and her voice took on that softness again, full of awe. "Wow, what a guy. Protecting two girls' secrets and your feelings. It's a double Darcy! Maybe a triple!"

Jensy allowed a little moan to escape her lips. "Oh, Becks. Help me figure out what to say to Phil tomorrow. And I need to spend some time in prayer tonight. I have some serious groveling to do."

CHAPTER TWELVE

PHIL AND JENSY BOTH SAT THROUGH the Monday morning meeting as if it weren't horribly awkward. But she felt enough awkwardness to cover both of them. She deliberately chose a seat near David Summers so she could face front and not have to watch Phil, or make eye contact with him.

After the meeting drew to a close, David called out to both of them and stopped them from leaving. "Jensy and Phil. Hang on a second."

No escape. Well, she *had* prayed last night that God would help her broach the subject with Phil. Maybe forcing her to talk with him was the only way He was going to get her to do the right thing. She looked in Phil's direction, and his face was devoid of expression, but he completely ignored her. He looked directly, and only, at David.

David put a hand on each of their shoulders, forming a triangle that Jensy felt radiated the heat of humiliation (hers) and possibly anger (Phil's).

"I hate to put a rush on your efforts, but I'm going to need you two to make that presentation to Chrysalis this evening. I talked with Mr. Ruis this morning. He's going out of the country tomorrow and wants to see the final idea before he heads out. But you don't have that much to finish up, right? We simply need to show as complete an idea as we can with your storyboards. That way the production team can go to work on the ad while Ruis is in Japan."

Jensy had expected Phil to answer with more enthusiasm. But they both mumbled assent as if they had been chastised.

"Come on, now," David said. "I'm not asking much. Don't tell me you two have lost your mojo on this."

"Oh, no." Jensy brightened her expression. "I'm sorry. I need my morning coffee, that's all."

"Right." Phil gave the stiffest smile she'd ever seen from him. "No worries. We'll be fine."

David arched an eyebrow at them both. "Ooookay. Please pull it together and do *not* hesitate to let me know if you need help in some way. We'll head to Chrysalis at six tonight." He patted them each on the shoulder. "I'm counting on your excellent teamwork."

They walked out of the conference room together, and they stopped making eye contact. Phil focused on David's assistant, Monica.

"Okay if we use David's work room again, Monica?"

She checked her calendar. "You're good to go. All day."

"Thanks." He glanced at Jensy, and she tried to smile at him, but he looked away so quickly she doubted he even saw it. He looked at the file in his hands as he spoke. "So I'll grab my laptop and you do the same. See you back here in ten?"

"Right."

She headed to her desk and felt Rebecca's eyes on her.

"How'd it go, Jen?" The care in Rebecca's voice almost made Jensy cry with self-pity.

"Ugh, I feel like I'm wearing a huge 'Loser' sign around my neck and being illuminated by a glaring beam of shame."

Rebecca snorted lightly. "Well, okay, as long as you're not being melodramatic about it."

"I know. I'm an idiot."

"No, I'm sorry, Jen. But lighten up. You need to apologize to him, that's all. It won't be as bad as you think it is."

"What won't be as bad as she thinks it is?" It was Alfie, who had come around the corner and put his arm across Jensy's shoulders. "What's wrong?"

"It's Phil," Rebecca said, before Jensy could stop her.

"Is it now?" Alfie crooked his head to look more closely at Jensy. "Is that big bad playboy being mean to you? Do I need to go defend your honor, maybe slap his face with my glove? Come to fisticuffs with him?" He patted his chest and then his pants pockets. "Shoot, it seems I've left my gloves, and possibly my fisticuffs, in my other pants."

"See, Jen?" Rebecca said. "You're not an idiot. Alfie's the idiot."

She loved her friends, and they actually brought a smile to her otherwise dreary face. She looked at Alfie. "He's not the creep I said he was, Alfie. I thought I was avoiding gossip, but I'm knee deep in gossip here, and I need to go apologize to Phil. He's a good guy."

"There you go," Rebecca said. "Say something like that to him. And maybe give him another kiss."

Both Alfie and Jensy gasped.

"Well, you little minx!" Alfie said.

"Becks!" Jensy grabbed her laptop and backed away from them both. She pointed at them. "Do *not* discuss me while I'm gone."

PHIL WAS ALREADY IN the workroom when Jensy arrived. She had been praying as she headed there, but she didn't feel the calm she was hoping for.

Still, she knew this was all on her. He had done nothing wrong. She had to humble herself, apologize, and accept whatever his reaction might be.

He spoke as soon as she walked in. He looked at his computer screen and tapped on the touchpad to bring up what they needed.

"I think we can easily get this finished. We're pretty much there, with just a few rough spots to iron out."

She nodded. "Yes. I think you're right."

She inhaled, asked once more for a blessing, then exhaled.

"I think you're right . . . you're *in* the right. And I would like to ask you to forgive me."

He stopped tapping. He slowly turned his head and looked at her without saying a word.

She simply stared at him for a moment. He was really such a handsome man, and now she was overwhelmed with the knowledge of how kind he actually was. His reaction to her accusations had been downright noble.

She was *not* going to cry. So she swallowed before speaking.

"I've been unkind and judgmental of you, Phil. I chose that

behavior based on lies I was told by people I trusted. But they were wrong, and I was wrong and stupid and wrong—"

"You already said 'wrong.'"

She stopped. He wasn't smiling. "Yes, well I was especially wrong. And *so* stupid, and I know I already said stupid, but I was a teenager in love with someone who was terrible, and I didn't have a clue that he was terrible. But I know now that Mike lied about you and about himself and Emily and Samantha. I know what happened. And I'm so sorry, and I hope we can still be friends and work together without things being so uncomfortable. And I hope you can forgive me. I'm supposed to be a Christian, and I treated you in such an un-Christian way."

After what felt like a lifetime, he sighed.

"Jensy, you didn't give me a chance. It would have been nice to be able to get to know each other as adults, since we never really knew each other when we were kids."

"I know. You're right. But you were so cocky that first day. You fit right in with the image Mike gave me of you."

"I was only cocky with you because you were such a prig. I'm a Christian, too, but you definitely brought out the . . . well, the lack of graciousness in me."

Were they getting there? She felt a flash of hope.

"I understand that. Will you forgive me?"

He looked at his laptop. After a moment he nodded. "Yes. Thank you for apologizing."

The relief flooded through her. But it was short lived.

"So let's finish up this project," he said, "and agree to be professional co-workers from here on out. There's no reason we can't work together to finish this up and even work on future projects, if that's what David wants us to do." He put out his hand to her. "Agreed?"

She wasn't sure why, but this outcome broke her heart. She shook his hand and gave him a friendly smile. "Agreed."

But she knew that something that had blossomed was now dead. If Phil hadn't been standing right there, shaking her hand, she would have broken down and cried.

CHAPTER THIRTEEN

PHIL, JENSY, AND DAVID SUMMERS STOOD at the front of the Chrysalis conference room, Phil's laptop projecting on the big screen. Jensy was proud of what they had produced. She and Phil had been the professionals he proposed they be, despite what had happened between them. With a nod and a determination to move on like an adult, Jensy smiled when the lights came up.

With the presentation ended, Teodore Ruis applauded, which led to applause from his board members.

David bowed his head in acceptance. "We're so glad you enjoyed it. If this is the concept you like, we can have the ad completed for your approval when you return from Japan, Teodore. My excellent designers—" he gestured towards Jensy and Phil—"and my production team will be sure to tailor it with any changes you prefer."

"No, no changes," Ruis said. "Exactly like that. I liked the graphics when you first showed them to me, but we really needed that human touch. That's exactly the blend I was hoping for."

David put his hand on Jensy's shoulder. "This is Jensy St. Martin. She's the human touch you needed."

"Excellent, Ms. St. Martin." Ruis gave her a fatherly smile, and she was unable to shake off the feeling that Phil was being slighted.

"Thank you, sir." She stood without knowing what in the world she was about to do. "But I have to tell you, my . . . partner here, Phil Quinn, is at least half responsible for this end product. He—"

"Yes, of course," Ruis said. "Thank you, as well, Mr. Quinn."

"Because really, Mr. Ruis, he's excellent at what he does." She absolutely could not stop her mouth from talking. "He's creative and cutting edge, and he *does* have a human touch, as well. It's not just me. He's far more human than I am, and I mean that in a good way. He might seem cocky, but that's not really him. He's a very kind person, and you can count on him to take the noble path, every time."

David widened his eyes at her. "Thank you, Jensy."

"Even if he's wronged. It's amazing." She became aware that she was sweating, but still she stumbled all over the words as they cascaded from her like well-meaning toads jumping from a very stupid cave. "And don't ever believe anything you hear about him unless it's good. All good things. That's . . . that's Phil."

When she finally ran out of steam, she registered a roomful of people staring at her. She knew the smile she gave them was weak, and as she sank to her seat she looked from David's puzzled face to Phil's. And beneath all of her burning heat of shame, she sensed something better because of what she saw. Phil's hand hid most of his face. But his eyes were unmistakable. They twinkled at her with the brightness of a very amused smile.

DAVID HAD THEM RETURN to the office while he stayed to meet further with Ruis. "Ask the driver to come back for me in an hour. Go ahead and leave for the evening. You both did very well." He gave Jensy extra attention. "Maybe get a good night's sleep, eh, Jensy?"

"I will. Thanks." She still felt the blush in her face. Would David ever consider her a professional again?

They reached the car downstairs and Phil opened the back door for Jensy, but before she got in, he put his finger to his lips, thinking.

"Um, we're only five blocks from the office," he said. "Would you be interested in walking?"

She studied his face. He looked upbeat enough, and she was still replaying that smile in her memory. "Sure."

Phil closed the door and passed his laptop through the front window to the driver. "Blake, would you mind taking that to the office and putting it on my desk?" He looked over his shoulder at Jensy. "You still have the whole presentation at the office on your laptop, right?"

She nodded and then heard Blake laugh. "Don't worry, Phil. I'll get this to Summers without corporate spies heading me off on my way and stealing it from me."

"I don't know," Phil said. "You lost my burger when you picked up our dinner the other night."

Blake gave him a rakish grin. "I didn't lose it, moron. I ate it."

Jensy sighed. She had known Blake for years and had never developed this kind of laid-back camaraderie with him. Phil had a gift. And she was too uptight.

Phil laughed. "David said to ask you to return for him in an hour. We're going to walk back."

After Blake drove away, they walked for a short while in silence. She felt the ball was in Phil's court, so she kept her mouth shut. She had said enough foolish things for one day.

"So, how did you figure everything out? About Emily and Mike." He looked straight ahead as he spoke.

"Rebecca saw my reunion invitation from Williams. She decided to RSVP for me on Facebook, and she saw Emily's married name."

He looked over at her. "Oh, she kept Mike's name?" He cocked his head to the side. "Huh. I'm surprised. Maybe she still loved him."

"You didn't see her name when you RSVP'd?"

He gave her a sly smile. "You checked to see if I was going?"

"No. Rebecca checked." She gave him a little shove. "I was completely indifferent about that."

He nodded, providing no response.

She didn't want to keep up that pretense, though. "Well, I wasn't *completely* indifferent. But it was Becks' idea to check on you."

"I like Becks. She has guts."

For some reason she loved that he said that. But she chuckled. "Because she was willing to check on you?"

"No. Because she puts herself out there. She makes herself vulnerable."

"How do you mean?"

"I heard you two talking about that weird guy she met at one of those meet-ups. He sounded pretty dicey, but she gave him a few chances. I mean, maybe she thought she didn't have a lot of guys to choose from, which I think is wrong. But I think it was more that she didn't want to be too judgmental."

Jensy couldn't help but feel he was saying this to chastise her for being so judgmental with him, but he stopped and put his hand on her arm. "Wait. That didn't come out the way I meant it. I really did mean that about Rebecca. The guy was a total wreck, from what I heard, so I'm glad she gave up on him. Sometimes a loser really is a loser. I think she'll eventually find a good guy."

"I do too. But for now, she's hoping to focus on progressing at Summers. We should try to help her in that, if we can."

"Even better," he said.

They crossed another street in silence before he walked a little closer to her and spoke near her ear. "So, you weren't completely indifferent about whether or not I was going to the reunion?"

She smiled. "Not completely."

More silence, and then, "Phil, thank you for not throwing the truth in my face."

She was afraid he would ask her what truth she meant, forcing her to spell out how badly Mike betrayed her and how blind and naive she had been all these years. But he did none of that. He spoke in a matter-of-fact tone.

"No one needs that kind of hurt."

"But weren't you hurt? I mean, both your sister and your girlfriend. At least I had a ten-year buffer of ignorance before I realized what happened, but you had it right there in your life. I think Mike might be a sociopath."

"Yeah, I was hurt. And angry. And I still have to work to let it go sometimes, especially about his taking advantage of Samantha. But you can't carry that stuff around long-term. It'll destroy you. And I've decided to not waste a lot of time trying to figure out people like Mike. God sorts all of that out."

She folded her arms around herself and looked down at the sidewalk as they strolled. "You were so wrong, when you first started at Summers."

"About what?"

She stopped walking and looked up into his eyes. "At the first meeting you attended. I was so rude to you, and you said you were much worse than I thought you were."

There was that twinkle in his eye again. "And you said that wasn't possible."

"Ugh. I *was* a prig, as you said. And you weren't a bad person at all."

He took her by the shoulders. "Look. Stop beating yourself up. You were working with what you thought was the truth. I didn't help that any by teasing you. And we've already been through this. We're going to work together fine—no hard feelings."

His reference to their working together brought a swift burn to her eyes, and she had to fight to keep tears from forming.

"But—"

And it was no good. She quickly looked at the ground so he wouldn't see her cry. "But I don't . . . I don't want to work with you."

The kindness in his voice told her he could read her mood. "No?"

She shook her head, still looking down. "I mean, yes, I want to work with you. But, well, we seemed to have something . . . more."

He said nothing at first, and she simply couldn't look up at him.

"Why, Ms. St. Martin, are you flirting with me? Is that what's going on here?"

The smile that comment provoked gave her a shot of courage. "I'm afraid so."

She was surprised when she looked up to kiss him, that he had already met her halfway.

CHAPTER FOURTEEN

Seven months later Phil held Jensy's hand as they walked toward the ballroom at Alexandria's Hotel Monaco.

"We're going to cause quite a stir." Jensy lifted her eyebrows at Phil.

"This is good," he said. "It's what I've worked toward for years — getting my design degree, moving to Manhattan, then back to Washington, getting the job at Summers, all so I could nab you and make a big entrance at our high school reunion."

"Well played." Jensy leaned toward him to kiss his cheek.

"Oh, my goodness!"

They turned to face Bobbie Something — Jensy couldn't remember her last name — the perpetual class president, who stared at them wide-eyed and grinning.

"Phil Quinn and Jensy St. Martin! I remember both of you like it was yesterday!" She frowned. "But you two weren't together when we were in school, were you?"

Phil gave a melodramatic gasp and faced Jensy. "Wait a minute! *You* went to Williams, too?"

Jensy laughed. "I did!"

Bobbie chuckled and lowered her eyes to half-mast. "Phil, now I *really* remember you. You were always such a tease. Well, welcome, you two. Take your nametags to help everyone remember you." She looked at them a moment longer. "What a nice couple you make! You should have dated in high school."

Phil smiled at her. "We should have, Bobbie."

They went through a similar moment of surprise and confusion with each person they met — at least with each person with whom either of them had been high school friends. Jensy assumed Phil was joking about their causing a stir, but their being a couple after all these years actually provoked more interest than she expected.

She had entered very little information about herself on the reunion's Facebook page, and Phil had followed suit. Once they started dating and became a united front, neither of them felt compelled to share much of their private circumstances.

Jensy was relieved that the reaction to their dating status had calmed by the time Emily walked into the ballroom. Emily Blanton Pierpont, Phil's high school sweetheart, Mike's ex-wife, who had indicated she wouldn't be attending the reunion, had apparently changed her mind. Jensy had to shake off the feeling that she was doing something wrong, being there with Phil. She was glad that no one was giving them a lot of attention as a couple when Emily arrived.

Emily was still lovely, albeit a bit sad around the eyes. Jensy was chatting with a couple of her old girlfriends when she first saw her. She watched Bobbie greet her with her usual enthusiasm, and then she saw Emily spot Phil, who stood laughing with some of his fellow baseball team members.

Emily wasted no time in approaching Phil, and Jensy felt the slightest hint of concern. From this distance she could see the two of them simultaneously, and they were still a striking couple. Phil was such a forgiving person. Jensy watched the surprise in his expression when Emily spoke to him, and his friends suddenly made themselves scarce.

"You okay, Jen?" One of her friends drew her attention back to their conversation, but when the woman followed Jensy's gaze, she said, "Oh, wow. Emily. You want to go over there and make your presence known?"

Hearing that question shook Jensy out of her reverie. It would be so awkward if Phil glanced over and saw her watching them. She smiled at her friend. "No, of course not. Everything's fine."

"Really? Gosh, I don't know if I could be that cool. I mean, it's been years, but you read her update, right? You do the math and it's pretty clear. She went after Mike Pierpont when you guys were together, and now she's flashing that smile at Phil—"

Jensy put up her hand. "Phil's not Mike. He's not remotely like

Mike. And Emily is probably quite a bit different now, too."

"I guess so. She's coming over here with Phil, so we'll see."

Jensy turned to see them walking over together. Both of them were smiling. This was . . . a *good* sign? Maybe?

"Look who decided to come," Phil said to Jensy. He flashed his eyes at her and completely settled her concerns. His eyes said, "Is this awkward or what?" And she saw something else in his eyes, but she wasn't quite sure what it was.

"Emily!" Jensy said. "You look great." She gave her as warm a smile as she could.

"Thank you so much for saying that, Jensy." Before the usual, polite comments could be made around the group, Emily glanced at Phil and at the women in the group, and then she looked directly at Jensy. "I was wondering if I could have a word with you."

"Me? Uh, sure."

They walked out of the ballroom together and sat in the spacious lounging area in the lobby.

"I'm sorry to pull you away so abruptly," Emily said. "I've never been one for beating around the bush."

Ugh, what was Jensy about to get hit with? "That's okay. What's . . . up?"

"First of all, I want to apologize. For what I did in high school. With Mike."

"Thank you, Emily, but that was so long ago. And we were all kids."

Emily shook her head. "Ten years isn't that long ago, really. What I did to you—and to Phil—was horrible. And I never set out to get Mike to marry me or any of that. Our parents thought it was the best solution after, well, after I found out I was pregnant. I was stupid and selfish and impulsive, and I hurt a lot of people, and I deserved everything bad that happened after."

As deep as she had felt in gossip mode before, Jensy found she didn't want to hear about the bad things that had happened after. She felt no joy hearing that. "None of us is perfect, right? Please, don't keep carrying that guilt. If you want me to forgive you, I do."

"And I apologize for . . . for what happened moments ago. With

Phil."

Jensy's stomach sank. "Moments ago?"

Emily sighed and looked at her lap. "As I said, ten years isn't really all that long. Not to me. I wasn't going to come tonight, because I didn't really tell people from school about what happened. About Mike and the baby—my son Teddy. We both kind of cut off ties and tried to start a life together. But we didn't last long. Mike couldn't stand the way we forced him to give up his plans for college and all. So he took off. He comes into town about once a year. It's hard for Teddy."

Her voice caught, and Jensy almost placed her hand on Emily's shoulder to comfort her.

Then Emily straightened and continued. "But then I saw that Phil was coming. You know how it is, the high school sweetheart thing."

No, Jensy didn't know. Her high school sweetheart had cheated on her and lied to her, and she had only found out this year. And tonight she was learning he deserted his wife and son so he could continue to indulge his own desires, free of responsibility. So her idea of a high school sweetheart was a tad warped. But she lifted up a quick prayer that she would truly have a forgiving heart. "What do you mean? What about the high school sweetheart thing?"

Now Emily looked embarrassed. "I'm sorry. I had no idea he had fallen in love with you. Phil, I mean. I was a fool, anyway, to even think he would have an interest in rekindling anything with someone like me."

But Jensy hadn't heard anything beyond "he had fallen in love with you." Had Phil *said* that to Emily?

"Anyway," Emily said, standing and holding out her hand. "I'm trying to clean up my messes more quickly these days, so I just wanted to tell you I'm sorry for going after your man in high school and then almost doing the same thing tonight. You two are perfect for each other. You're both kind and forgiving, and I'll bet neither of you will ever cheat on the other."

Not exactly romance poetry, but Jensy would take it. She stood and shook Emily's hand. "Thanks, Emily. I hope your life is blessed. And your son's."

She was surprised when Emily turned and walked to the hotel

lobby and out the door. She truly had severed all ties with her high school friends, it appeared. Jensy watched her and experienced an odd mixture of sadness and relief.

"Weird?"

She turned to see Phil walking toward her. He enveloped her in his arms. "You okay? What did she say?"

Jensy tilted her head. "She apologized about Mike. And then she said she came here to see you."

He nodded. "Yeah. That made me kind of sad for her."

Jensy pushed away from him, gently. "Hey. Did you tell her you were in love with me?"

He gave her a subtle grimace. "A little, yeah."

"Phil! You've never said that to me. How could you tell that to Emily before you even told me?" She wasn't sure if it was right for her to be perturbed, but she was.

He shrugged as if he had been caught going through her purse.

"I didn't know until I told her. But, you know, it's just something you say."

Jensy gasped but then gave him a squinty-eyed study. They had been together long enough for her to know Phil didn't tend to make insensitive comments.

"Just something you say?"

"Yeah." He took her hand, and they walked to a railing that allowed them to look downstairs, where another event was taking place. Phil leaned on the railing and spoke without looking at her. She leaned on the railing, too, but she watched him as he spoke.

"You know how it is. You're with someone for quite a while, and you realize you have an amazing number of interests in common, not only professionally but personally, too. And you enjoy each other's families so much you actually look *forward* to family gatherings. And you resolve your arguments by risking hurt and being vulnerable and then finding out the other person is risking as much as you are and trusts you that much. And you watch the person's new niece so her brother and sister-in-law can have date nights, and you see what it would be like if that kid were yours—yours and hers. And you like what you see. And you both embrace your faith. And it's the *same* faith!"

Jensy felt the sting of tears and let them come. He turned his head and looked at her. Now she realized what the expression on Phil's face was when he and Emily approached her. As he told her, he had suddenly realized something.

He said, "Yeah, you know how it is. When those things happen, and they happen with someone who makes your heart jump every time you see her again, it's just something you say."

He leaned toward her and kissed her. "I love you. I'm *in* love with you."

Jensy kissed him back, and as they turned to each other, she reached up and put her arms around him. "You make a good case. It appears I'm in love with you, too."

The music from the ballroom streamed out to them. The band had taken a break, and "You're Beautiful," a James Blunt song from their high school days, played through the speakers. It was about a man meeting eyes with a beautiful woman on the subway and sadly realizing he would likely never see her again.

Phil started swaying to the music with her, humming softly. They looked at each other and smiled. Jensy studied his striking looks. He *was* beautiful—but not because of his face or physique. She considered the list Phil had recited, and he was absolutely right.

There was no denying their physical attraction. But she felt blessed to know there was more to them—so much more—than that.

The End

You can contact the authors or
learn more about them on their websites:

Miralee Ferrell: www.miraleeferrell.com
Kimberly Rose Johnson: www.kimberlyrjohnson.com
Debby Mayne: www.debbymayne.com
Trish Perry: www.trishperry.com